New York Times bestse  master Ed McBain ha
ern fiction and had th
one-of-a-kind series. I
turing new tales from these be

Lawrence Block

Jeffery Deaver

John Farris

Stephen King

Ed McBain

Sharyn McCrumb

Walter Mosley

Joyce Carol Oates

Anne Perry

Donald E. Westlake

TRANSGRESSIONS

Edited by Ed McBain

FOREVER
Jeffery Deaver

KELLER'S ADJUSTMENT
Lawrence Block

A TOM DOHERTY ASSOCIATES BOOK
NEW YORK

Copyright Acknowledgments

"Forever," copyright © 2005 by Jeffery Deaver
"Keller's Adjustment," copyright © 2005 Lawrence Block

This is a work of fiction. All the characters and events portrayed in these novellas are either fictitious or are used fictitiously.

TRANSGRESSIONS

The novellas collected in this volume and the three forthcoming volumes of *Transgressions* were previously published in 2005 as a single-volume hardcover edition under the title *Transgressions*.

A Forge Book
Published by Tom Doherty Associates, LLC
175 Fifth Avenue
New York, NY 10010

www.tor.com

Forge® is a registered trademark of Tom Doherty Associates, LLC.

ISBN-13: 978-0-765-34750-3
ISBN-10: 0-765-34750-4

First mass market edition: August 2006

Printed in the United States of America

0 9 8 7 6 5 4 3 2 1

Contents

Introduction

When I was writing novellas for the pulp magazines back in the 1950s, we still called them "novelettes," and all I knew about the form was that it was long and it paid half a cent a word. This meant that if I wrote 10,000 words, the average length of a novelette back then, I would sooner or later get a check for five hundred dollars. This was not bad pay for a struggling young writer.

A novella today can run anywhere from 10,000 to 40,000 words. Longer than a short story (5,000 words) but much shorter than a novel (at least 60,000 words) it combines the immediacy of the former with the depth of the latter, and it ain't easy to write. In fact, given the difficulty of the form, and the scarcity of markets for novellas, it is surprising that any writers today are writing them at all.

But here was the brilliant idea.

Round up the best writers of mystery, crime, and suspense novels, and ask them to write a brand-new novella for a collection of similarly superb novellas to be published anywhere in the world for the very first time. Does that sound keen, or what? In a perfect world, *yes*, it *is* a wonderful idea, and here is your novella, sir, thank you very much for asking me to contribute.

But many of the bestselling novelists I approached had never written a novella in their lives. (Some of them had never even written a short story!) Up went the hands in mock horror. "What! A novella? I wouldn't even know how to *begin* one." Others thought that writing a novella ("*How* long did you say it had to be?") would constitute a wonderful challenge, but bestselling novelists are busy people with publishing contracts to fulfill and deadlines to meet, and however intriguing the invitation may have seemed at first, stark reality reared its ugly head, and so . . .

"Gee, thanks for thinking of me, but I'm already three months behind deadline," or . . .

"My publisher would *kill* me if I even

dreamed of writing something for another house," or . . .

"Try me again a year from now," or . . .

"Have you asked X? Or Y? Or Z?"

What it got down to in the end was a matter of timing and luck. In some cases, a writer I desperately wanted was happily between novels and just happened to have some free time on his/her hands. In other cases, a writer had an idea that was too short for a novel but too long for a short story, so yes, what a wonderful opportunity! In yet other cases, a writer wanted to introduce a new character he or she had been thinking about for some time. In each and every case, the formidable task of writing fiction that fell somewhere between 10,000 and 40,000 words seemed an exciting challenge, and the response was enthusiastic.

Except for length and a loose adherence to crime, mystery, or suspense, I placed no restrictions upon the writers who agreed to contribute. The results are as astonishing as they are brilliant. The novellas that follow are as varied as the writers who concocted them, but they all exhibit the same devoted passion and the same extraordinary writing. More than that, there is an underlying sense here that the writer is attempting something new and unexpected, and willing to share his or her own surprises with us. Just as their names are in alphabetical order on the book cover, so do their stories follow in reverse alphabetical order: I have no favorites among them. I love them all equally.

Enjoy!

ED MCBAIN
Weston, Connecticut
August 2004

TRANSGRESSIONS

JEFFERY DEAVER

Jeffery Deaver has had a rapid and much-deserved rise to the top of the bestseller lists. His novels have always been riveting reads, especially those he wrote about Rune, a woman living and working in New York City. Seen through her eyes, the urban landscape is a wondrous—and sometimes frightening—place indeed. Fans of his work know that this is to be expected, or he can take the most commonplace career or event—news reporting, marriage—and turn it upside down with one of the surprising plot twists that have become his trademark. These days, he writes such bestsellers as *Praying for Sleep, A Maiden's Grave, Hard News,* and *The Bone Collector,* featuring the brilliant quadriplegic detective Lincoln Rhyme and his assistant Amelia Sachs. *The Bone Collector* was the basis for the successful movie of the same name starring Denzel Washington and Angelina Jolie. His readership expands with each new novel, and with each new short story he writes. His most recent novels are *The Cold Moon* and *The Twelfth Card.*

FOREVER

Jeffery Deaver

Mathematics is not a careful march down a well-cleared highway, but a journey into a strange wilderness, where the explorers often get lost.
—W. S. ANGLIN, "Mathematics and History"

∞

An old couple like that, the man thought, acting like kids.

Didn't have a clue how crazy they looked.

Peering over the boxwood hedge he was trimming, the gardener was looking at Sy and Donald Benson on the wide, back deck of their house, sitting in a rocking love seat and drinking champagne. Which they'd had plenty of. That was for sure.

Giggling, laughing, loud.

Like kids, he thought contemptuously.

But enviously too a little. Not at their wealth—oh, he didn't resent that; he made a good living tending the grounds of the Bensons' neighbors, who were just as rich.

No, the envy was simply that even at this

age they looked like they were way in love and happy.

The gardener tried to remember when he'd laughed like that with his wife. Must've been ten years. And holding hands like the Bensons were doing? Hardly ever since their first year together.

The electric hedge trimmer beckoned but the man lit a cigarette and continued to watch them. They poured the last of the champagne into their glasses and finished it. Then Donald leaned forward, whispering something in the woman's ear and she laughed again. She said something back and kissed his cheek.

Gross. And here they were, totally ancient. Sixties, probably. It was like seeing his own parents making out. Christ . . .

They stood up and walked to a metal table on the edge of the patio and piled dishes from their lunch on a tray, still laughing, still talking. With the old guy carrying the tray, they both headed into the kitchen, the gardener wondering if he'd drop it, he was weaving so much. But, no, they made it inside all right and shut the door.

The man flicked the butt into the grass and turned back to examine the boxwood hedge.

A bird trilled nearby, a pretty whistle. The

gardener knew a lot about plants but not so much about wildlife and he wasn't sure what kind of bird this was.

But there was no mistaking the sound that cut through the air a few seconds later and made the gardener freeze where he stood, between a crimson azalea and a purple. The gunshot, coming from inside the Bensons' house, was quite distinctive. Only a moment later he heard a second shot.

The gardener stared at the huge Tudor house for three heartbeats, then, as the bird resumed its song, he dropped the hedge trimmer and sprinted back to his truck where he'd left his cell phone.

∞

The county of Westbrook, New York, is a large trapezoid of suburbs elegant and suburbs mean, parks, corporate headquarters and light industry—a place where the majority of residents earn their keep by commuting into Manhattan, some miles to the south.

Last year this generally benign-looking county of nearly 900,000 had been the site of 31 murders, 107 rapes, 1,423 robberies, 1,575 aggravated assaults, 4,360 burglaries, 16,955 larcenies, and 4,130 automobile thefts, resulting in a crime rate of 3,223.3

per 100,000 population, or 3.22 percent for
these so-called "index crimes," a standard-
ized list of offenses used nationwide by statisticians to compare one community to
another, and each community to its own
past. This year Westbrook County was faring
poorly compared with last. Its year-to-date
index crime rate was already hovering near
4.5 percent and the temper-inflaming
months of summer were still to come.

These facts—and thousands of others
about the pulse of the county—were readily
available to whoever might want them,
thanks largely to a slim young man, eyes as
dark as his neatly cut and combed hair, who
was presently sitting in a small office on the
third floor of the Westbrook County Sheriff's Department, the Detective Division. On
his door were two signs. One said, DET. TAL-
BOT SIMMS. The other read, FINANCIAL
CRIMES/STATISTICAL SERVICES.

The Detective Division was a large open
space, surrounded by a U of offices. Tal and
the support services were on one ascending
stroke of the letter, dubbed the "Unreal
Crimes Department" by everybody on the
other arm (yes, the "Real Crimes Department," though the latter was officially la-
beled Major Crimes and Tactical Services).

This April morning Tal Simms sat in his

immaculate office, studying one of the few items spoiling the smooth landscape of his desktop: a spreadsheet—evidence in a stock scam perpetrated in Manhattan. The Justice Department and the SEC were jointly running the case but there was a small local angle that required Tal's attention.

Absently adjusting his burgundy-and-black striped tie, Tal jotted some notes in his minuscule, precise handwriting as he observed a few inconsistencies in the numbers on the spreadsheet. Hmm, he was thinking, a .588 that should've been a .743. Small but extremely incriminating. He'd have to—

His hand jerked suddenly as a deep voice boomed outside his door, "It was a goddamn suicide. Waste of time."

Erasing the errant pencil tail from the margins of the spreadsheet, Tal saw the bulky form of the head of Homicide—Detective Greg LaTour—stride through the middle of the pen, past secretaries and communications techs, and push into his own office, directly across from Tal's. With a loud clunk the detective dropped a backpack on his desk.

"What?" somebody called. "The Bensons?"

"Yeah, that was them," LaTour called. "On Meadowridge in Greeley."

"Came in as a homicide."

"Well, it fucking wasn't."

Technically, it *was* a homicide—all non-accidental deaths were, even suicides, reflected Tal Simms, whose life was devoted to making the finest of distinctions. But to correct the temperamental Greg LaTour you had to either be a good friend or have a good reason and Tal fell into none of these categories.

"Gardener working next door heard a coupla shots, called it in," LaTour grumbled. "Some blind rookie from Greeley P.D. responded."

"Blind?"

"Had to be. Looked at the scene and thought they'd been murdered. Why don't the local boys stick to traffic?"

Like everyone else in the department Tal had been curious about the twin deaths. Greeley was an exclusive enclave in Westbrook and—Tal had looked it up—had never been the scene of a double murder. He wondered if the fact that the incident was a double *suicide* would bring the event slightly back toward the statistical norm.

Tal straightened the spreadsheet and his notepad, set his pencil in its holder, then walked over to the Real Crimes portion of the room. He stepped through LaTour's doorway.

"So, suicide?" Tal asked.

The hulking homicide detective, sporting a goatee and weighing nearly twice what Tal did, said, "Yeah. It was so fucking obvious to me. . . . But we got the crime scene boys in to make sure. They found GSR on—"

"Global—?" Tal interrupted.

"GSR. Gunshot residue. On both their hands. Her first, then him."

"How do you know?"

LaTour looked at Tal with a well, duh blink. "He was lying on top of her."

"Oh. Sure."

LaTour continued. "There was a note too. And the gardener said they were acting like teenagers—drunk on their asses, staggering around."

"Staggering."

"Old folks. Geezers, he said. Acting like kids."

Tal nodded. "Say, I was wondering. You happen to do a questionnaire?"

"Questionnaire?" he asked. "Oh, your questionnaire. Right. You know, Tal, it was just a suicide."

Tal nodded. "Still, I'd like to get that data."

"Data plural," LaTour said, pointing a finger at him and flashing a big, phony grin. Tal had once sent around a memo that included the sentence "The data were very helpful." When another cop corrected him Tal had said, "Oh, *data*'s plural; *datum*'s singular." The ensuing ragging taught him a pointed lesson about correcting fellow cops' grammar.

"Right," Tal said wearily. "Plural. It'd—"

LaTour's phone rang and he grabbed it. "'Lo? . . . I don't know, couple days we'll have the location . . . Naw, I'll go in with SWAT. I wanta piece of him personal. . . ."

Tal looked around the office. A Harley poster. Another, of a rearing grizzly—"Bear" was LaTour's nickname. A couple of flyblown certificates from continuing education courses. No other decorations. The desk, credenza, and chairs were filled with an irritating mass of papers, dirty coffee cups, magazines, boxes of ammunition, bullet-riddled targets, depositions, crime lab reports, a scabby billy club. The big detective continued into the phone, "When? . . . Yeah, I'll let you know." He slammed the phone down and glanced back at Tal. "Anyway. I didn't think you'd want it, being a suicide. The questionnaire, you know. Not like a murder."

"Well, it'd still be pretty helpful."

LaTour was wearing what he usually did, a black leather jacket cut like a sport coat and blue jeans. He patted the many pockets involved in the outfit. "Shit, Tal. Think I lost it. The questionnaire, I mean. Sorry. You have another one?" He grabbed the phone, made another call.

"I'll get you one," Tal said. He returned to his office, picked up a questionnaire from a neat pile on his credenza and returned to LaTour. The cop was still on the phone, speaking in muted but gruff tones. He glanced up and nodded at Tal, who set the sheet on his desk.

LaTour mouthed, Thank you.

Tal waited a moment and asked, "Who else was there?"

"What?" LaTour frowned, irritated at being interrupted. He clapped his hand over the mouthpiece.

"Who else was at the scene?"

"Where the Bensons offed themselves? Fuck, I don't know. Fire and Rescue. That Greeley P.D. kid." A look of concentration that Tal didn't believe. "A few other guys. Can't remember." The detective returned to his conversation.

Tal walked back to his office, certain that the questionnaire was presently being slam-dunked into LaTour's wastebasket.

He called the Fire and Rescue Department but couldn't track down anybody

who'd responded to the suicide. He gave up
for the time being and continued working
on the spreadsheet.

After a half hour he paused and
stretched. His eyes slipped from the spreadsheet to the pile of blank questionnaires. A
Xeroxed note was stapled neatly to each
one, asking the responding or case officer
to fill it out in full and explaining how helpful the information would be. He'd ago-
nized over writing that letter (numbers
came easy to Talbot Simms, words hard).
Still, he knew the officers didn't take the
questionnaire seriously. They joked about it.
They joked about *him* too, calling him "Einstein" or "Mr. Wizard" behind his back.

1. *Please state nature of incident:*

He found himself agitated, then angry,
tapping his mechanical pencil on the
spreadsheet like a drumstick. Anything not
filled out properly rankled Talbot Simms;
that was his nature. But an unanswered
questionnaire was particularly irritating.
The information the forms harvested was
important. The art and science of statistics
not only compiles existing information but
is used to make vital decisions and predict
trends. Maybe a questionnaire in this case
would reveal some fact, some *datum*, that

would help the county better understand elderly suicides and save lives.

4. *Please indicate the sex, approximate age,
and apparent nationality and/or race of each
victim:*

The empty lines on the questions were
like an itch—aggravated by hot-shot La-
Tour's condescending attitude.

"Hey, there, Boss." Shellee, Tal's fire-
cracker of a secretary, stepped into his office. "*Finally* got the Templeton files. Sent
'em by mule train from Albany's my guess."
With massive blonde ringlets and the feistiness of a truck-stop waitress compressed into
a five-foot, hundred-pound frame, Shellee
looked as if she'd sling out words with a
twangy Alabaman accent but her intonation
was pure Hahvahd Square Bostonian.

"Thanks." He took the dozen folders she
handed off, examined the numbers on the
front of each and rearranged them in ascending order on the credenza behind his desk.

"Called the SEC again and they promise,
promise, promise they'll have us the—Hey,
you leaving early?" She was frowning, looking at her watch, as Tal stood, straightened
his tie and pulled on the thin, navy-blue
raincoat he wore to and from the office.

"Have an errand."

A frown of curiosity filled her round face, which was deceptively girlish (Tal knew she had a twenty-one-year-old daughter and a husband who'd just retired from the phone company). "Sure. You do? Didn't see anything on your calender."

The surprise was understandable. Tal had meetings out of the office once or twice a month at the most. He was virtually always at his desk, except when he went out for lunch, which he did at twelve-thirty every day, joining two or three friends from a local university at the Corner Tap Room up the street.

"Just came up."

"Be back?" Shellee asked.

He paused. "You know, I'm not really sure." He headed for the elevator.

∞

The white-columned Colonial on Meadowridge had to be worth six, seven million. Tal pulled his Honda Accord into the circular drive, behind a black sedan, which he hoped belonged to a Greeley P.D. officer, somebody who might have the information he needed. Tal took the questionnaire and two pens from his briefcase, made sure the tips were retracted then slipped them into his shirt pocket. He walked up the flagstone

path to the house, the door to which was un-
locked. He stepped inside and identified
himself to a man in jeans and work shirt,
carrying a clipboard. It was his car in the
drive, he explained. He was here to meet
the Bensons' lawyer about liquidating their
estate and knew nothing about the Bensons
or their death, other than what he'd heard
about the suicides.

He stepped outside, leaving Tal alone in
the house.

As he walked through the entry foyer and
into the spacious first floor a feeling of disquiet came over him. It wasn't the queasy
sense that somebody'd just died here; it was
that the house was such an unlikely setting
for death. He looked over the yellow-and-
pink floral upholstery, the boldly colorful
abstracts on the walls, the gold-edged china
and prismatic glasses awaiting parties, the
collection of crystal animals, the Moroccan
pottery, shelves of well-thumbed books,
framed snapshots on the walls and mantle.
Two pairs of well-worn slippers—a man's
size and a woman's—sat poignantly together by the back door. Tal imagined the
couple taking turns to be the first to rise,
make coffee and brave the dewy cold to collect *The New York Times* or the Westbrook
Ledger.

The word that came to him was "home." The idea of the owners here shooting themselves was not only disconcerting, it was downright eerie.

Tal noticed a sheet of paper weighted down by a crystal vase and blinked in surprise as he read it.

To our friends:
We're making this decison with great contentment in hearts, joyous in the knowldge that we'll be together forever.

Both Sy and Don Benson had signed it. He stared at the words for a moment then wandered to the den, which was cordoned off with crime scene tape. He stopped cold, gasping faintly.

Blood.

On the couch, on the carpet, on the wall.

He could clearly see where the couple had been when they'd died; the blood explained the whole scenario to him. Brown, opaque, dull. He found himself breathing shallowly, as if the stains were giving off toxic fumes.

Tal stepped back into the living room and decided to fill out as much of the questionnaire as he could. Sitting on a couch he clicked a pen point out and picked up a book from the coffee table to use as a writing surface. He read the title: *Making the Final Journey: The Complete Guide to Suicide and Euthanasia.*

Okay . . . I don't think so. He replaced the book and made a less troubling lap desk from a pile of magazines. He filled out some of the details, then he paused, aware of the front door opening. Footsteps sounded on the foyer tile and a moment later a stocky man in an expensive suit walked into the den. He frowned.

"Sheriff's Department," Tal said and showed his ID, which the man looked at carefully.

"I'm their lawyer. George Metzer," he said slowly, visibly shaken. "Oh, this is terrible. Just terrible. I got a call from somebody in your department. My secretary did, I mean. . . . You want to see some ID?"

Tal realized that a Real Cop would have asked for it right up front. "Please."

He looked over the driver's license and nodded, then gazed past the man's pudgy hand and looked again into the den. The blood stains were like brown laminate on cheap furniture.

"Was there a note?" the lawyer asked, putting his wallet away.

Tal walked into the dining room. He nodded toward the note.

Together forever . . .

The lawyer looked it over, shook his head again. He glanced into the den and blinked, seeing the blood. Turned away.

Tal showed Metzer the questionnaire. "Can I ask you a few questions? For our statistics department? It's anonymous. We don't use names."

"Sure, I guess."

Tal began querying the man about the couple. He was surprised to learn they were only in their mid sixties, he'd assumed La-Tour's assessment had been wrong and the Bensons were older.

"Any children?"

"No. No close relatives at all. A few cousins they never see. . . . Never *saw*, I mean. They had a lot of friends, though. They'll be devastated."

He got some more information, and finally felt he had nearly enough to process the data, but one more question needed an answer.

9. Apparent motives for the incident:

"You have any idea why they'd do this?" Tal asked.

"I know exactly," Metzer said. "Don was ill."

Tal glanced down at the note again and noticed that the writing was unsteady and a few of the words were misspelled. LaTour'd said something about them drinking but Tal remembered seeing a wicker basket full of medicine bottles sitting on the island in the kitchen. He mentioned this then asked, "Did one of them have some kind of palsy? Nerve disease?"

The lawyer said, "No, it was heart problems. Bad ones."

In space number nine Tal wrote: *Illness*. Then he asked, "And his wife?"

"No, Sy was in good health. But they were very devoted to each other. Totally in love. She must've decided she didn't want to go on without him."

"Was it terminal?"

"Not the way he described it to me," the lawyer said. "But he could've been bedridden for the rest of his life. I doubt Don could've handled that. He was so active, you know."

Tal signed the questionnaire, folded and slipped it into his pocket.

The round man gave a sigh. "I should've guessed something was up. They came to my office a couple of weeks ago and made a few changes to the will and they gave me instructions for their memorial service. I thought it was just because Don was going to have the surgery, you know, thinking about what would happen *if*. . . . But I should've read between the lines. They were planning it then, I'll bet."

He gave a sad laugh. "You know what they wanted for their memorial service? See, they weren't religious so they wanted to be cremated then have their friends throw a big party at their country club and scatter their ashes on the green at the eighteenth hole." He grew somber again. "It never occurred to me they had something like this in mind. They seemed so happy, you know? . . . Crazy fucked-up life sometimes, huh? Anyway, I've got to meet with this guy outside. Here's my card. Call me, you got any other questions, Detective."

Tal walked around the house one more time. He glanced at the calendar stuck to the refrigerator with two magnets in the shape of lobsters. *Newport Rhode Island* was written in white across the bright red tails. In the calendar box for yesterday there was a note to take the car in to have the oil changed. Two days before that Sy'd had a hair appointment.

Today's box was empty. And there was nothing in any of the future dates for the rest of April. Tal looked through the remaining months. No notations. He made a circuit of the first floor, finding nothing out of the ordinary.

Except, someone might suggest, maybe the troubled spirits left behind by two people alive that morning and now no longer so.

Tal Simms, mathematician, empirical scientist, statistician, couldn't accept any such presence. But he hardly needed to, in order to feel a churning disquiet. The stains of dark blood that had spoiled the reassuring comfort of this homey place were as chilling as any ghost could be.

∞

When he was studying math at Cornell ten years earlier Talbot Simms dreamed of being a John Nash, a Pierre de Fermat, a Euler, a Bernoulli. By the time he hit grad school and looked around him, at the other students who wanted to be the same, he realized two things: one, that his love of the beauty of mathematics was no less than it had ever been but, two, he was utterly sick of academics.

What was the point? he wondered. Writing articles that a handful of people would read? Becoming a professor? He could have done so easily thanks to his virtually perfect test scores and grades but to him that life was like a Mobius strip—the twisted ribbon with a single surface that never ends. Teaching more teachers to teach . . .

No, he wanted a practical use for his skills and so he dropped out of graduate school. At the time there was a huge demand for statisticians and analysts on Wall Street, and Tal joined up. In theory the job seemed a perfect fit—numbers, numbers and more numbers, and a practical use for them. But he soon found something else: Wall Street mathematics was a fishy math. Tal felt pressured to skew his statistical analysis of certain companies to help his bank sell financial products to the clients. To Tal, 3 was no more nor less than 3. Yet his bosses sometimes wanted 3 to *appear* to be 2.9999 or 3.12111. There was nothing illegal about this—all the qualifications were disclosed to customers. But statistics, to Tal, helped us understand life; they weren't smoke screens to let predators sneak up on the unwary. Numbers were pure. And the glorious compensation he received didn't take the shame out of his prostitution.

On the very day he was going to quit, though, the FBI arrived in Tal's office—not for anything he or the bank had done—but to serve a warrant to examine the accounts of a client who'd been indicted in a stock scam. It turned out the agent looking over the figures was a mathematician and accountant. He and Tal had some fascinating discussions

while the man pored over the records, armed
with handcuffs, a large automatic pistol, and
a Texas Instruments calculator.

Here at last was a logical outlet for his
love of numbers. He'd always been interested in police work. As a slight, reclusive
only child he'd read not only books on loga-
rithms and trigonometry and Einstein's the-
ories but murder mysteries as well, Agatha
Christie and A. Conan Doyle. His analytical
mind would often spot the surprise villain
early in the story. After he'd met with the
agent, he called the Bureau's personnel department. He was disappointed to learn that
there was a federal government hiring
freeze in effect. But, undeterred, he called
the NYPD and other police departments
in the metro area—including Westbrook
County, where he'd lived with his family for
several years before his widower father got a
job teaching math at UCLA.

Westbrook, it turned out, needed someone
to take over their financial crimes investigations. The only problem, the head of county
personnel admitted, was that the officer
would also have to be in charge of gathering
and compiling statistics. But, to Tal Simms,
numbers were numbers and he had no problem with the piggy-backed assignments.

One month later, Tal kissed Wall Street

good-bye and moved into a tiny though pristine Tudor house in Bedford Plains, the county seat.

There was one other glitch, however, which the Westbrook County personnel office had neglected to mention, probably because it was so obvious: To be a member of the sheriff's department financial crimes unit he had to become a cop.

The four-month training was rough. Oh, the academic part about criminal law and procedure went fine. The challenge was the physical curriculum at the academy, which was a little like army basic training. Tal Simms, who was five-foot-nine and had hovered around 153 pounds since high school, had fiercely avoided all sports except volleyball, tennis, and the rifle team, none of which had buffed him up for the Suspect Takedown and Restraint course. Still, he got through it all and graduated in the top 1.4 percent of his class. The swearing-in ceremony was attended by a dozen friends from local colleges and Wall Street, as well as his father, who'd flown in from the Midwest where he was a professor of advanced mathematics at the University of Chicago. The stern man was unable to fathom why his son had taken this route but, having largely abandoned the boy for the world of numbers in his early years, Simms senior had forfeited all rights to nudge Tal's career in one direction or another.

As soon as he started work Tal learned that financial crimes were rare in Westbrook. Or, more accurately, they tended to be adjunct to federal prosecutions and Tal found himself sidelined as an investigator. He was, however, in great demand as a statistician.

Finding and analyzing data are more vital than the public thinks. Certainly crime statistics determine budget and staff hiring strategies. But, more than that, statistics can diagnose a community's ills. If the national monthly average for murders of teenagers by other teenagers in neighborhoods with a mean income of $26,000 annual is .03, and Kendall Heights in southern Westbrook was home to 1.1 such killings per month, why? And what could be done to fix the problem?

Hence, the infamous questionnaire.

Now, 6:30 P.M., armed with the one he'd just completed, Tal returned to his office from the Benson house. He inputted the information from the form into his database and placed the questionnaire itself into his to-be-filed basket. He stared at the information on the screen for a moment then began to log off. But he changed his mind and went online to the Internet and searched some databases. Then he read the brief official report on the Bensons' suicides.

He jumped when someone walked into his office. "Hey, Boss." Shellee blinked. "Thought you were gone."

"Just wanted to finish up a few things here."

"I've got that stuff you wanted."

He glanced at it. The title was, "Supplemental reports. SEC case 04-5432."

"Thanks," he said absently, staring at his printouts.

"Sure." She eyed him carefully. "You need anything else?"

"No, go on home. . . . 'Night." When she turned away, though, he glanced at the computer screen once more and said, "Wait, Shell. You ever work in Crime Scene?"

"Never did. Bill watches that TV show. It's icky."

"You know what I'd have to do to get Crime Scene to look over the house?"

"House?"

"Where the suicide happened. The Benson house in Greeley."

"The—"

"Suicides. I want Crime Scene to check it out. All they did was test for gunshot residue and take some pictures. I want a complete search. But I don't know what to do."

"Something funny about it?"

He explained, "Just looked up a few things. The incident profile was out of range. I think something weird was going on there."

"I'll make a call. Ingrid's still down there, I think."

She returned to her desk and Tal rocked back in his chair.

The low April sun shot bars of ruddy light into his office, hitting the large, blank wall and leaving a geometric pattern on the white paint. The image put in mind the blood on the walls and couch and carpet of the Bensons' house. He pictured too the shaky lettering of their note.

Together forever . . .

Shellee appeared in the doorway. "Sorry, Boss. They said it's too late to twenty-one-twenty-four it."

"To?—"

"That's what they said. They said you need to declare a twenty-one-twenty-four to get Crime Scene in. But you can't do it now."

"Oh. Why?"

"Something about it being too contaminated now. You have to do it right away or get some special order from the sheriff himself. Anyway, that's what they told me, Boss."

Even though Shellee worked for three

other detectives Tal was the only one who received this title—a true endearment, coming from her. She was formal, or chill, with the other cops in direct proportion to the number of times they asked her to fetch coffee or snuck peeks at her ample breasts.

Outside, a voice from the Real Crimes side of the room called out, "Hey, Bear, you get your questionnaire done?" A chortle followed.

Greg LaTour called back, "Naw, I'm taking mine home. Had front-row Knicks tickets but I figured, fuck, it'd be more fun to fill out paperwork all night."

More laughter.

Shellee's face hardened into a furious mask. She started to turn but Tal motioned her to stop.

"Hey, guys, tone it down." The voice was Captain Dempsey's. "He'll hear you."

"Naw," LaTour called, "Einstein left already. He's probably home humping his calculator. Who's up for Sal's?"

"I'm for that, Bear."

"Let's do it. . . ."

Laughter and receding footsteps.

Shellee muttered, "It just frosts me when they talk like that. They're like kids in the schoolyard."

True, they were, Tal thought. Math whizzes know a lot about bullies on playgrounds.

But he said, "It's okay."

"No, Boss, it's *not* okay."

"They live in a different world," Tal said. "I understand."

"Understand how people can be cruel like that? Well, I surely don't."

"You know that thirty-four percent of homicide detectives suffer from depression? Sixty-four percent get divorced. Twenty-eight percent are substance abusers."

"You're using those numbers to excuse 'em, Boss. Don't do it. Don't let 'em get away with it." She slung her purse over her shoulder and started down the hall, calling "Have a nice weekend, Boss. See you Monday."

"And," Tal continued, "six point three percent kill themselves before retirement." Though he doubted she could hear.

∞

The residents of Hamilton, New York, were educated, pleasant, reserved and active in politics and the arts. In business too; they'd chosen to live here because the enclave was the closest exclusive Westbrook community to Manhattan. Industrious bankers and lawyers

could be at their desks easily by eight o'clock
in the morning.

The cul-de-sac of Montgomery Way, one
of the nicest streets in Hamilton, was in fact
home to two bankers and one lawyer, as well
as one retired couple. These older residents, at number 205, had lived in their
house for twenty-four years. It was a six
thousand-square-foot stone Tudor with
leaded-glass windows and a shale roof, surrounded by five acres of clever landscaping.

Samuel Ellicott Whitley had attended law
school while his wife worked in the advertis-
ing department of Gimbel's, the department store near the harrowing intersection
of Broadway, Sixth Avenue, and Thirty-
Fourth Street. He'd finished school in '57
and joined Brown, Lathrop & Soames on
Broad Street. The week after he was named
partner, Elizabeth gave birth to a daughter,
and after a brief hiatus, resumed classes at
Columbia's graduate business school. She
later took a job at one of the country's
largest cosmetics companies and rose to be
a senior vice president.

But the lives of law and business were behind the Whitleys now and they'd moved
into the life of retirement as gracefully and
comfortably as she stepped into her Dior
gowns and he into his Tripler's tux.

Tonight, a cool, beautiful April Sunday, Elizabeth hung up the phone after a conversation with her daughter, Sandra, and piled the dinner dishes in the sink. She poured herself another vodka and tonic. She stepped outside onto the back patio, looking out over the azure dusk crowning the hemlocks and pine. She stretched and sipped her drink, feeling tipsy and completely content.

She wondered what Sam was up to. Just after they'd finished dinner he'd said that he'd had to pick up something. Normally she would have gone with him. She worried because of his illness. Afraid not only that his undependable heart would give out but that he might faint at the wheel or drive off the road because of the medication. But he'd insisted that she stay home; he was only going a few miles.

Taking a long sip of her drink, she cocked her head, hearing an automobile engine and the hiss of tires on the asphalt. She looked toward the driveway. But she couldn't see anything. Was it Sam? The car, though, had not come up the main drive but had turned off the road at the service entrance and eased through the side yard, out of sight of the house. She squinted but with the foliage and the dim light of dusk she couldn't see who it was.

Logic told her she should be concerned. But Elizabeth was comfortable sitting here with her glass in hand, under a deep blue evening sky. Feeling the touch of cashmere on her skin, happy, warm . . . No, life was perfect. What could there possibly be to worry about?

∞

Three nights of the week—or as Tal would sometimes phrase it, 42.8751 percent of his evenings—he'd go out. Maybe on a date, maybe to have drinks and dinner with friends, maybe to his regular poker game (the others in the quintet enjoyed his company, though they'd learned it could be disastrous to play with a man who could remember cards photographically and calculate the odds of drawing to a full house like a computer).

The remaining 57.1249 percent of his nights he'd stay home and lose himself in the world of mathematics.

This Sunday, nearly 7:00 P.M., Tal was in his small library, which was packed with books but was as ordered and neat as his office at work. He'd spent the weekend running errands, cleaning the house, washing the car, making the obligatory—and ever awkward—call to his father in Chicago, dining with a couple up the road who'd made good their threat to set him up with a cousin (e-mail addresses had been unenthusiastically exchanged over empty mousse dishes). Now, classical music playing on the radio, Tal had put the rest of the world aside and was working on a proof.

This is the gold ring that mathematicians constantly seek. One might have a brilliant insight about numbers but without completing the proof—the formal argument that verifies the premise—that insight remains merely a theorem; it's pure speculation.

The proof that had obsessed him for months involved perfect numbers. These are positive numbers whose divisors (excluding the number itself) add up to that number. The number 6, for instance, is perfect because it's divisible only by 1, 2, and 3 (not counting 6), and 1, 2, and 3 also add up to 6.

The questions Tal had been trying to answer: How many even perfect numbers are there? And, more intriguing, are there any *odd* perfect numbers? In the entire history of mathematics no one has been able to offer a proof that an odd perfect number exists (or that it can't exist).

Perfect numbers have always intrigued mathematicians—theologians too. St. Au-

gustine felt that God intentionally chose a
perfect number of days—six—to create the
world. Rabbis attach great mystical signifi-
cance to the number 28, the days in the
moon's cycle. Tal didn't consider perfect
numbers in such a spiritual or philosophical
way. For him they were simply a curious
mathematical construct. But this didn't min-
imize their importance to him; proving theorems about perfect numbers (or any other
mathematical enigmas) might lead other insights about math and science . . . and perhaps life in general.

He now hunched over his pages of neat
calculations, wondering if the odd perfect
number was merely a myth or if it was real
and waiting to be discovered, hiding somewhere in the dim distance of numbers approaching infinity.

Something about this thought troubled
him and he leaned back in his chair. It took
a moment to realize why. Thinking of infinity reminded him of the suicide note Don
and Sy Benson had left.

Together forever . . .

He pictured the room where they'd died,
the blood, the chilling sight of the grim
how-to guide they'd bought. *Making the Final Journey.*

Tal stood and paced. Something definitely wasn't right. For the first time in years he decided to return to the office on a Sunday night. He wanted to look up some background on suicides of this sort.

A half hour later he was walking past the surprised desk sergeant who had to think for a moment or two before he recognized him.

"Officer . . ."

"Detective Simms."

"Right. Yessir."

Ten minutes later he was in his office, tapping on the keyboard, perusing information about suicides in Westbrook County. At first irritated that the curious events of today had taken him away from his mathematical evening, he soon found himself lost in a very different world of numbers—those that defined the loss of life by one's own hand in Westbrook County.

∞

Sam Whitley emerged from the kitchen with a bottle of old Armagnac and joined his wife in the den.

It had been her husband arriving fifteen minutes ago, after all, driving up the back driveway for reasons he still hadn't explained.

Elizabeth now pulled her cashmere sweater around her shoulders and lit a vanilla-scented candle, which sat on the table in front of her. She glanced at the bottle in his hand and laughed.

"What?" her husband asked.

"I was reading some of the printouts your doctor gave you."

He nodded.

"And it said that some wine is good for you."

"I read that too." He wiped dust off the bottle, examined the label.

"That you should have a glass or two every day. But cognac wasn't on the list. I don't know how good *that* is for your health."

Sam laughed too. "I feel like living dangerously."

He expertly opened the bottle, whose cork stopper was close to disintegrating.

"You were always good at that," his wife said.

"I never had many talents—only the important skills." He handed her a glass of the honey-colored liquor and then he filled his. They downed the drink. He poured more.

"So what've you got there?" she asked, feeling even warmer now, giddier, happier. She was nodding toward a bulge in the side pocket of his camel-hair sport coat, the jacket he always wore on Sundays.

"A surprise."

"Really? What?"

He tapped her glass and they drank again. He said, "Close your eyes."

She did. "You're a tease, Samuel." She felt him sit next to her, sensed his body close. There was a click of metal.

"You know I love you." His tone overflowed with emotion. Sam occasionally got quite maudlin. Elizabeth had long ago learned, though, that among the long list of offenses in the catalog of masculine sins sentiment was the least troublesome.

"And I love you, dear," she said.

"Ready?"

"Yes, I'm ready."

"Okay. . . . Here."

Another click of metal . . .

Then Elizabeth felt something in her hand. She opened her eyes and laughed again.

"What . . . Oh, my God, is this—?" She examined the key ring he'd placed in her palm. It held two keys and bore the distinctive logo of a British MG sports car. "You . . . you found one?" she stammered. "Where?"

"That import dealer up the road, believe it or not. Two miles from here! It's a nineteen-fifty-four. He called a month ago but it needed some work to get in shape."

"So that's what those mysterious calls were about. I was beginning to suspect another woman," she joked.

"It's not the same color. It's more bur-
gundy."

"As if that matters, honey."

The first car they'd bought as a married
couple had been a red MG, which they'd
driven for ten years until the poor thing had
finally given out. While Liz's friends were
buying Lexuses or Mercedes, she refused to
join the pack and continued to drive her ancient Cadillac, holding out for an old MG
like their original car.

She flung her arms around his shoulders
and leaned up to kiss him.

Lights from an approaching car flashed
into the window, startling them.

"Caught," she whispered, "just like when
my father came home early on our first
date. Remember?" She laughed flirtatiously,
feeling just like a carefree, rebellious Sarah
Lawrence sophomore in a pleated skirt and
Peter-Pan collared blouse—exactly who
she'd been forty-two years ago when she
met this man, the one she would share her
life with.

∞

Tal Simms was hunched forward, jotting
notes, when the dispatcher's voice clattered
thought the audio monitor, which was
linked to the 911 system, in the darkened

detective pen. "All units in the vicinity of Hamilton. Reports of a possible suicide in progress."

Tal froze. He pushed back from his computer monitor and rose to his feet, staring at the speaker, as the electronic voice continued. "Neighbor reports a car engine running in the closed garage at two-oh-five Montgomery Way. Any units in the vicinity, respond."

Tal Simms looked up at the speaker and hesitated only a moment. Soon, he was sprinting out of the building. He was halfway out of the parking lot, doing seventy in his Toyota, when he realized that he'd neglected to put his seat belt on. He reached for it but lost the car to a skid and gave up and sped toward the suburb of Hamilton on the Hudson, five miles away from the office.

You couldn't exactly call any of Westbrook County desolate but Hamilton and environs were surrounded by native-wood parks and the estates of very wealthy men and women who liked their privacy; most of the land here was zoned five or ten acres and some homes were on much larger tracts. The land Tal was now speeding past was a deserted mess of old forest, vines, brambles, jutting rocks. It was not far from here, he reflected, that Washington Irving had thought up the macabre tale of the Headless Horseman.

Normally a cautious, patient driver, Tal wove madly from lane to lane, laying on the horn often. But he didn't consider the illogic of what he was doing. He pictured chocolate-brown blood in the Bensons' den, pictured the unsteady handwriting of their last note.

We'll be together forever . . .

He raced through downtown Hamilton at nearly three times the speed limit. As if the Headless Horseman himself were galloping close behind.

∞

His gray sedan swerved down the long driveway leading to the Whitley house, bounding off the asphalt and taking out a bed of blooming white azaleas.

He grimaced at the damage as he skidded to a stop in front of the doorway.

Leaping from his car, he noticed a Hamilton Village police car and a boxy county ambulance pull up. Two officers and two medical technicians jogged to meet him and they all sprinted to the garage door. He smelled fumes and could hear the rattle of a car engine inside.

As a uniformed cop banged on the door, Tal noticed a handwritten note taped to the front.

WARNING: The garage is filled with dangrous fumes. We've left the remote control on the groun in front of the flower pot. Please use it to the door and let it air out before entring.

"No!" Tal dropped the note and began tugging futilely at the door, which was locked from the inside. In the dark they couldn't immediately find the remote so a fireman with an axe ran to the side door and broke it open with one swing.

But they were too late.

To save either of them.

Once again it was a multiple suicide. Another husband and wife.

Samuel and Elizabeth Whitley were in the garage, reclining in an open convertible, a old-fashioned MG sports car. While one officer had shut off the engine and firemen rigged a vent fan, the medical techs had pulled them out of the car and rested them on the driveway. They'd attempted to revive them but the efforts were futile. The couple had been very efficient in their planning; they'd sealed the doors, vents, and windows of the garage with duct tape. Shades had been drawn, so no one could look inside and interrupt their deaths. Only the unusual rattle of the engine had alerted a dog-walking neighbor that something was wrong.

Talbot Simms stared at them, numb. No blood this time but the deaths were just as horrible to him—seeing the bodies and noting the detachment in their planning: the thoughtfulness of the warning note, its cordial tone, the care in sealing the garage. And the underlying uneasiness; like the Bensons' note, this one was written in unsteady writing and there were misspellings—"dangrous"— and a missing word or two: "use it to the door . . ."

The uniformed officers made a circuit of the house to make certain nobody else was inside and had been affected by the carbon monoxide. Tal too entered but hesitated at first when he smelled a strong odor of fumes. But then he realized that the scent wasn't auto exhaust but smoke from the fireplace. Brandy glasses and a dusty bottle sat on the table in front of a small couch. They'd had a final romantic drink together in front of a fire—and then died.

"Anybody else here?" Tal asked the cops as they returned to the main floor.

"No, it's clean. Neatest house I've ever seen. Looks like it was just scrubbed. Weird, cleaning the house to kill yourself."

In the kitchen they found another note, the handwriting just as unsteady as the warning about the gas.

To our friends and family:
We do this with great joy in hearts and with love for everone in our family and everyone we've known. Don't feel any sorrow; weve never been happier.

The letter ended with the name, address, and phone number of their attorney. Tal lifted his mobile phone from his pocket and called the number.

"Hello."

"Mr. Wells, please. This is Detective Simms with the county police."

A hesitation. "Yes, sir?" the voice asked.

The pause was now on Tal's part. "Mr. Wells?"

"That's right."

"You're the Whitleys' attorney?"

"That's right. What's this about?"

Tal took a deep breath. "I'm sorry to tell you that they've . . . passed away. It was a suicide. We found your name in their note."

"My, God, no. . . . What happened?"

"How, you mean? In their garage. Their car exhaust."

"When?"

"Tonight. A little while ago."

"No! . . . Both of them? Not both of them?"

"I'm afraid so," Tal replied.

There was a long pause. Finally the lawyer, clearly shaken, whispered, "I should've guessed."

"How's that? Had they talked about it?"

"No, no. But Sam was sick."

"Sick?"

"His heart. It was pretty serious."

Just like Don Benson.

More common denominators.

"His wife? Was she sick too?"

"Oh, Elizabeth. No. She was in pretty good health. . . . Does the daughter know?"

"They have a daughter?" This news instantly made the deaths exponentially more tragic.

"She lives in the area. I'll call her." He sighed. "That's what they pay me for. . . . Well, thank you, Officer. . . . What was your name again?"

"Simms."

"Thank you."

Tal put his phone away and started slowly through the house. It reminded him of the

Bensons'. Tastefully opulent. Only more so. The Whitleys were, he guessed, much richer.

Glancing at the pictures on the wall, many of which showed a cute little girl who'd grown into a beautiful young woman.

He was grateful that the lawyer would be making the call to their daughter.

Tal walked into the kitchen. No calendars here.

He looked again at the note.

Joy . . . Never been happier.

Nearby was another document. He looked it over and frowned. Curious. It was a receipt for the purchase of a restored MG automobile. Whitley'd paid for a deposit on the car earlier but had given the dealer the balance today.

Tal walked to the garage and hesitated before entering. But he steeled up his courage and stepped inside, glanced at the tarps covering the bodies. He located the vehicle identification number. Yes, this was the same car as on the receipt.

Whitley had bought an expensive restored antique vehicle today, driven it home and then killed himself and his wife.

Why?

There was motion in the driveway. Tal watched a long, dark-gray van pull up outside. LEIGHEY'S FUNERAL HOME was printed on the side. Already? Had the officers called or the lawyer? Two men got out of the hearse and walked up to a uniformed officer. They seemed to know each other.

Then Tal paused. He noticed something familiar. He picked up a book on a table in the den. *Making the Final Journey.*

The same book the Bensons had.

Too many common denominators. The suicide book, the heart diseases, spouses also dying.

Tal walked into the living room and found the older trooper filling out a form— not *his* questionnaire, Tal noticed. He asked one of the men from the funeral home, "What're you doing with the bodies?"

"Instructions were cremation as soon as possible."

"Can we hold off on that?"

"Hold off?" he asked and glanced at the Hamilton officer. "How do you mean, Detective?"

Tal said, "Get an ~~autopsy?~~"

"Why?"

"Just wondering if we can."

"You're county," the heavy-set cop said. "You're the boss. Only, I mean, you know— you can't do it halfway. Either you declare a twenty-one-twenty-four or you don't."

Oh, *that.* He wondered what exactly it was.

A glance at the sports car. "Okay, I'll do that. I'm declaring a twenty-four-twenty-one."

"You mean twenty-one-twenty-four. . . . You sure about this?" the officer asked, looking uncertainly toward the funeral home assistant, who was frowning; even he apparently knew more about the mysterious 2124 than Tal did.

The statistician looked outside and saw the other man from the funeral home pull a stretcher out of the back of the hearse and walk toward the bodies.

"Yes," he said firmly. "I'm sure." And tapped loudly on the window, gesturing for the man to stop.

∞

The next morning, Monday, Tal saw the head of the Crime Scene Unit walk into the Detective pen and head straight toward LaTour's office. He was carrying a half dozen folders.

He had a gut feeling that this was the Whitley scene report and was out of his office fast to intercept him. "Hey, how you doing? That about the Whitley case?"

"Yeah. It's just the preliminary. But there was an expedite on it. Is Greg in? LaTour?"

"I think it's for me."

"You're . . ."

"Simms."

"Oh, yeah," the man said, looking at the request attached to the report. "I didn't notice. I figured it was LaTour. Being head of Homicide, you know." He handed the files to Tal.

A 2124, it turned out, was a declaration that a death was suspicious. Like hitting a fire alarm button, it set all kinds of activities in motion—getting Crime Scene to search the house, collect evidence, record friction-ridge prints and extensively photograph and video the scene; scheduling autopsies, and alerting the prosecutor's office that a homicide investigation case file had been started. In his five years on the job Tal had never gotten so many calls before 10:00 as he had this morning.

Tal glanced into the captain's office then LaTour's. Nobody seemed to notice that a statistician who'd never issued a parking ticket in his life was clutching crime scene files.

Except Shellee, who subtly blessed herself and winked.

Tal asked the Crime Scene detective, "Preliminary, you said. What else're you waiting for?"

"Phone records, handwriting confirmation of the note and autopsy results. Hey,

I'm really curious. What'd you find that made you think this was suspicious? Fits the classic profile of every suicide I've ever worked."

"Some things."

"Things," the seasoned cop said, nodding slowly. "Things. Ah. Got a suspect?"

"Not yet."

"Ah. Well, good luck. You'll need it."

Back in his office Tal carefully filed away the spreadsheet he'd been working on then opened the CSU files. He spread the contents out on his desk.

We begin with inspiration, a theorem, an untested idea: There is a perfect odd number. There is a point at which pi repeats. The universe is infinite.

A mathematician then attempts to construct a proof that shows irrefutably that his position either is correct or cannot be correct.

Tal Simms knew how to create such proofs with numbers. But to prove the theorem that there was something suspicious about the deaths of the Bensons and the Whitleys? He had no idea how to do this and stared at the hieroglyphics of the crime scene reports, increasingly discouraged. He had basic academy training, of course, but, beyond that, no investigation skills or experience.

But then he realized that perhaps this wasn't quite accurate. He did have one talent that might help: the cornerstone of his profession as a mathematician—logic.

He turned his analytical mind to the materials on his desk as he examined each item carefully. He first picked the photos of the Whitleys' bodies. All in graphic, colorful detail. They troubled him a great deal. Still, he forced himself to examine them carefully, every inch. After some time he concluded that nothing suggested that the Whitleys had been forced into the car or had struggled with any assailants.

He set the photos aside and read the documents in the reports themselves. There were no signs of any break-in, though the front and back doors weren't locked, so someone might have simply walked in. But with the absence of signs of physical assault an intrusion seemed unlikely. And their jewelry, cash, and other valuables were untouched.

One clue, though, suggested that all was not as it seemed. The Latents team found that both notes contained, in addition to Sam Whitley's, Tal's and the police officers' prints, smudges that were probably from gloved hands or fingers protected by a cloth or tissue. The team had also found glove prints in the den where the couple had had their last drink, in the room where the note had been found, and in the garage.

Gloves? Tal wondered. Curious.

The team had also found fresh tire prints on the driveway. The prints didn't match the MG, the other cars owned by the victims or the vehicles driven by the police, medical team, or the funeral home. The report concluded that the car had been there within the three hours prior to death. The tread marks were indistinct, so that the brand of tire couldn't be determined, but the wheelbase meant the vehicle was a small one.

A search of the trace evidence revealed several off-white cotton fibers—one on the body of Elizabeth Whitley and one on the living room couch—that didn't appear to match what the victims were wearing or any of the clothes in their closets. An inventory of drugs in the medicine cabinets and kitchen revealed no antidepressants, which suggested, even if tenuously, that mood problems and thoughts of suicide might not have occurred in the Whitley house recently.

He rose, walked to his doorway and called Shellee in.

"Hi, Boss. Havin' an exciting morning, are we?"

He rolled his eyes. "I need you to do something for me."

"Are you . . . ? I mean, you look tired."

"Yes, yes, I'm fine. It's just about this case."

"What case?"

"The suicide."

"Oh."

"I need to find out if anybody's bought a book called *Making the Final Journey*. Then a subhead—something about suicide and euthanasia."

"A book. Sure."

"I don't remember exactly. But *Making the Journey* or *Making the Final Journey* is the start of the title."

"Okay. And I'm supposed to check on—?"

"If anybody bought it."

"I mean, everywhere? There're probably a lot of—"

"For now, just in Westbrook County. In the last couple of weeks. Bookstores. And that online place, the big one, Booksource dot com."

"Hey, when I call, is it okay to play cop?"

Tal hesitated. But then he said, "Oh, hell, sure. You want, you can be a detective."

"Yippee," she said. "Detective Shellee Bingham."

"And if they *haven't* sold any, give them my name and tell them if they *do*, call us right away."

"We need a warrant or anything?" Detective Shellee asked, thoughtful now.

Did they? he wondered.

"Hmm. I don't know. Let's just try it without and see what they say."

Five minutes later Tal felt a shadow over him and he looked up to see Captain Ronald Dempsey's six-foot-three form fill the doorway in his ubiquitous striped shirt, his sleeves ubiquitously rolled up.

The man's round face smiled pleasantly. But Tal thought immediately: I'm busted.

"Captain."

"Hey, Tal." Dempsey leaned against the doorjamb, looking over the desktop. "Got a minute?"

"Sure do."

Tal had known that the brass would find out about the 2124, of course, and he'd planned to talk to Dempsey about it soon; but he'd hoped to wait until his proof about the suspicious suicide was somewhat further developed.

"Heard about the twenty-one-twenty-four at the Whitleys'."

"Sure."

"What's up with *that*?"

Tal explained about the two suicides, the common denominators.

Dempsey nodded. "Kind of a coincidence, sure. But you know, Tal, we don't have a lot of resources for full investigations. Like, we've only got one dedicated homicide crime scene unit."

"Didn't know that."

"And there was a shooting in Rolling Hills Estates last night. Two people shot up bad, one died. The unit was late running that scene 'cause you had them in Hamilton."

"I'm sorry about that, Captain."

"It's also expensive. Sending out CS."

"Expensive? I didn't think about that."

"Thousands, I'm talking. Crime scene bills everything back to us. Every time they go out. Then there're lab tests and autopsies and everything. The M.E. too. You know what an autopsy costs?"

"They *bill* us?" Tal asked.

"It's just the more we save for the county the better we look, you know."

"Right. I guess it would be expensive."

"You bet." No longer smiling, the captain adjusted his sleeves. "Other thing is, the way I found out: I heard from their daughter. Sandra Whitley. She was going to make funeral arrangements and then she hears about the M.E. autopsy. Phew . . . she's pissed off. Threatening to sue. . . . I'm going to have to answer questions. So. Now, what *exactly* made you twenty-one-twenty-four the scene, Tal?"

He scanned the papers on his desk, uneasy, wondering where to start. "Well, a couple of things. They'd just bought—"

"Hold on there a minute," the captain said, holding up a finger.

Dempsey leaned out the door and shouted, "LaTour! . . . Hey, LaTour?"

"What?" came the grumbling baritone.

"Come over here. I'm with Simms."

Tal heard the big man make his way toward the Unreal Crimes side of the detective pen. The ruddy, goateed face appeared in the office. Ignoring Tal, he listened as the captain explained about the Whitleys' suicide.

"Another one, huh?"

"Tal declared a twenty-one-twenty-four."

The homicide cop nodded noncommitally. "Uh-huh. Why?"

The question was directed toward Dempsey, who turned toward Tal.

"Well, I was looking at the Bensons' deaths and I pulled up the standard statistical profile on suicides in Westbrook County. Now, when you look at all the attributes—"

"Attributes?" LaTour asked, frowning, as if tasting sand.

"Right. The attributes of the Bensons' death—and the Whitleys' too now—they're way out of the standard range. Their deaths are outliers."

"Out-liars? The fuck's that?"

Tal explained. In statistics an outlier was an event significantly different from a group of similar events. He gave a concrete example. "Say you're analyzing five murderers. Three perps killed a single victim each, one of them killed two victims, and the final man was a serial killer who'd murdered twenty people. To draw any meaningful conclusions from that, you need to treat the last one as an outlier and analyze him separately. Otherwise, your analysis'll be mathematically correct but misleading. Running the numbers, the mean—the average—number of victims killed by each suspect is five. But that exaggerates the homicidal nature of the first four men and underplays the last one. See what I mean?"

The frown on LaTour's face suggested he didn't. But he said, "So you're saying these two suicides're different from most of the others in Westbrook."

"*Significantly* different. Fewer than six percent of the population kill themselves when they're facing a possibly terminal illness. That number drops to two point six percent when the victim has medical insurance and down to point nine when the net worth of the victim is over one million dollars. It drops even further when the victims are married and are in the relatively young category of sixty-five to seventy-five, like these folks. And love-pact deaths are only two percent of suicides nationwide and ninety-one percent of those involve victims under the age of twenty-one. . . . Now, what do you think the odds are that two heart patients would take their own lives, and their wives', in the space of two days?"

"I don't really know, Tal," LaTour said, clearly uninterested. "What else you got? Suspicious, I mean."

"Okay, the Whitleys'd just bought a car earlier that day. Rare, antique MG. Why do that if you're going to kill yourself?"

LaTour offered, "They needed a murder weapon. Didn't want a gun. Probably there was something about the MG that meant something to them. From when they were younger, you know. They wanted to go out that way."

"Makes sense," Dempsey said, tugging at a sleeve.

"There's more," Tal said and explained about the gloves, the fiber, the smudges on the note. And the recent visitor's tire prints.

"Somebody else was there around the time they killed themselves. Or just after."

LaTour said, "Lemme take a look."

Tal pushed the reports toward him. The big cop examined everything closely. Then shook his head. "I just don't see it," he said to the captain. "No evidence of a break-in or struggle . . . The note?" He shrugged. "Looks authentic. I mean, Documents'll tell us for sure but look—" He held up the Whitleys' checkbook ledger and the suicide note, side by side. The script was virtually identical. "Smudges from gloves on paper? We see that on every piece of paper we find at a scene. Hell, half the pieces of paper *here* have smudges on them that look like smeared FRs—"

"FRs?"

"Friction ridges," LaTour muttered. "*Fingerprints.* Smudges—from the manufacturer, stockers, browsing customers."

"The fiber?" He leaned forward and lifted a tiny white strand off Tal's suit jacket. "This's the same type the Crime Scene found. Cotton worsted. See it all the time. The fibers at the Whitleys' could've come from anywhere. It might've come from you." Shuffling sloppily through the files with his massive paws. "Okay, the gloves and the tread marks? Those're Playtex kitchen gloves; I recognize the ridges. No perps ever use them because the wear patterns can be traced. . . ." He held up the checkbook ledger again. "Lookit the check the wife wrote today. To Esmerelda Constanzo 'For cleaning services.' The housekeeper was in yesterday, cleaned the house wearing the gloves—maybe she even straightened up the stack of paper they used later for the suicide note, left the smudges then. The tread marks? That's about the size of a small import. Just the sort that a cleaning woman'd be driving. They were hers. Bet you any money."

Though he didn't like the man's message, Tal was impressed at the way his mind worked. He'd made all those deductions— extremely *logical* deductions—based on a three-minute examination of the data.

"Got a case needs lookin' at," LaTour grumbled and tossed the report onto Tal's desk. He clomped back to his office.

Breaking the silence that followed, Dempsey said, "Hey, I know you don't get out into the field much. Must get frustrating to sit in the office all day long, not doing . . . you know . . ."

Real police work? Tal wondered if that's what the captain was hesitating to say.

"More active stuff" turned out to be the

captain's euphemism. "You probably feel sometimes like you don't fit in."

He's probably home humping his calculator. . . .

"We've all felt that way sometimes. Honest. But being out in the field's not what it's cracked up to be. Not like TV, you know. And you're the best at what you do, Tal. Statistician. Man, that's a hard job. An *important* job. Let's face it—" Lowering his voice. "—guys like Greg wouldn't know a number if it jumped out and bit 'em on the ass. You've got a real special talent."

Tal weathered the condescension with a faint smile, which obscured the anger beneath his flushed face. The speech was clearly out of a personnel management training manual. Dempsey had just plugged in "statistician" for "traffic detail" or "receptionist."

"Okay, now, don't you have some numbers to crunch? We've got that midyear assignment meeting coming up and nobody can put together a report like you, my friend."

∞

Monday evening's drive to the Whitleys' house took considerably longer than his Headless Horseman race night before, since he drove the way he usually did: within the speed limit and perfectly centered in his lane (and with the belt firmly clasped this time).

Noting with a grimace how completely he'd destroyed the shrubs last night, Tal parked in front of the door and ducked under the crime scene tape. He stepped inside, smelling again the sweet, poignant scent of the woodsmoke from the couple's last cocktail hour.

Inside their house, he pulled on latex gloves he'd bought at a drugstore on the way here (thinking only when he got to the checkout lane: Damn, they probably have hundreds of these back in the Detective pen). Then he began working his way though the house, picking up anything that Crime Scene had missed that might shed some light on the mystery of the Whitleys' deaths.

Greg LaTour's bluntness and Captain Dempsey's pep talk, in other words, had no effect on him. All intellectually honest mathematicians welcome the disproving of their theorems as much as the proving. But the more LaTour had laid out the evidence that the 2124 was wrong, the more Tal's resolve grew to get to the bottom of the deaths.

There *was* an odd perfect number out there, and there *was* something unusual about the deaths of the Bensons and the Whitleys; Tal was determined to write the proof.

Address books, DayTimers, receipts, letters, stacks of papers, piles of business cards for lawyers, repairmen, restaurants, investment advisors, accountants. He felt a chill as he read one for some new age organization, the Lotus Research Foundation for Alternative Treatment, tucked in with all the practical and mundane cards—evidence of the desperation of rational people frightened by impending death.

A snap of floorboard, a faint clunk. A metallic sound. It startled him and he felt uneasy—vulnerable. He'd parked in the front of the house; whoever'd arrived would know he was here. The police tape and crime scene notice were clear about forbidding entry; he doubted that the visitor was a cop.

And, alarmed, he realized that a corollary of his theorem that the Whitleys had been murdered was, of course, that there had to be a murderer.

He reached for his hip and realized, to his dismay, that he'd left his pistol in his desk at the office. The only suspects Tal had ever met face to face were benign accountants or investment bankers and even then the confrontation was usually in court. He never carried the gun—about the only regulation he ever broke. Palms sweating, Tal looked around for something he could use to protect himself. He was in the bedroom, surrounded by books, clothes, furniture. Nothing he could use as a weapon.

He looked out the window.

A twenty-foot drop to the flagstone patio.

Was he too proud to hide under the bed?

Footsteps sounded closer, walking up the stairs. The carpet muted them but the old floorboards creaked as the intruder got closer.

No, he decided, he wasn't too proud for the bed. But that didn't seem to be the wisest choice. Escape was better.

Out the window.

Tal opened it, swung the leaded-glass panes outward. No grass below; just a flagstone deck dotted with booby traps of patio furniture.

He heard the metallic click of a gun. The steps grew closer, making directly for the bedroom.

Okay, jump. He glanced down. Aim for the padded lawn divan. You'll sprain your ankle but you won't get shot.

He put his hand on the windowsill, was

about to boost himself over when a voice filled the room, a woman's voice. "Who the hell're you?"

Tal turned fast, observing a slim blonde in her mid or late thirties, eyes narrow. She was smoking a cigarette and putting a gold lighter back into her purse—the metallic sound he'd assumed was a gun. There was something familiar—and troubling—about her and he realized that, yes, he'd seen her face—in the snapshots on the walls. "You're their daughter."

"Who are you?" she repeated in a gravelly voice.

"You shouldn't be in here. It's a crime scene."

"You're a cop? Let me see some ID." She glanced at his latex-gloved hand on the window, undoubtedly wondering what he'd been about to do.

He offered her the badge and identification card.

She glanced at them carefully. "You're the one who did it?"

"What?"

"You had them taken to the morgue? Had them goddamn *butchered?*"

"I had some questions about their deaths. I followed procedures."

More or less.

"So you *were* the one. Detective Talbot Simms." She'd memorized his name from the brief look at his ID. "I'll want to be sure you're personally named in the suit."

"You're not supposed to be here," Tal repeated. "The scene hasn't been released yet."

He remembered this from a cop show on TV.

"Fuck your scene."

A different response than on the TV show.

"Let me see some ID," Tal said stepping forward, feeling more confident now.

The staring match began.

He added cheerfully, "I'm happy to call some officers to take you downtown." This—from another show—was a bit inaccurate; the Westbrook Sheriff's Department wasn't downtown at all. It was in a strip mall next to a large Stop 'N' Shop grocery.

She reluctantly showed him her driver's license. Sandra Kaye Whitley, thirty-six. He recognized the address, a very exclusive part of the county.

"What was so fucking mysterious about their deaths? They killed themselves."

Tal observed something interesting about her. Yes, she was angry. But she wasn't sad.

"We can't talk about an open case."

"What *case*?" Sandra snapped. "You keep saying that."

"Well, it was a murder, you know."

Her hand paused then continued carrying her cigarette to her lips. She asked coolly, "Murder?"

Tal said, "Your father turned the car ignition on. Technically he murdered your mother."

"That's bullshit."

Probably it was. But he sidestepped the issue. "Had they ever had a history of depression?"

She debated for a moment then answered. "My father's disease was serious. And my mother didn't want to live without him."

"But his illness wasn't terminal, was it?"

"Not exactly. But he *was* going to die. And he wanted to do it with dignity."

Tal felt he was losing this contest; she kept him on the defensive. He tried to think more like Greg LaTour. "What exactly're you doing here?"

"It's my family's house," she snapped. "*My* house. I grew up here. I wanted to see it. They *were* my parents, you know."

He nodded. "Of course. . . . I'm sorry for your loss. I just want to make sure that everything's what it seems to be. Just doing my job."

She shrugged and stubbed the cigarette out in a heavy crystal ashtray on the dresser.

She noticed, sitting next to it, a picture of her with her parents. For a long moment she stared at it then looked away, hiding tears from him. She wiped her face then turned back. "I'm an attorney, you know. I'm going to have one of my litigation partners look at this situation through a microscope, Detective."

"That's fine, Ms. Whitley," Tal said. "Can I ask what you put in your purse earlier?"

She blinked. "Purse?"

"When you were downstairs."

A hesitation. "It's nothing important."

"This is a crime scene. You can't take anything. That's a felony. Which I'm sure you knew. Being an attorney, as you say."

Was it a felony? he wondered.

At least Sandra didn't seem to know it *wasn't*.

"You can give it to me now and I'll forget about the incident. Or we can take that trip downtown."

She held his eye for a moment, slicing him into tiny pieces, as she debated. Then she opened her purse. She handed him a small stack of mail. "It was in the mailbox to be picked up. But with that yellow tape all over the place the mailman couldn't come by. I was just going to mail it."

"I'll take it."

She held the envelopes out to him with a hand that seemed to be quivering slightly. He took them in his gloved hands.

In fact, he'd had no idea that she'd put anything in her purse; he'd had a flash of intuition. Talbot Simms suddenly felt a rush of excitement; statisticians never bluff.

Sandra looked around the room and her eyes seemed mournful again. But he decided it was in fact anger. She said icily, "You *will* be hearing from my litigation partner, Detective Simms. Shut the lights out when you leave, unless the county's going to be paying the electric bill."

∞

"I'm getting coffee, Boss. You want some?"

"Sure, thanks," he told Shellee.

It was the next morning and Tal was continuing to pore over the material he'd collected. Some new information had just arrived: the Whitleys' phone records for the past month, the autopsy results, and the handwriting analysis of the suicide note.

He found nothing immediately helpful about the phone records and set them aside, grimacing as he looked for someplace to rest them. There wasn't any free space on his desk and so he stacked them, as orderly as he could, on top of another stack. It made him feel edgy, the mess, but there wasn't anything else he could do, short of moving a table or another desk into his office—and he could imagine the ribbing he'd take for that.

Data plural . . . humping his calculator . . .

Tal looked over the handwriting expert's report first. The woman said that she could state with 98 percent certainty that Sam Whitley had written the note, though the handwriting had been unsteady and the spelling flawed, which was unusual for a man of his education.

The garage is filled with dangrous fumes.

This suggested some impairment, possible severe, she concluded.

Tal turned to the autopsy results. Death was, as they'd thought, due to carbon monoxide poisoning. There were no contusions, tissue damage, or ligature marks to suggest they'd been forced into the car. There was alcohol in the blood, .010 percent in Sam's system, 0.019 in Elizabeth's, neither particularly high. But they both had medication in their bloodstreams too.

Present in both victims were unusually large quantities of 9-fluoro, 7-chloro-1, 3-dihydro-1-methyl-5-phenyl-2H-

1,4-benzodiazepin,
5-hydroxytryptamine and
N-(1-phenethyl-4-piperidyl)
propionanilide citrate.

This was, the M.E.'s report continued, an analgesic/anti-anxiety drug sold under the trade name Luminux. The amount in their blood meant that the couple had recently taken nearly three times the normally prescribed strength of the drug, though, it did not, the M.E. concluded, make them more susceptible to carbon monoxide poisoning or otherwise directly contribute to their deaths.

Looking over his desk—too goddamn many papers!—he finally found another document and carefully read the inventory of the house, which the Crime Scene Unit had prepared. The Whitleys had plenty of medicine—for Sam's heart problem, as well as for Elizabeth's arthritis and other maladies—but no Luminux.

Shellee brought him the coffee. Her eyes cautiously took in the cluttered desktop.

"Thanks," he muttered.

"Still lookin' tired, Boss."

"Didn't sleep well." Instinctively he pulled his striped tie straight, kneaded the knot to make sure it was tight.

"It's fine, Boss," she whispered, nodding at his shirt. Meaning: Quit fussing.

He winked at her.

Thinking about common denominators . . .

The Bensons' suicide note too had been sloppy, Tal recalled. He rummaged though the piles on his desk and found their lawyer's card then dialed the man's office and was put through to him.

"Mr. Metzer, this's Detective Simms. I met you at the Bensons' a few days ago."

"Right. I remember."

"This is a little unusual but I'd like permission to take a blood sample."

"From me?" he asked in a startled voice.

"No, no, from the Bensons."

"Why?"

He hesitated, then decided to go ahead with the lie. "I'd like to update our database about medicines and diseases of recent suicides. It'll be completely anonymous."

"Oh. Well, sorry, but they were cremated this morning."

"They were? That was fast."

"I don't know if it was fast or it was slow. But that's what they wanted. It was in their instructions to me. They wanted to be cremated as soon as possible and the contents of the house sold—"

"Wait. You're telling me—"

"—the contents of the house sold immediately."

"When's that going to happen?"

"It's probably already done. We've had dealers in the house since Sunday morning. I don't think there's much left."

Tal remembered the man at the Whitleys' house—there to arrange for the liquidation of the estate. He wished he'd known about declaring 2124s when he'd been to the Bensons' house.

Common denominators . . .

"Do you still have the suicide note?"

"I didn't take it. I imagine it was thrown out when the service cleaned the house."

This's all way too fast, Tal thought. He looked over the papers on his desk. "Do you know if either of them was taking a drug called Luminux?"

"I don't have a clue."

"Can you give me Mr. Benson's cardiologist's name?"

A pause then the lawyer said, "I suppose it's okay. Yeah. Dr. Peter Brody. Over in Glenstead."

Tal was about to hang up but then a thought occurred to him. "Mr. Metzer, when I met you on Friday, didn't you tell me the Bensons weren't religious?"

"That's right. They were atheists. . . . What's this all about, Detective?"

"Like I say—just getting some statistics together. That's all. Thanks for your time."

He got Dr. Brody's number and called the doctor's office. The man was on vacation and his head nurse was reluctant to talk about patients, even deceased ones. She did admit, though, that Brody had not prescribed Luminux for them.

Tal then called the head of Crime Scene and learned that the gun the Bensons had killed themselves with was in an evidence locker. He asked that Latents look it over for prints. "Can you do a rush on it?"

"Happy to. It's comin' outa your budget, Detective," the man said cheerfully. "Be about ten, fifteen minutes."

"Thanks."

As he waited for the results on the gun, Tal opened his briefcase and noticed the three letters Sandra Whitley had in her purse at her parents' house. Putting on a pair of latex gloves once again, he ripped open the three envelopes and examined the contents.

The first one contained a bill from their lawyer for four hours of legal work, performed that month. The project, the bill summarized, was for "estate planning services."

Did he mean redoing the will? Was this another common denominator? Metzer had said that the Bensons had just redone theirs.

The second letter was an insurance form destined for the Cardiac Support Center at Westbrook Hospital, where Sam had been a patient.

Nothing unusual here.

But then he opened the third letter.

He sat back in his chair, looking at the ceiling then down at the letter once more.

Debating.

Then deciding that he didn't have any choice. When you're writing a mathematical proof you go anywhere the numbers take you. Tal rose and walked across the office, to the Real Crimes side of the pen. He leaned into an open door and knocked on the jamb. Greg LaTour was sitting back in his chair, boots up. He was reading a document. "Fucking liar," he muttered and put a large check mark next to one of the paragraphs. Looking up, he cocked an eyebrow.

Humping his calculator . . .

Tal tried to be pleasant. "Greg. You got a minute?"

"Just."

"I want to talk to you about the case."

"Case?" The man frowned. "Which case?"

"The Whitleys."

"Who?"

"The suicides."

"From Sunday? Yeah, okay. Drew a blank. I don't think of suicides as cases." LaTour's meaty hand grabbed another piece of paper. He looked down at it.

"You said that the cleaning lady'd probably been there? She'd left the glove prints? And the tire treads."

It didn't seem that he remembered at first. Then he nodded. "And?"

"Look." He showed LaTour the third letter he'd found at the Whitleys. It was a note to Esmerelda Constanzo, the Whitleys' cleaning lady, thanking her for her years of help and saying they wouldn't be needing her services any longer. They'd enclosed the check that LaTour had spotted in the register.

"They'd put the check in the mail," Tal pointed out. "That means she wasn't there the day they died. Somebody else wore the gloves. And I got to thinking about it? Why would a cleaning lady wear kitchen gloves to clean the rest of the house? Doesn't make sense."

LaTour shrugged. His eyes dipped to the document on his desk and then returned once more to the letter Tal held.

The statistician added, "And that means the car wasn't hers either. The tread marks. Somebody else was there around the time they died."

"Well, Tal—"

"Couple other things," he said quickly. "Both the Whitleys had high amounts of a prescription drug in their bloodstream. Some kind of narcotic. Luminux. But there were no prescription bottles for it in their house. And their lawyer'd just done some estate work for them. Maybe revising their wills."

"You gonna kill yourself, you gonna revise your will. That ain't very suspicious."

"But then I met the daughter."

"Their daughter?"

"She broke into the house, looking for something. She'd pocketed the mail but she might've been looking for something else. Maybe she got scared when she heard we didn't buy the suicide—"

"*You.* Not we."

Tal continued, "And she wanted to get rid of any evidence about the Luminux. I didn't search her. I didn't think about it at the time."

"What's this with the drugs? They didn't OD."

"Well, maybe she got them doped up, had

them change their will and talked them into killing themselves."

"Yeah, right," LaTour muttered. "That's outa some bad movie."

Tal shrugged. "When I mentioned murder she freaked out."

"Murder? Why'd you mention murder?" He scratched his huge belly, looking for the moment just like his nickname.

"I meant murder-suicide. The husband turning the engine on."

LaTour gave a grunt—Tal hadn't realized that you could make a sound like that condescending.

"And, you know, she had this attitude."

"Well, now, Tal, you *did* send her parents to the county morgue. You know what they do to you there, don'tcha? Knives and saws. That's gotta piss the kid off a little, you know."

"Yes, she was pissed. But mostly, I think, 'cause I was there, checking out what'd happened. And you know what she didn't seem upset about?"

"What's that?"

"Her parents. Them dying. She *seemed* to be crying. But I couldn't tell. It could've been an act."

"She was in shock. Skirts get that way."

Tal persisted, "Then I checked on the first

couple. The Bensons? They were cremated right after they died and their estate liquidated in a day or two."

"Liquidated?" LaTour lifted an eyebrow and finally delivered a comment that was neither condescending nor sarcastic. "And cremated that fast, hm? Seems odd, yeah. I'll give you that."

"And the Bensons' lawyer told me something else. They were atheists, both of them. But their suicide note said they'd be together forever or something like that. Atheists aren't going to say that. I'm thinking maybe *they* might've been drugged too. With that Luminux."

"What does their doctor?—"

"No, he didn't prescribe it. But maybe somebody slipped it to them. Their suicide note was unsteady too, sloppy, just like the Whitleys'."

"What's the story on *their* doctor?"

"I haven't got that far yet."

"Maybe, maybe, maybe." LaTour squinted. "But that gardener we talked to at the Benson place? He said they'd been boozing it up. You did the blood work on the Whitleys. They been drinking?"

"Not too much. . . . Oh, one other thing. I called their cell phone company and checked the phone records—the Whitleys'.

They received a call from a pay phone forty minutes before they died. Two minutes long. Just enough time to see if they're home and say you're going to stop by. And who calls from pay phones anymore? Everybody's got cells, right?"

Reluctantly LaTour agreed with this.

"Look at it, Greg: Two couples, both rich, live five miles from each other. Both of 'em in the country club set. Both husbands have heart disease. Two murder-suicides a few days apart. What do you think about that?"

In a weary voice LaTour asked, "Outliers, right?"

"Exactly.

"You're thinking the bitch—"

"Who?" Tal asked.

"The daughter."

"I didn't say that."

"I'm not gonna quote you in the press, Tal."

"Okay," he conceded, "she's a bitch."

"You're thinking she's got access to her folks, there's money involved. She's doing something funky with the will or insurance."

"It's a theorem."

"A what?" LaTour screwed up his face.

"It's a hunch is what I'm saying."

"Hunch. Okay. But you brought up the Bensons. The Whitley daughter isn't going to off *them* now, is she? I mean, why would she?"

Tal shrugged. "I don't know. Maybe she's the Bensons' goddaughter and she was in their will too. Or maybe her father was going into some deal with Benson that'd tie up all the estate money so the daughter'd lose out and she had to kill them both."

"Maybe, maybe, maybe," LaTour repeated.

Shellee appeared in the doorway and, ignoring LaTour, said, "Latents called. They said the only prints on the gun were the Bensons' and a few smears from cloth or paper."

"What fucking gun?" he asked.

"I will thank you not to use that language to me," Shellee said icily.

"I was talking to *him*," LaTour snapped and cocked an eyebrow at Tal.

Tal said, "The gun the Bensons killed themselves with. Smears—like on the Whitleys' suicide note."

Shellee glanced at the wall poster behind the desk then back to the detective. Tal couldn't tell whether the distasteful look was directed at LaTour himself or the blonde in a red-white-and-blue bikini lying provocatively across the seat and teardrop gas tank of the Harley. She turned and walked back to her desk quickly, as if she'd been holding her breath while she was inside the cop's office.

"Okay. . . . This's getting marginally fucking interesting." LaTour glanced at the huge gold watch on his wrist. "I gotta go. I got some time booked at the range. Come with me. Let's go waste some ammunition, talk about the case after."

"Think I'll stay here."

LaTour frowned, apparently unable to understand why somebody wouldn't jump at the chance to spend an hour punching holes in a piece of paper with a deadly weapon. "You don't shoot?"

"It's just I'd rather work on this."

Then enlightenment dawned. Tal's office was, after all on the Unreal Crimes side of the pen. He had no interest in cop toys.

You're the best at what you do, statistician. Man, that's a hard job. . . .

"Okay," LaTour said. "I'll check out the wills and the insurance policies. Gimme the name of the icees."

"The?—"

"The corpses, the stiffs . . . the losers who killed 'emselves, Tal. And their lawyers."

Tal wrote down the information and handed the neat note to LaTour, who stuffed it into his plaid shirt pocket behind two large cigars. He ripped open a desk drawer and took out a big, chrome automatic pistol.

Tal asked, "What should I do?"

"Get a P-I-I team and—"

"A what?"

"You go to the same academy as me, Tal? Post-Incident Interviewing team," he said as if he was talking to a three-year-old. "Use my name and Doherty'll put one together for you. Have 'em talk to all the neighbors around the Bensons' and the Whitleys' houses. See if they saw anybody around just before or after the TOD. Oh, that's—"

"Time of death."

LaTour gave him a thumbs up. "We'll talk this afternoon. I'll see you back here, how's four?"

"Sure. Oh, and maybe we should find out what kind of car the Whitleys' daughter drove. See if the wheelbase data match."

"That's good thinking, Tal," he said, looking honestly impressed. Grabbing some boxes of 9mm cartridges, LaTour walked heavily out of the Detective Division.

Tal returned to his desk and arranged for the P-I-I team. Then he called DMV, requesting information on Sandra Whitley's car. He glanced at his watch. One P.M. He realized he was hungry; he'd missed his regular lunch with his buddies from the university. He walked down to the small canteen on the second floor, bought a cheese sandwich and a diet soda and returned to his desk. As he ate he continued to pore over the pages of the crime scene report and the documents and other evidence he himself had collected at the house.

Shellee walked past his office, then stopped fast and returned. She stared at him then barked a laugh.

"What?" he asked.

"This is too weird, you eating at your desk."

Hadn't he ever done that? he wondered. He asked her.

"No. Not once. Ever. . . . And here you are, going to crime scenes, cluttering up your desk. . . . Listen, Boss, on your way home?"

"Yes?"

"Watch out for flying pigs. The sky's gotta be full of 'em today."

∞

"Hi," Tal said to the receptionist.

Offering her a big smile. Why not? She had sultry, doe eyes, a heart-shaped face and the slim, athletic figure of a Riverdance performer.

Margaret Ludlum—according to the name plate—glanced up and cocked a pale, red eyebrow. "Yes?"

"It's Maggie, right?"

"Can I help you?" she asked in a polite but detached tone. Tal offered a second assault of a smile then displayed his badge and ID, which resulted in a cautious frown on her freckled face.

"I'm here to see Dr. Sheldon." This was Sam Whitley's cardiologist, whose card he'd found in the couple's bedroom last night.

"It's . . ." She squinted at the ID card.

"Detective Simms."

"Sure. Just hold on. Do you have—"

"No. An appointment? No. But I need to talk to him. It's important. About a patient. A former patient. Sam Whitley."

She nodded knowingly and gave a slight wince. Word of the deaths would have spread fast, he assumed.

"Hold on, please."

She made a call and a few minutes later a balding man in his fifties stepped out into the waiting room and greeted him. Dr. Anthony Sheldon led Tal back into a large office, whose walls were filled with dozens of diplomas and citations. The office was large and beautifully decorated, as one would expect for a man who probably made a few thousand dollars an hour.

Gesturing for Tal to sit across the desk, Sheldon dropped into his own high-backed chair.

"We're looking into their deaths," Tal said. "I'd like to ask you a few questions if I could."

"Yeah, sure. Anything I can do. It was . . . I mean, we heard it was a suicide, is that right?"

"It appeared to be. We just have a few unanswered questions. How long had you treated them?"

"Well, first, not *them*. Only Sam Whitley. He'd been referred to me by his personal GP."

"That's Ronald Weinstein," Tal said. Another nugget from the boxes of evidence that'd kept him up until three A.M. "I just spoke to him."

Tal had learned a few facts from the doctor, though nothing particularly helpful, except that Weinstein had not prescribed Luminux to either of the Whitleys, nor had he ever met the Bensons. Tal continued to Sheldon, "How serious was Sam's cardiac condition?"

"Fairly serious. Hold on—let me make sure I don't misstate anything."

Sheldon pressed a buzzer on his phone.

"Yes, Doctor?"

"Margaret, bring me the Whitley file, please."

So, not Maggie.

"Right away."

A moment later the woman walked briskly into the room, coolly ignoring Tal.

He decided that he liked the Celtic dancer part. He liked "Margaret" better than "Maggie."

The tough-as-nails part gave him some pause.

"Thanks."

Sheldon looked over the file. "His heart was only working at about fifty per cent efficiency. He should've had a transplant but wasn't a good candidate for one. We were going to replace valves and several major vessels."

"Would he have survived?"

"You mean the procedures? Or afterward?"

"Both."

"The odds weren't good for either. The surgeries themselves were the riskiest. Sam wasn't a young man and he had severe deterioration in his blood vessels. If he'd survived that, he'd have a fifty-fifty chance for six months. After that, the odds would've improved somewhat."

"So it wasn't hopeless."

"Not necessarily. But, like I told him, there was also a very good chance that even if he survived he'd be bedridden for the rest of his life."

Tal said, "So you weren't surprised to hear that he'd killed himself?"

"Well, I'm a doctor. Suicide doesn't make sense to most of us. But he was facing a very risky procedure and a difficult, painful recovery with an uncertain outcome. When I heard that he'd died, naturally I was troubled, and guilty too—thinking maybe I didn't explain things properly to him. But I have to say that I wasn't utterly shocked."

"Did you know his wife?"

"She came to most of his appointments."

"But she was in good health?"

"I don't know. But she seemed healthy."

"They were close?"

"Oh, very devoted to each other."

Tal looked up. "Doctor, what's Luminux?"

"Luminux? A combination antidepressant, pain-killer and anti-anxiety medication. I'm not too familiar with it."

"Then you didn't prescribe it to Sam or his wife?"

"No—and I'd never prescribe anything to a spouse of a patient unless she was a patient of mine too. Why?"

"They both had unusually high levels of the drug in their bloodstreams when they died."

"Both of them?"

"Right."

Dr. Sheldon shook his head. "That's odd. . . . Was that the cause of death?"

"No, it was carbon monoxide."

"Oh. Their car?"

"In the garage, right."

The doctor shook his head. "Better way to go than some, I suppose. But still . . ."

Another look at the notes he'd made from his investigation. "At their house I found an insurance form for the Cardiac Support Center here at the hospital. What's that?"

"I suggested he and Liz see someone there. They work with terminal and high-risk patients, transplant candidates. Counseling and therapy mostly."

"Could they have prescribed the drug?"

"Maybe. They have MDs on staff."

"I'd like to talk to them. Who should I see?"

"Dr. Peter Dehoeven is the director. They're in building J. Go back to the main lobby, take the elevator to three, turn left and keep going."

He thanked the doctor and stepped back into the lobby. Cell phone calls weren't allowed in the hospital so he asked Margaret if he could use one of the phones on her desk. She gestured toward it distractedly and turned back to her computer. It was

3:45 and Tal had to meet Greg LaTour in fifteen minutes.

One of the Homicide Division secretaries came on the line and he asked her to tell LaTour that he'd be a little late.

But she said, "Oh, he's gone for the day."

"Gone? We had a meeting."

"Didn't say anything about it."

He hung up, angry. Had LaTour just been humoring him, agreeing to help with the case to get Tal out of his hair?

He made another call—to the Cardiac Support Center. Dr. Dehoeven was out but Tal made an appointment to see him at eight-thirty in the morning. He hung up and nearly asked Margaret to clarify the way to the Cardiac Support Center. But Sheldon's directions were solidly implanted in his memory and he'd only bring up the subject to give it one more shot with sweet Molly Malone. But why bother? He knew to a statistical certainty that he and this redhaired lass would never be step-dancing the night away then lying in bed till dawn discussing the finer point of perfect numbers.

∞

"All the valves?" Seventy-two-year-old Robert Covey asked his cardiologist, who was sitting across from him. The name on the white jacket read *Dr. Lansdowne* in scripty stitching, but with her frosted blonde hair in a Gwyneth Paltrow bun and sly red lipstick, he thought of her only as "Dr. Jenny."

"That's right." She leaned forward. "And there's more."

For the next ten minutes she proceeded to give him the lowdown on the absurd medical extremes he'd have to endure to have a chance of seeing his seventy-third birthday.

Unfair, Covey thought. Goddamn unfair to've been singled out this way. His weight, on a six-foot-one frame, was around 180, had been all his adult life. He gave up smoking forty years ago. He'd taken weekend hikes every few months with Veronica until he lost her and then had joined a hiking club where he got even more exercise than he had with his wife, outdistancing the widows who'd try to keep up with him as they flirted relentlessly.

Dr. Jenny asked, "Are you married?"

"Widower."

"Children?"

"I have a son."

"He live nearby?"

"No, but we see a lot of each other."

"Anybody else in the area?" she asked.

"Not really, no."

The doctor regarded him carefully. "It's tough, hearing everything I've told you today. And it's going to get tougher. I'd like you to talk to somebody over at Westbrook Hospital. They have a social services department there just for heart patients. The Cardiac Support Center."

"Shrink?"

"Counselor/nurses, they're called."

"They wear short skirts?" Covey asked.

"The men don't," the doctor said, deadpan.

"Touché. Well, thanks, but I don't think that's for me."

"Take the number anyway. If nothing else, they're somebody to talk to."

She took out a card and set it on the desk. He noticed that she had perfect fingernails, opalescent pink, though they were very short—as befit someone who cracked open human chests on occasion.

Covey asked her a number of questions about the procedures and what he could expect, sizing up his odds. Initially she seemed reluctant to quantify his chances but she sensed finally that he could indeed handle the numbers and told him. "Sixty-forty against."

"Is that optimistic or pessimistic?"

"Neither. It's realistic."

He liked that.

There were more tests that needed to be done, the doctor explained, before any procedures could be scheduled. "You can make the appointment with Janice."

"Sooner rather than later?"

The doctor didn't smile when she said, "That would be the wise choice."

He rose. Then paused. "Does this mean I should stop having strenuous sex?"

Dr. Jenny blinked and a moment later they both laughed.

"Ain't it grand being old? All the crap you can get away with."

"Make that appointment, Mr. Covey."

He walked toward the door. She joined him. He thought she was seeing him out but she held out her hand; he'd neglected to take the card containing the name and number of the Cardiac Support Center at Westbrook Hospital.

"Can I blame my memory?"

"No way. You're sharper than me." The doctor winked and turned back to her desk.

He made the appointment with the receptionist and left the building. Outside, still clutching the Cardiac Support Center card, he noticed a trash container on the sidewalk. He veered toward it and lifted the card like a Frisbee, about to sail the tiny rec-

tangle into the pile of soda empties and
limp newspapers. But then he paused.

Up the street he found a pay phone.
Worth more than fifty million dollars,
Robert Covey believed that cell phones were
unnecessary luxuries. He set the card on the
ledge, donned his reading glasses and began fishing in his leather change pouch for
some coins.

∞

Dr. Peter Dehoeven was a tall blond man
who spoke with an accent that Tal couldn't
quite place.

European—Scandinavian or German
maybe. It was quite thick at times and that,
coupled with his oddly barren office suggested that he'd come to the U.S. recently.
Not only was it far sparser than the cardiologist Dr. Anthony Sheldon's but the walls fea-
tured not a single framed testament to his
education and training.

It was early the next morning and Dehoeven was elaborating on the mission of his
Cardiac Support Center. He told Tal that
the CSC counselors helped seriously ill patients change their diets, create exercise
regimens, understand the nature of heart
disease, deal with depression and anxiety,
find care-givers, and counsel family mem-

bers. They also helped with death and dying issues—funeral plans, insurance, wills. "We live to be older nowadays, yes?" Dehoeven explained, drifting in and out of his accent. "So we are having longer to experience our bodies' failing than we used to. That means, yes, we must confront our mortality for a longer time too. That is a difficult thing to do. So we need to help our patients prepare for the end of life."

When the doctor was through explaining CSC's mission Tal told him that he'd come about the Whitleys. "Were you surprised when they killed themselves?" Tal found his hand at his collar, absently adjusting his tie knot; the doctor's hung down an irritating two inches from his buttoned collar.

"Surprised?" Dehoeven hesitated. Maybe the question confused him. "I didn't think about being surprised or not. I didn't know Sam personal, yes? So I can't say—"

"You never met him?" Tal was surprised.

"Oh, we're a very big organization. Our counselors work with the patients. Me?" He laughed sadly. "My life is budget and planning and building our new facility up the street. That is taking most of my time now. We're greatly expanding, yes? But I will find out who was assigned to Sam and his wife." He called his secretary for this information.

The counselor turned out to be Claire McCaffrey, who, Dehoeven explained, was both a registered nurse and a social worker/counselor. She'd been at the CSC for a little over a year. "She's good. One of the new generation of counselors, experts in aging, yes? She has her degree in that."

"I'd like to speak to her."

Another hesitation. "I suppose this is all right. Can I ask why?"

Tal pulled a questionnaire out of his briefcase and showed it to the doctor. "I'm the department statistician. I track all the deaths in the county and collect information about them. Just routine."

"Ah, routine, yes? And yet we get a personal visit." He lifted an eyebrow in curiosity.

"Details have to be attended to."

"Yes, of course." Though he didn't seem quite convinced that Tal's presence here was completely innocuous.

He called the nurse. It seemed that Claire McCaffrey was about to leave to meet a new patient but she could give him fifteen or twenty minutes.

Dehoeven explained where her office was. Tal asked, "Just a couple more questions."

"Yessir?"

"Do you prescribe Luminux here?"

"Yes, we do often."

"Did Sam have a prescription? We couldn't find a bottle at their house."

He typed on his computer. "Yes. Our doctors wrote several prescriptions for him. He started on it a month ago."

Tal then told Dehoeven how much drugs the Whitleys had in their blood. "What do you make of that?"

"Three times the usual dosage?" He shook his head. "I couldn't tell you."

"They'd also been drinking a little. But I'm told the drug didn't directly contribute to their death. Would you agree?"

"Yes, yes," he said quickly. "It's not dangerous. It makes you drowsy and giddy. That's all."

"Drowsy *and* giddy both?" Tal asked. "Is that unusual?" The only drugs he'd taken recently were aspirin and an antiseasickness medicine that didn't work for him, as a disastrous afternoon date on a tiny sailboat on Long Island Sound had proven.

"No, not unusual. Luminux is our anti-anxiety and mood-control drug of choice here at the Center. It was just approved by the FDA. We were very glad to learn that, yes? Cardiac patients can take it without fear of aggravating their heart problems."

"Who makes it?"

He pulled a thick book off his shelf and

read through it. "Montrose Pharmaceuticals in Paramus, New Jersey."

Tal wrote this down. "Doctor," he asked, "did you have another patient here . . . Don Benson?"

"I'm not knowing the name but I know very little of the patients here, as I was saying to you, yes?" He nodded out the window through which they could hear the sound of construction—the new CSC facility that was taking all his time, Tal assumed. Dehoeven typed on the computer keyboard. "No, we are not having any patients named Benson."

"In the past?"

"This is for the year, going back." A nod at the screen. "Why is it you are asking?"

Tal tapped the questionnaire. "Statistics." He put the paper away, rose and shook the doctor's hand. He was directed to the nurse's office, four doors up the hall from Dehoeven's.

Claire McCaffrey was about his age, with wavy brunette hair pulled back in a ponytail. She had a freckled, pretty face—girl next door—but seemed haggard.

"You're the one Dr. Dehoeven called about? Officer—?"

"Simms. But call me Tal."

"I go by Mac," she said. She extended her hand and a charm bracelet jangled on her right wrist as he gripped her strong fingers. He noticed a small gold ring in the shape of an ancient coin on her right hand. There was no jewelry at all on her left, he observed. "Mac," he reflected. A Celtic theme today, recalling Margaret, Dr. Sheldon's somber step-dancer.

She motioned him to sit. Her office was spacious—a desk and a sitting area with a couch and two armchairs around a coffee table. It seemed more lived-in than her boss's, he noted, comfortable. The decor was soothing—crystals, glass globes, and reproductions of Native American artifacts, plants and fresh flowers, posters and paintings of seashores and deserts and forests.

"This is about Sam Whitley, right?" she asked in a troubled monotone.

"That's right. And his wife."

She nodded, distraught. "I was up all night about it. Oh, it's so sad. I couldn't believe it." Her voice faded.

"I just have a few questions. I hope you don't mind."

"No, go ahead."

"Did you see them the day they died?" Tal asked.

"Yes, I did. We had our regular appointment."

"What exactly did you do for them?"

"What we do with most patients. Making sure they're on a heart-friendly diet, helping with insurance forms, making sure their medication's working, arranging for help in doing heavy work around the house. . . . Is there some problem? I mean, official problem?"

Looking into her troubled eyes, he chose not to use the excuse of the questionnaire as a front. "It was unusual, their deaths. They didn't fit the standard profile of most suicides. Did they say anything that'd suggest they were thinking about killing themselves?"

"No, of course not," she said quickly. "I would've intervened. Naturally."

"But?" He sensed there was something more she wanted to say.

She looked down, organized some papers, closed a folder.

"It's just . . . See, there was one thing. I spent the last couple of days going over what they said to me, looking for clues. And I remember they said how much they'd enjoyed working with me."

"That was odd?"

"It was the way they put it. It was the past tense, you know. Not *enjoy* working with me. It was *enjoyed* working with me. It didn't strike me as odd or anything at the time. But now we know . . ." A sigh. "I should've listened to what they were saying."

Recrimination. Like the couples' lawyers, like the doctors, Nurse McCaffrey would probably live with these deaths for a long, long time.

Perhaps forever . . .

"Did you know," he asked, "they just bought a book about suicide? *Making the Final Journey.*"

"No, I didn't know that," she said, frowning.

Behind her desk Nurse McCaffrey—Mac—had a picture of an older couple with their arms around each other, two snapshots of big, goofy black labs, and one picture of her with the dogs. No snaps of boyfriends or husbands—or girlfriends. In Westbrook County, married or cohabitating couples comprised 74 percent of the adult population, widows 7 percent, widowers 2 percent and unmarried/divorced/noncohabitating were 17 percent. Of that latter category only 4 percent were between the ages of twenty-eight and thirty-five.

He and Mac had at least one thing in common; they were both members of the Four Percent Club.

She glanced at her watch and he focused on her again. "They were taking Luminux, right?"

She nodded. "It's a good anti-anxiety

drug. We make sure the patients have it available and take it if they have a panic attack or're depressed."

"Both Sam and his wife had an unusually large amount in their bloodstreams when they died."

"Really?"

"We're trying to find what happened to the prescription, the bottle. We couldn't find it at their house."

"They had it the other day, I know."

"Are you sure?"

"Pretty sure. I don't know how much they had left on the prescription. Maybe it was gone and they threw the bottle out."

Raw data, Tal thought. Wondering what to make of these facts. Was he asking the right questions? Greg LaTour would know.

But LaTour was not here. The mathematician was on his own. He asked, "Did the Whitleys ever mention Don and Sy Benson?"

"Benson?"

"In Greeley."

"Well, no. I've never heard of them."

Tal asked, "Had anybody else been to the house that day?"

"I don't know. We were alone when I was there."

"Did you happen to call them from a pay phone that afternoon?"

"No."

"Did they mention they were expecting anyone else?"

She shook her head.

"And you left when?"

"At four. A little before."

"You sure of the time?"

"Yep. I know because I was listening to my favorite radio program in the car on my way home. The Opera Hour on NPR." A sad laugh. "It was highlights from *Madame Butterfly.*"

"Isn't that about the Japanese woman who . . ." His voice faded.

"Kills herself." Mac looked up at a poster of the Grand Tetons, then one of the surf in Hawaii. "My whole life's been devoted to prolonging people's lives. This just shattered me, hearing about Sam and Liz." She seemed close to tears then controlled herself. "I was talking to Dr. Dehoeven. He just came over here from Holland. They look at death differently over there. Euthanasia and suicide are a lot more acceptable. . . . He heard about their deaths and kind of shrugged. Like it wasn't any big deal. But I can't get them out of my mind."

Silence for a moment. Then she blinked and looked at her watch again. "I've got a

new patient to meet. But if there's anything
I can do to help, let me know." She rose,
then paused. "Are you . . . what *are* you exactly? A homicide detective?"

He laughed. "Actually, I'm a mathematician."

"A—"

But before he could explain his curious
pedigree his pager went off, a sound Tal was
so unaccustomed to that he dropped his
briefcase then knocked several files off the
nurse's desk as he bent to retrieve it. Thinking: Good job, Simms, way to impress a fellow member of the Westbrook County Four
Percent Club.

∞

"He's in there and I couldn't get him out.
I'm spitting nails, Boss."

In a flash of panic Tal thought that
Shellee, fuming as she pointed at his office,
was referring to the sheriff himself, who'd
descended from the top floor of the county
building to fire Tal personally for the 2124.

But, no, she was referring to someone else.

Tal stepped inside and lifted an eyebrow
to Greg LaTour. "Thought we had an appointment yester—"

"So where you been?" LaTour grumbled.

"Sleepin' in?" The huge man was finishing Tal's cheese sandwich from yesterday, sending a cascade of bread crumbs everywhere.

And resting his boots on Tal's desk.

It had been LaTour's page that caught him with Mac McCaffrey. The message: "Office twenty minutes. LaTour."

The slim cop looked unhappily at the scuff marks on the desktop.

LaTour noticed but ignored him. "Here's the thing. I got the information on the wills. And, yeah, they were both changed—"

"Okay, that's suspicious—"

"Lemme finish. No, it's *not* suspicious. The beneficiaries weren't any crazy housekeepers or Moonie guru assholes controlling their minds. The Bensons didn't have any kids so all they did was add a few charities and create a trust for some nieces and nephews—for college. A hundred thousand each. Small potatoes. The Whitley girl didn't get diddly-squat from them.

"Now, the Whitleys gave their daughter—bitch or not—a third of the estate in the first version of the will. She still gets the same for herself in the new version but she also gets a little more so she can set up a Whitley family library." LaTour looked up. "Now *there's* gonna be a fucking fun place to spend Sunday afternoons. . . . Then they added some new chartites too and got rid of some other ones. . . . Oh, and if you were going to ask, they were *different* charities from the ones in the Bensons' will."

"I wasn't."

"Well, you should have. Always look for connections, Tal. That's the key in homicide. Connections between facts."

"Just like—"

"—don't say fucking statistics."

"Mathematics. Common denominators."

"Whatever," LaTour muttered. "So, the wills're out as motives. Same with—"

"The insurance polices."

"I was going to say. Small policies and most of the Bensons' goes to paying off a few small debts and giving some bucks to retired employees of the husband's companies. It's like twenty, thirty grand. Nothing suspicious there . . . Now, what'd you find?"

Tal explained about Dr. Sheldon, the cardiologist, then about Dehoeven, Mac, and the Cardiac Support Center.

LaTour asked immediately, "Both Benson and Whitley, patients of Sheldon?"

"No, only Whitley. Same for the Cardiac Support Center."

"Fuck. We . . . what'sa matter?"

"You want to get your boots off my desk."

Irritated, LaTour swung his feet around

to the floor. "We need a connection, I was saying. Something—"

"I might have one," Tal said quickly. "Drugs."

"What, the old folks were dealing?" The sarcasm had returned. He added, "You still harping on that Lumicrap?"

"Lum*inux*. Makes you drowsy *and* happy. Could mess up your judgment. Make you susceptible to suggestions."

"That you blow your fucking brains out? One hell of a suggestion."

"Maybe not—if you were taking three times the normal dosage . . ."

"You think somebody slipped it to 'em?"

"Maybe." Tal nodded. "The counselor from the Cardiac Support unit left the Whitleys' at four. They died around eight. Plenty of time for somebody to stop by, put some stuff in their drinks. Whoever called them from that pay phone."

"Okay, the Whitleys were taking it. What about the Bensons?"

"They were cremated the day after they died, remember? We'll never know."

LaTour finished the sandwich. "You don't mind, do you? It was just sitting there."

He glanced at the desktop. "You got crumbs everywhere."

The cop leaned forward and blew them to the floor. He sipped coffee from a mug that'd left a sticky ring on an evidence report file. "Okay, your—what the fuck do you call it? Theory?"

"Theorem."

"Is that somebody slipped 'em that shit? But who? And why?"

"I don't know that part yet."

"Those *parts*," LaTour corrected. "Who and why. Parts plural."

Tal sighed.

"You think you could really give somebody a drug and tell 'em to kill themselves and they will?"

"Let's go find out," Tal said.

"Huh?"

The statistician flipped through his notes. "The company that makes the drug? It's over in Paramus. Off the Parkway. Let's go talk to 'em."

"Shit. All the way to Jersey."

"You have a better idea?"

"I don't need any fucking ideas. This's your case, remember?"

"Maybe *I* twenty-one-twenty-foured it. But it's *everybody's* case now. Let's go."

∞

She would've looked pretty good in a short skirt, Robert Covey thought, but unfortunately she was wearing slacks.

"Mr. Covey, I'm from the Cardiac Support Center."

"Call me Bob. Or you'll make me feel as old as your older brother."

She was a little short for his taste but then he had to remind himself that she was here to help him get some pig parts stuck into his chest and rebuild a bunch of leaking veins and arteries—or else die with as little mess as he could. Besides, he claimed that he had a rule he'd never date a woman a third his age. (When the truth was that after Veronica maybe he joked and maybe he flirted but in his heart he was content never to date at all.)

He held the door for her and gestured her inside with a slight bow. He could see her defenses lower a bit. She was probably used to dealing with all sorts of pricks in this line of work and was wary during their initial meeting, but Covey limited his grousing to surly repairmen and clerks and waitresses who thought because he was old he was stupid.

There was, he felt, no need for impending death to skew his manners. He invited her in and directed her to the couch in his den.

"Welcome, Ms. McCaffrey—"

"How 'bout Mac? That's what my mother used to call me when I was good."

"What'd she call you when you were bad?"

"Mac then too. Though she managed to get two syllables out of it. So, go ahead."

He lifted an eyebrow. "With what?"

"With what you were going to tell me. That you don't need me here. That you don't need any help, that you're only seeing me to humor your cardiologist, that you don't want any hand-holding, that you don't want to be coddled, that you don't want to change your diet, you don't want to exercise, you don't want to give up smoking and you don't want to stop drinking your—" She glanced at the bar and eyed the bottles. "—your port. So here're the ground rules. Fair enough, no hand-holding, no coddling. That's my part of the deal. But, yes, you'll give up smoking—"

"Did before you were born, thank you very much."

"Good. And you will be exercising and eating a cardio-friendly diet. And about the port—"

"Hold on—"

"I think we'll limit you to three a night."

"Four," he said quickly.

"Three. And I suspect on most nights you only have two."

"I can live with three," he grumbled. She'd been right about the two (though, okay, sometimes a little bourbon joined the party).

Damn, he liked her. He always had liked strong women. Like Veronica.

Then she was on to other topics. Practical things about what the Cardiac Support Center did and what it didn't do, about care givers, about home care, about insurance.

"Now, I understand you're a widower. How long were you married?"

"Forty-nine years."

"Well, now, that's wonderful."

"Ver and I had a very nice life together. Pissed me off we missed the fiftieth. I had a party planned. Complete with a harpist and open bar." He raised an eyebrow. "Vintage port included."

"And you have a son?"

"That's right. Randall. He lives in California. Runs a computer company. But one that actually makes money. Imagine that! Wears his hair too long and lives with a woman—he oughta get married—but he's a good boy."

"You see him much?"

"All the time."

"When did you talk to him last?"

"The other day."

"And you've told him all about your condition?"

"You bet."

"Good. Is he going to get out here?"

"In a week or so. He's traveling. Got a big deal he's putting together."

She was taking something out of her purse. "Our doctor at the clinic prescribed this." She handed him a bottle. "Luminux. It's an anti-anxiety agent."

"I say no to drugs."

"This's a new generation. You're going through a lot of stuff right now. It'll make you feel better. Virtually no side effects—"

"You mean it won't take me back to my days as a beatnik in the Village?" She laughed and he added, "Actually, think I'll pass."

"It's good for you." She shook out two pills into a small cup and handed them to him. She walked to the bar and poured a glass of water.

Watching her, acting like she lived here, Covey scoffed, "You ever negotiate?"

"Not when I know I'm right."

"Tough lady." He glanced down at the pills in his hand. "I take these, that means I can't have my port, right?"

"Sure you can. You know, moderation's the key to everything."

"You don't seem like a moderate woman."

"Oh, hell no, I'm not. But I don't practice what I preach." And she passed him the glass of water.

∞

Late afternoon, driving to Jersey.

Tal fiddled with the radio trying to find the Opera Hour program that Nurse Mac had mentioned.

LaTour looked at the dash as if he was surprised the car even had a radio.

Moving up and down the dial, through the several National Public Radio bands, he couldn't find the show. What time had she'd said it came on? He couldn't remember. He wondered why he cared what she listened to. He didn't even like opera that much. He gave up and settled on all news, all the time. LaTour stood that for five minutes then put the game on.

The homicide cop was either preoccupied or just a natural-born bad driver. Weaving, speeding well over the limit, then braking to a crawl. Occasionally he'd lift his middle finger to other drivers in a way that was almost endearing.

Probably happier on a motorcycle, Tal reflected.

LaTour tuned in the game on the radio. They listened for a while, neither speaking.

"So," Tal tried. "Where you live?"

"Near the station house."

Nothing more.

"Been on the force long?"

"A while."

New York seven, Boston three. . . .

"You married?" Tal had noticed that he wore no wedding band.

More silence.

Tal turned down the volume and repeated the question.

After a long moment LaTour grumbled, "That's something else."

"Oh." Having no idea what the cop meant.

He supposed there was a story here—a hard divorce, lost children.

And six point three percent kill themselves before retirement . . .

But whatever the sad story might be, it was only for Bear's friends in the Department, those on the Real Crimes side of the pen.

Not for Einstein, the calculator humper.

They fell silent and drove on amid the white noise of the sportscasters.

Ten minutes later LaTour skidded off the parkway and turned down a winding side road.

Montrose Pharmaceuticals was a small series of glass and chrome buildings in a land-
scaped industrial park. Far smaller than
Pfizer and the other major drug companies
in the Garden State, it nonetheless must've
done pretty well in sales—to judge from the
number of Mercedes, Jaguars, and Porsches
in the employee parking lot.

Inside the elegant reception area, Westbrook County Sheriff's Department badges
raised some eyebrows. But, Tal concluded, it
was LaTour's bulk and hostile gaze that cut
through whatever barriers existed here to
gaining access to the inner sanctum of the
company's president.

In five minutes they were sitting in the office of Daniel Montrose, an earnest, balding
man in his late forties. His eyes were as
quick as his appearance was rumpled and
Tal concluded that he was a kindred soul; a
scientist, rather than a salesperson. The
man rocked back and forth in his chair,
peering at them through stylish glasses with
a certain distraction. Uneasiness too.

Nobody said anything for a moment and
Tal felt the tension in the office rise appre-
ciably. He glanced at LaTour, who simply sat
in the leather-and-chrome chair, looking
around the opulent space. Maybe stone-

walling was a technique that real cops used to get people to start talking.

"We've been getting ready for our sales conference," Montrose suddenly volunteered. "It's going to be a good one."

"Is it?" Tal asked.

"That's right. Our biggest. Las Vegas this year." Then he clammed up again.

Tal wanted to echo, "Vegas?" for some reason. But he didn't.

Finally LaTour said, "Tell us about Luminux."

"Luminux. Right, Luminux . . . I'd really like to know, I mean, if it's not against any rules or anything, what you want to know for. I mean, and what are you doing here? You haven't really said."

"We're investigating some suicides."

"Suicides?" he asked, frowning. "And Luminux is involved?"

"Yes indeedy," LaTour said with all the cheer that the word required.

"But . . . it's based on a mild diazepam derivative. It'd be very difficult to fatally overdose on it."

"No, they died from other causes. But we found—"

The door swung open and a strikingly beautiful woman walked into the office. She blinked at the visitors and said a very unsor-rowful, "Sorry. Thought you were alone." She set a stack of folders on Montrose's desk.

"These are some police officers from Westbrook County," the president told her.

She looked at them more carefully. "Po-lice. Is something wrong?"

Tal put her at forty. Long, serpentine face with cool eyes, very beautiful in a European fashion-model way. Slim legs with runner's calves. Tal decided that she was like Shel-don's Gaelic assistant, an example of some predatory genus very different from Mac McCaffrey's.

Neither Tal nor LaTour answered her question. Montrose introduced her—Karen Billings. Her title was a mouthful but it had something to do with product support and patient relations.

"They were just asking about Luminux. There've been some problems, they're claiming."

"Problems?"

"They were just saying . . ." Montrose pushed his glasses higher on his nose. "Well, what *were* you saying?"

Tal continued, "A couple of people who killed themselves had three times the nor-mal amount of Luminux in their systems."

"But that can't kill them. It couldn't have.

I don't see why . . ." Her voice faded and she looked toward Montrose. They eyed each other, poker-faced. She then said coolly to LaTour, "What exactly would you like to know?"

"First of all, how could they get it into their bloodstream?" LaTour sat back, the chair creaking alarmingly. Tal wondered if he'd put his feet up on Montrose's desk.

"You mean how could it be administered?"

"Yeah."

"Orally's the only way. It's not available in an IV form yet."

"But could it be mixed in food or a drink?"

"You think somebody did that?" Montrose asked. Billings remained silent, looking from Tal to LaTour and back again with her cautious, swept-wing eyes.

"Could it be done?" Tal asked.

"Of course," the president said. "Sure. It's water soluble. The vehicle's bitter—"

"The—?"

"The inert base we mix it with. The drug itself is tasteless but we add a compound to make it bitter so kids'll spit it out if they eat it by mistake. But you can mask that with sugar or—"

"Alcohol?"

Billings snapped, "Drinking isn't recommended when taking—"

LaTour grumbled, "I'm not talking about the fucking fine print on the label. I'm talking about could you hide the flavor by mixing it in a drink?"

She hesitated. Then finally answered, "One could." She clicked her nails together in impatience or anger.

"So what's it do to you?"

Montrose said, "It's essentially an anti-anxiety and mood-elevating agent, not a sleeping pill. It makes you relaxed. You get happier."

"Does it mess with your thinking?"

"There's some cognitive dimunition."

"English?" LaTour grumbled.

"They'd feel slightly disoriented—but in a happy way."

Tal recalled the misspellings in the note. "Would it affect their handwriting and spelling?"

Dangrous . . .

"It could, yes."

Tal said. "Would their judgment be affected?"

"Judgment?" Billings asked harshly. "That's subjective."

"Whatta you mean?"

"There's no quantifiable measure for one's ability to judge something."

"No? How 'bout if *one* puts a gun to *one*'s

head and pulls the trigger?" LaTour said. "I call that *bad* judgment. Any chance we agree on that?"

"What the fuck're you getting at?" Billings snapped.

"Karen," Montrose said, pulling off his designer glasses and rubbing his eyes.

She ignored her boss. "You think they took our drug and decided to kill themselves? You think we're to blame for that? This drug—"

"This drug that a couple of people popped—maybe *four* people—and then killed themselves. Whatta we say about that from a statistical point of view?" LaTour turned to Tal.

"Well within the percentile of probability for establishing a causal relationship between the two events."

"There you go. Science has spoken."

Tal wondered if they were playing the good-cop/bad-cop routine you see in movies. He tried again. "Could an overdose of Luminux have impaired their judgment?"

"Not enough so that they'd decide to kill themselves," she said firmly. Montrose said nothing.

"That your opinion too?" LaTour muttered to him.

The president said, "Yes, it is."

Tal persisted, "How about making them susceptible?"

Billings leapt in with, "I don't know what you mean. . . . This is all crazy."

Tal ignored her and said levelly to Montrose, "Could somebody persuade a person taking an overdose of Luminux to kill themselves?"

Silence filled the office.

Billings said, "I strongly doubt it."

"But you ain't saying no." LaTour grumbled.

A glance between Billings and Montrose. Finally he pulled his wire-rims back on, looked away and said, "We're not saying no."

∞

They next morning Tal and LaTour arrived at the station house at the same time, and the odd couple walked together through the Detective Division pen into Tal's office.

They looked over the case so far and found no firm leads.

"Still no who," LaTour grumbled. "Still no why."

"But we've got a how," Tal pointed out. Meaning the concession about Luminux making one suggestible.

"Fuck *how*. I want *who*."

At just that moment they received a possible answer.

Shellee stepped into Tal's office. Pointedly ignoring the homicide cop, she said, "You're back. Good. Got a call from the P-I-I team in Greeley. They said a neighbor saw a woman in a small, dark car arrive at the Bensons' house about an hour before they died. She was wearing sunglasses and a tan or beige baseball cap. The neighbor didn't recognize her."

"Car?" LaTour snapped.

It's hard to ignore an armed, 250-pound, goateed man named Bear but Shellee was just the woman for the job.

Continuing to speak to her boss, she said, "They weren't sure what time she got there but it was before lunch. She stayed maybe forty minutes then left. That'd be an hour or so before they killed themselves." A pause. "The car was a small sedan. The witness didn't remember the color."

"Did you ask about the—" LaTour began.

"They didn't see the tag number," she told Tal. "Now, that's not all. DMV finally calls back and tells me that Sandra Whitley drives a blue BMW 325."

"Small wheelbase," Tal said.

"And, getting better 'n' better, Boss.

Guess who's leaving town before her parents' memorial service."

"Sandra?"

"How the hell d'you find that out?" La-Tour asked.

She turned coldly to him. "Detective Simms asked to me organize all the evidence from the Whitley crime scene. Because, like he says, having facts and files out of order is as bad as not having them at all. I found a note in the Whitley evidence file with an airline locator number. It was for a flight from Newark today to San Francisco, continuing on to Hawaii. I called and they told me it was a confirmed ticket for Sandra Whitley. Return is open."

"Meaning the bitch might not be coming back at all," LaTour said. "Going on vacation without saying goodbye to the folks? That's fucking harsh."

"Good job," Tal told Shellee.

Eyes down, a faint smile of acknowledgment.

LaTour dropped into one of Tal's chairs, belched softly and said, "You're doing such a good job, Sherry, here, look up whatever you can about this shit." He offered her the notes on Luminux.

"It's Shellee," she snapped and glanced at Tal, who mouthed, "Please."

She snatched them from LaTour's hand and clattered down the hall on her dangerous heels.

LaTour looked over the handwritten notes she'd given them and growled, "So what about the why? A motive?"

Tal spread the files out of his desk—all the crime scene information, the photos, the notes he'd taken.

What were the common denominators? The deaths of two couples. Extremely wealthy. The husbands ill, yes, but not hopelessly so. Drugs that make you suggestible.

A giddy lunch then suicide, a drink beside a romantic fire then suicide . . .

Romantic . . .

"Hmm," Tal mused, thinking back to the Whitleys'.

"What hmm?"

"Let's think about the wills again."

"We tried that," LaTour said.

"But what if they were *about* to be changed?"

"Whatta you mean?"

"Try this for an assumption: Say the Whitleys and their daughter had some big fight in the past week. They were going to change their will again—this time to cut her out completely."

"Yeah, but their lawyer'd know that."

"Not if she killed them before they talked to him. I remember smelling smoke from the fire when I walked into the Whitley house. I thought they'd built this romantic fire just before they killed themselves. But maybe they hadn't. Maybe Sandra burned some evidence—something about changing the will, memos to the lawyer, estate planning stuff. Remember, she snatched the mail at the house. One was to the lawyer. Maybe that was why she came back—to make sure there was no evidence left. Hell, wished I'd searched her purse. I just didn't think about it."

"Yeah, but offing her own *parents?*" La-Tour asked skeptically.

"Seventeen point two percent of murderers are related to their victims." Tal added pointedly, "I know that because of my questionnaires, by the way."

LaTour rolled his eyes. "What about the Bensons?"

"Maybe they met in some cardiac support group, maybe they were in the same country club. Whitley might've mentioned something about the will to them. Sandra found out and had to take them out too."

"Jesus, you say 'maybe' a lot."

"It's a theorem, I keep saying. Let's go prove it or disprove it. See if she's got an alibi. And we'll have forensics go through the fireplace."

"If the ash is intact," LaTour said, "they can image the printing on the sheet. Those techs're fucking geniuses."

Tal called Crime Scene again and arranged to have a team return to the Whitleys' house. Then he said, "Okay, let's go visit our suspect."

∞

"Hold on there."

When Greg LaTour charged up to you, muttering the way he'd just done, you held on there.

Even tough Sandra Whitley.

She'd been about to climb into the BMW sitting outside her luxurious house. Suitcases sat next to her.

"Step away from the car," LaTour said, flashing his badge.

Tal said, "We'd like to ask you a few questions, ma'am."

"You again! What the hell're you talking about?" Her voice was angry but she did as she was told.

"You're on your way out of town?" LaTour took her purse off her shoulder. "Just keep your hands at your sides."

"I've got a meeting I can't miss."

"In Hawaii?"

Sandra was regaining the initiative. "I'm an attorney, like I told you. I *will* find out how you got that information and for your sake there better've been a warrant involved."

Did they *need* a warrant? Tal wondered.

"Meeting in Hawaii?" LaTour repeated. "With an open return?"

"What're you implying?"

"It's a little odd, don't you think. Flying off to the South Seas a few days after your parents die? Not going to the funeral?"

"Funerals're for the survivors. I've made peace with my parents and their deaths. They wouldn't've wanted me to blow off an important meeting. Dad was as much a businessman as a father. I'm as much a businesswoman as a daughter."

Her eyes slipped to Tal and she gave a sour laugh. "Okay, you got me, Simms." Emphasizing the name was presumably to remind him again that his name would be prominently included in the court documents she filed. She nodded to the purse. "It's all in there. The evidence about me escaping the country after—what?—stealing my parents' money? What *exactly* do you think I've done?"

"We're not accusing you of anything. We just want to—"

"—ask you a few questions."

"So ask, goddamn it."

LaTour was reading a lengthy document he'd found in her purse. He frowned and handed it to Tal, then asked her, "Can you tell me where you were the night your parents died?"

"Why?"

"Look, lady, you can cooperate or you can clam up and we'll—"

"Go downtown. Yadda, yadda, yadda. I've heard this before."

LaTour frowned at Tal and mouthed, "What's downtown?" Tal shrugged and returned to the document. It was a business plan for a company that was setting up an energy joint venture in Hawaii. Her law firm was representing it. The preliminary meeting seemed to be scheduled for two days from now in Hawaii. There was a memo saying that the meetings could go on for weeks and recommended that the participants get open-return tickets.

Oh.

"Since I have to get to the airport now," she snapped, "and I don't have time for any bullshit, okay, I'll tell you where I was on the night of the quote crime. On an airplane. I flew back on United Airlines from San Francisco, the flight that got in about 11 P.M. My boarding pass is probably in there—" A contemptuous nod at the purse LaTour held. "And if it isn't, I'm sure there's a record of the flight at the airline. With security being what it is nowadays, picture IDs and everything, that's probably a pretty solid alibi, don't you think?"

Did seem to be, Tal agreed silently. And it got even more solid when LaTour found the boarding pass and ticket receipt in her purse.

Tal's phone began ringing and he was happy for the chance to escape from Sandra's searing fury. He heard Shellee speak from the receiver. "Hey, Boss, 's'me."

"What's up?"

"Crime Scene called. They went through all the ash in the Whitleys' fireplace, looking for a letter or something about changing the will. They didn't find anything about that at all. Something had been burned but it was all just a bunch of information on companies—computer and biotech companies. The Crime Scene guy was thinking Mr. Whitley might've just used some old junk mail or something to start the fire."

Once again: Oh.

Then: Damn.

"Thanks."

He nodded LaTour aside and told him what Crime Scene had reported.

"Shit on the street," he whispered. "Jumped a little fast here . . . Okay, let's go kiss some ass. Brother."

The groveling time was quite limited—. Sandra was adamant about catching her plane. She sped out of the driveway, leaving behind a blue cloud of tire smoke.

"Aw, she'll forget about it," LaTour said.

"You think?" Tal asked.

A pause. "Nope. We're way fucked." He added, "We still gotta find the mysterious babe in the sunglasses and hat." They climbed into the car and LaTour pulled into traffic.

Tal wondered if Mac McCaffrey might've seen someone like that around the Whitleys' place. Besides, it'd be a good excuse to see her again. Tal said, "I'll look into that one."

"You?" LaTour laughed.

"Yeah. Me. What's so funny about that?"

"I don't know. Just you never investigated a case before."

"So? You think I can't interview witnesses on my own? You think I should just go back home and hump my calculator?"

Silence. Tal hadn't meant to say it.

"You heard that?" LaTour finally asked, no longer laughing.

"I heard."

"Hey, I didn't mean it, you know."

"Didn't mean it?" Tal asked, giving an exaggerated squint. "As in you didn't mean for me to hear you? Or as in you don't actually believe I have sex with adding machines?"

"I'm sorry, okay? . . . I bust people's chops sometimes. It's the way I am. I do it to everybody. Fuck, people do it to me. They call me Bear 'causa my gut. They call you Einstein 'cause you're smart."

"Not to my face."

LaTour hesitated. "You're right. Not to your face. . . . You know, you're too polite, Tal. You can give me a lot more shit. I wouldn't mind. You're too uptight. Loosen up."

"So it's *my* fault that I'm pissed 'cause you dump on me?"

"It was . . ." He began defensively but then he stopped. "Okay, I'm sorry. I am. . . . Hey, I don't apologize a lot, you know. I'm not very good at it."

"That's an apology?"

"I'm doing the best I can . . . Whatta you want?"

Silence.

"All right," Tal said finally.

LaTour sped the car around a corner and wove frighteningly through the heavy traffic. Finally he said, "It's okay, though, you know."

"What's okay?"

"If you want to."

"Want to what?" Tal asked.

"You know, you and your calculator. . . . Lot safer than some of the weird shit you see nowadays."

"LaTour," Tal said, "you can—"

"You just seemed defensive about it, you know. Figure I probably hit close to home, you know what I'm saying?"

"You can go fuck yourself."

The huge cop was laughing hard. "Shit, don'tcha feel like we're finally breaking the ice here? I think we are. Now, I'll drop you off back at your car, Einstein, and you can go on this secret mission all by your lonesome."

∞

His stated purpose was to ask her if she'd ever seen the mysterious woman in the baseball cap and sunglasses, driving a small car, at the Whitleys' house.

Lame, Tal thought.

Lame *and* transparent—since he could've asked her that on the phone. He was sure the true mission here was so obvious that it was laughable: To get a feel for what would happen if he asked Mac McCaffrey out to dinner. Not to actually *invite* her out at this point, of course; she was, after all, a potential witness. No, he just wanted to test the waters.

Tal parked along Elm Street and climbed out of the car, enjoying the complicated smells of the April air, the skin-temperature breeze, the golden snowflakes of fallen forsythia petals covering the lawn.

Walking toward the park where he'd arranged to meet her, Tal reflected on his recent romantic life.

Fine, he concluded. It was fine.

He dated 2.66 women a month. The median age of his dates in the past 12 months was approximately 31 (a number skewed somewhat by the embarrassing—but highly memorable—outlier of a Columbia University senior). And the mean IQ of the women was around 140 or up—and that latter statistic was a very sharp bell curve with a very narrow standard deviation; Talbot Simms went for intellect before anything else.

It was this latter criteria, though, he'd come to believe lately, that led to the tepid adjective "fine."

Yes, he'd had many interesting evenings with his 2⅔ dates every month. He'd discussed with them Cartesian hyperbolic doubt. He'd argue about the validity of ana-

lyzing objects in terms of their primary qualities. ("No way! *I'm* suspicious of secondary
qualities too. . . . I mean, how 'bout that?
We have a lot in common!") They'd draft
mathematical formulae in crayon on the paper table coverings at the Crab House.
They'd discuss Fermat's Last Theorem until
2:00 or 3:00 A.M. (These were not wholly academic encounters, of course; Tal Simms
happened to have a full-size chalkboard in
his bedroom).

He was intellectually stimulated by most
of these women. He even learned things
from them.

But he didn't really have a lot of fun.

Mac McCaffrey, he believed, would be fun.

She'd sounded surprised when he'd
called. Cautious too at first. But after a
minute or two she'd relaxed and had
seemed almost pleased at the idea that he
wanted to meet with her.

He now spotted her in the park next to
the Knickerbocker Home, which appeared
to be a nursing facility, where she suggested
they get together.

"Hey," he said.

"Hi there. Hope you don't mind meeting
outside. I hate to be cooped up."

He recalled the Sierra Club posters in her
office. "No, it's beautiful here."

Her sharp green eyes, set in her freckled face, looked away and took in the sights of the park. Tal sat down and they made small talk for five minutes or so. Finally she asked, "You started to tell me that you're, what, a mathematician?"

"That's right."

She smiled. There was crookedness to her mouth, an asymmetry, which he found charming. "That's pretty cool. You could be on a TV series. Like *CSI* or *Law and Order*, you know. Call it *Math Cop*."

They laughed. He glanced down at her shoes, old black Reeboks, and saw they were nearly worn out. He noticed too a bare spot on the knee of her jeans. It'd been rewoven. He thought of cardiologist Anthony Sheldon's designer wardrobe and huge office, and reflected that Mac worked in an entirely different part of the health care universe.

"So I was wondering," she asked. "Why this interest in the Whitleys' deaths?"

"Like I said. They were out of the ordinary."

"I guess I mean, why are *you* interested? Did you lose somebody? To suicide, I mean."

"Oh, no. My father's alive. My mother passed away a while ago. A stroke."

"I'm sorry. She must've been young."

"Was, yes."

She waved a bee away. "Is your dad in the area?"

"Nope. Professor in Chicago."

"Math?"

"Naturally. Runs in the family." He told her about Wall Street, the financial crimes, statistics.

"All that adding and subtracting. Doesn't it get, I don't know, boring?"

"Oh, no, just the opposite. Numbers go on forever. Infinite questions, challenges. And remember, math is a lot more than just calculations. What excites me is that numbers let us understand the world. And when you understand something you have control over it."

"Control?" she asked, serious suddenly. "Numbers won't keep you from getting hurt. From dying."

"Sure they can," he replied. "Numbers make car brakes work and keep airplanes in the air and let you call the fire department. Medicine, science."

"I guess so. Never thought about it." Another crooked smile. "You're pretty enthusiastic about the subject."

Tal asked, "Pascal?"

"Heard of him."

"A philosopher. He was a prodigy at math but he gave it up completely. He said math was so enjoyable it had to be related to sex. It was sinful."

"Hold on, mister," she said, laughing. "You got some math porn you want to show me?"

Tal decided that the preliminary groundwork for the date was going pretty well. But, apropos of which, enough about himself. He asked, "How'd you get into your field?"

"I always liked taking care of people . . . or animals," she explained. "Somebody's pet'd get hurt, I'd be the one to try to help it. I hate seeing anybody in pain. I was going to go to med school but my mom got sick and, without a father around, I had to put that on hold—where it's been for. . . . well, for a few years."

No explanation about the missing father. But he sensed that, like him, she didn't want to discuss dad. A common denominator among these particular members of the Four Percent Club.

She continued, looking at the nursing home door. "Why I'm doing *this* particularly? My mother, I guess. Her exit was pretty tough. Nobody really helped her. Except me, and I didn't know very much. The hospital she was in didn't give her any support. So after she passed I decided I'd go into the field myself. Make sure patients have a comfortable time at the end."

"It doesn't get you down?"

"Some times are tougher than others. But I'm lucky. I'm not all that religious but I do think there's something there after we die."

Tal nodded but he said nothing. He'd always wanted to believe in that *something* too but religion wasn't allowed in the Simms household—nothing, that is, except the cold deity of numbers his father worshiped—and it seemed to Tal that if you don't get hooked early by some kind of spiritualism, you'll rarely get the bug later. Still, people do change. He recalled that the Bensons had been atheists but apparently toward the end had come to believe differently.

Together forever . . .

Mac was continuing, speaking of her job at the Cardiac Support Center. "I like working with the patients. And I'm good, if I do say so myself. I stay away from the sentiment, the maudlin crap. I knock back some scotch or wine with them. Watch movies, pig out on low-fat chips and popcorn, tell some good death and dying jokes."

"No," Tal said, frowning. "Jokes?"

"You bet. Here's one: When I die, I want to go peacefully in my sleep, like my grandfather. . . . Not screaming like the passengers in the car with him."

Tal blinked then laughed hard. She was

pleased he'd enjoyed it, he could tell. He said, "Hey, there's a statistician joke. Want to hear it?"

"Sure."

"Statistics show that a person gets robbed every four minutes. And, man, is he getting tired of it."

She smiled. "That really sucks."

"Best we can do," Tal said. Then after a moment he added, "But Dr. Dehoéven said that your support center isn't all death and dying. There's a lot of things you do to help before and after surgery."

"Oh, sure," she said. "Didn't mean to neglect that. Exercise, diet, care giving, getting the family involved, psychotherapy."

Silence for a moment, a silence that, he felt, was suddenly asking: what exactly was he doing here?

He said, "I have a question about the suicides. Some witnesses said they saw a woman in sunglasses and a beige baseball cap, driving a small car, at the Bensons' house just before they killed themselves. I was wondering if you ever saw anyone like that around their house."

A pause. "Me?" she asked, frowning. "I wasn't seeing the Bensons, remember?"

"No, I mean at the Whitleys."

"Oh." She thought for a moment. "Their daughter came by a couple of times."

"No, it wasn't her."

"They had a cleaning lady. But she drove a van. And I never saw her in a hat."

Her voice had grown weaker and Tal knew that her mood had changed quickly. Probably the subject of the Whitleys had done it—raised the issue of whether there was anything else she might've done to keep them from dying.

Silence surrounded them, as dense as the humid April air, redolent with the scent of lilac. He began to think that it was a bad idea to mix a personal matter with a professional one—especially when it involved patients who had just died. Conversation resumed but it was now different, superficial, and, as if by mutual decision, they both glanced at their watches, said goodbye, then rose and headed down the same sidewalk in different directions.

∞

Shellee appeared in the doorway of Tal's office, where the statistician and LaTour were parked. "Found something," she said in her Beantown accent.

"Yeah, whatsat?" LaTour asked, looking

over a pile of documents that she was handing her boss.

She leaned close to Tal and whispered,
"He just gonna move in here?"

Tal smiled and said to her, "Thanks, Detective."

An eye-roll was her response.

"Where'd you get all that?" LaTour asked,
pointing at the papers but glancing at her
chest.

"The Internet," Shellee snapped as she
left. "Where else?"

"She got all that information from there?"
the big cop asked, taking the stack and flipping through it.

Tal saw a chance for a bit of cop-cop jibe,
now that, yeah, the ice was broken, and he
nearly said to LaTour, you'd be surprised,
there's a lot more on line than wicked-
sluts.com that you browse through in the
wee hours. But then he recalled the silence
when he asked about the cop's family life.

That's something else . . .

And he decided a reference to lonely
nights at home was out of line. He kept the
joke to himself.

LaTour handed the sheets to Tal. "I'm not
gonna read all this crap. It's got fucking
numbers in it. Gimme the bottom line."

Tal skimmed the information, much of

which might have contained numbers but was still impossible for him to understand. It was mostly chemical jargon and medical formulae. But toward the end he found a summary. He frowned and read it again.

"Jesus."

"What?"

"We maybe have our perps."

"No shit."

The documents Shellee had found were from a consumer protection Web site devoted to medicine. They reported that the FDA was having doubts about Luminux because the drug trials showed that it had hallucinogenic properties. Several people in the trials had had psychotic episodes believed to have been caused by the drug. Others reported violent mood swings. Those with serious problems were a small minority of those in the trials, less than a tenth of one percent. But the reactions were so severe that the FDA was very doubtful about approving it.

But Shellee also found that the agency had approved Luminux a year ago, despite the dangers.

"Okay, got it," LaTour said. "How's this for a maybe, Einstein? Montrose slipped some money to somebody to get the drug approved and then kept an eye on the patients taking it, looking for anybody who had bad reactions."

The cops speculated that he'd have those patients killed—making it look like suicide—so that no problems with Luminux ever surfaced. LaTour wondered if this was a realistic motive—until Tal found a printout that revealed that Luminux was Montrose's only money-maker, to the tune of $78 million a year.

Their other postulate was that it had been Karen Billings—as patient relations director—who might have been the woman in the hat and sunglasses at the Bensons and who'd left the tire tracks and worn the gloves at the Whitleys. She'd spent time with them, given them overdoses, talked them into buying the suicide manual and helped them—what had Mac said? That was it: Helped them "exit."

"Some fucking patient relations," LaTour said. "That's harsh." Using his favorite adjective. "Let's go see 'em."

Ignoring—with difficulty—the clutter on his desk, Tal opened the top drawer of his desk and pulled out his pistol. He started to mount it to his belt but the holster clip slipped and the weapon dropped to the floor. He winced as it hit. Grimacing, Tal bent down and retrieved then hooked it on successfully.

As he glanced up he saw LaTour watching him with a faint smile on his face. "Do me a favor. It probably won't come to it but if it does, lemme do the shooting, okay?"

∞

Nurse McCaffrey would be arriving soon.

No, "Mac" was her preferred name, Robert Covey reminded himself.

He stood in front of his liquor cabinet and finally selected a nice vintage port, a 1977. He thought it would go well with the Saga blue cheese and shrimp he'd had laid out for her, and the water crackers and nonfat dip for himself. He'd driven to the Stop 'N' Shop that morning to pick up the groceries.

Covey arranged the food, bottle and glasses on a silver tray. Oh, napkins. Forgot the napkins. He found some under the counter and set them out on the tray, which he carried into the living room. Next to it were some old scrapbooks he'd unearthed from the basement. He wanted to show her pictures—snapshots of his brother, now long gone, and his nieces, and his wife, of course. He also had many pictures of his son.

Oh, Randall . . .

Yep, he liked Mac a lot. It was scary how in minutes she saw right into him, perfectly.

It was irritating. It was good.

But one thing she couldn't see through was the lie he'd told her.

"You see him much?"

"All the time."

"When did you talk to him last?"

"The other day."

"And you've told him all about your condition?"

"You bet."

Covey called his son regularly, left messages on his phone at work and at home. But Randy never returned the calls. Occasionally he'd pick up, but it was always when Covey was calling from a different phone, so that the son didn't recognize the number (Covey even wondered in horror if the man bought a caller ID phone mostly to avoid his father).

In the past week he'd left two messages at his son's house. He'd never seen the place but pictured it being a beautiful high-rise somewhere in L.A., though Covey hadn't been to California in years and didn't even know if they had real high-rises there, the City of Angels being to earthquakes what trailer parks in the Midwest are to twisters.

In any case, whether his home was high-rise, low- or a hovel, his son had not returned a single call.

Why? he often wondered in despair. *Why?*

He looked back on his days as a young father. He'd spent much time at the office and traveling, yes, but he'd also devoted many, many hours to the boy, taking him to the Yankees games and movies, attending Randy's recitals and Little League.

Something had happened, though, and in his twenties he'd drifted away. Covey had thought maybe he'd gone gay, since he'd never married, but when Randy came home for Ver's funeral he brought a beautiful young woman with him. Randy had been polite but distant and a few days afterward he'd headed back to the coast. It had been some months before they'd spoken again.

Why? . . .

Covey now sat down on the couch, poured himself a glass of the port, slowly to avoid the sediment, and sipped it. He picked up another scrapbook and began flipping through it.

He felt sentimental. And then sad and anxious. He rose slowly from the couch, walked into the kitchen and took two of his Luminux pills.

In a short while the drugs kicked in and he felt better, giddy. Almost carefree.

The book sagged in his hands. He reflected on the big question: Should he tell Randy about his illness and the impending surgery? Nurse Mac would want him to, he knew. But Covey wouldn't do that. He wanted the young man to come back on his own or not at all. He wasn't going to use sympathy as a weapon to force a reconciliation.

A glance at the clock on the stove. Mac would be here in fifteen minutes.

He decided to use the time productively and return phone calls. He confirmed his next appointment with Dr. Jenny and left a message with Charley Hanlon, a widower up the road, about going to the movies next weekend. He also made an appointment for tomorrow about some alternative treatments the hospital had suggested he look into. "Long as it doesn't involve colonics, I'll think about it," Covey grumbled to the soft-spoken director of the program, who'd laughed and assured him that it did not.

He hung up. Despite the silky calm from the drug Covey had a moment's panic. Nothing to do with his heart, his surgery, his mortality, his estranged son, tomorrow's non-colonic treatment.

No, what troubled him: What if Mac didn't like blue cheese?

Covey rose and headed into the kitchen, opened the refrigerator and began to forage for some other snacks.

∞

"You can't go in there."

But in there they went.

LaTour and Tal pushed past the receptionist into the office of Daniel Montrose.

At the circular glass table sat the president of the company and the other suspect, Karen Billings.

Montrose leaned forward, eyes wide in shock. He stood up slowly. The woman too pushed back from the table. The head of the company was as rumpled as before; Billings was in a fierce crimson dress.

"You, don't move!" LaTour snapped.

The red-dress woman blinked, unable to keep the anger out of her face. Tal could hear the tacit rejoinder: Nobody talks to me that way.

"Why didn't you tell us about the problems with Luminux?"

The president exchanged a look with Billings.

He cleared his throat. "Problems?"

Tal dropped the downloaded material about the FDA issues with Luminux on Montrose's desk. The president scooped it up and read.

LaTour had told Tal to watch the man's eyes. The eyes tell if someone's lying, the homicide cop had lectured. Tal squinted and studied them. He didn't have a clue what was going on behind his expensive glasses.

LaTour said to Billings, "Can you tell me where you were on April seventh and the ninth?"

"What the fuck are you talking about?"

"Simple question, lady. Where were you?"

"I'm not answering any goddamn questions without our lawyer." She crossed her arms, sat back and contentedly began a staring contest with LaTour.

"Why didn't you tell us about this?" Tal nodded at the documents.

Montrose said to Billings, "The dimethylamino."

"They found out about that?" she asked.

"Yeah, we found out about it," LaTour snapped. "Surprise."

Montrose turned to Tal. "What exactly did you find in the victims' blood?"

Unprepared for the question, he frowned. "Well, Luminux."

"You have the coroner's report?"

Tal pulled it out of his briefcase and put it on the table. "There."

Montrose frowned in an exaggerated way. "Actually, it doesn't say 'Luminux.'"

"The fuck you talking about? It's—"

Montrose said, "I quote: '9-fluoro, 7-chloro-1,3-dihydro-1methyl-5-phenyl-2H-1, 4-benzodiazepin, 5-hydroxytrypta-mine and N-(1-phenethyl-4-piperidyl) pro-pionanilide citrate.'"

"Whatever," LaTour snapped, rolling his eyes. "That *is* Luminux. The medical examiner said so."

"That's right," Karen snapped right back. "That's the approved version of the drug."

LaTour started to say something but fell silent.

"Approved?" Tal asked uncertainly.

Montrose said, "Look at the formula for the early version."

"Early?"

"The one the FDA rejected. It's in that printout of yours."

Tal was beginning to see where this was headed and he didn't like the destination. He found the sheet in the printout and compared it to the formula in the medical examiner's report. They were the same except that the earlier version of the Luminux contained another substance, dimethyl-amino ethyl phosphate ester.

"What's—"

"A mild antipsychotic agent known as DEP. That's what caused the problems in the first version. In combination it had a slight psychedelic effect. As soon as we took it out the FDA approved the drug. That was a year ago. You didn't find any DEP in the bodies. The victims were taking the approved version of the drug. No DEP-enhanced Luminux was every released to the public."

Billings muttered, "And we've never had a single incidence of suicide among the six million people worldwide on the drug—a lot of whom are probably alive today because they were taking Luminux and *didn't* kill themselves."

Montrose pulled a large binder off his desk and dropped it on his desk. "The complete study and FDA approval. No detrimental side effects. It's even safe with alcohol in moderation."

"Though we don't recommend it," Billings snapped, just as icily as she had at their first meeting.

"Why didn't you tell us before?" LaTour grumbled.

"You didn't ask. All drugs go through a trial period while we make them safe." Montrose wrote a number on a memo pad. "If you still don't believe us—this's the FDA's number. Call them."

Billings's farewell was "You found your way in here. You can find your way out."

∞

Tal slouched in his office chair. LaTour was across from him with his feet up on Tal's desk again.

"Got a question," Tal asked. "You ever wear spurs?"

"Spurs? Oh, you mean like for horses? Why would I wear spurs? Or is that some kind of math nerd joke about putting my feet on your fucking desk?"

"You figure it out," Tal muttered as the cop swung his feet to the floor. "So where do we go from here? No greedy daughters, no evil drug maker. And we've pretty much humiliated ourselves in front of two *harsh* women. We're batting oh for two." The statistician sighed. "Maybe they *did* kill themselves. Hell, sometimes life is just too much for some people."

"You don't think that, though."

"I don't *feel* it but I do *think* it and I do better thinking. When I start feeling I get into trouble."

"And the world goes round and round," LaTour said. "Shit. It time for a beer yet?"

But a beer was the last thing on Tal's mind. He stared at the glacier of paper on his desk, the printouts, the charts, the lists, the photographs, hoping that he'd spot one fact, one *datum*, that might help them.

Tal's phone rang. He grabbed it. "'Lo?"

"Is this Detective Simms?" a meek voice asked.

"That's right."

"I'm Bill Fendler, with Oak Creek Books in Barlow Heights. Somebody from your office called and asked to let you know if we sold any copies of *Making the Final Journey: The Complete Guide to Suicide and Euthanasia.*"

Tal sat up. "That's right. Have you?"

"I just noticed the inventory showed one book sold in the last couple of days."

LaTour frowned. Tal held up a wait-a-minute finger.

"Can you tell me who bought it"

"That's what I've been debating. . . . I'm not sure it's ethical. I was thinking if you had a court order it might be better."

"We have reason to believe that somebody might be using that book to cover up a series of murders. That's why we're asking about it. Maybe it's not ethical. But I'm asking you, please, give me the name of the person who bought it."

A pause. The man said, "Okay. Got a pencil?"

Tal found one. "Go ahead."

The mathematician started to write the name. Stunned, he paused. "Are you sure?" he asked.

"Positive, Detective. The receipt's right here in front of me."

The phone sagged in Tal's hand. He finished jotting the name, showed it to LaTour. "What do we do now?" he asked.

LaTour lifted a surprised eyebrow. "Search warrant," he said. "That's what we do."

∞

The warrant was pretty easy, especially since LaTour was on good terms with nearly every judge and magistrate in Westbrook County personally, and a short time later they were halfway through their search of the modest bungalow located in even more modest Harrison Village. Tal and LaTour were in the bedroom, three uniformed county troopers were downstairs.

Drawers, closets, beneath the bed . . .

Tal wasn't exactly sure what they were looking for. He followed LaTour's lead. The big cop had considerable experience sniffing out hiding places, it seemed, but it was Tal who found the jacket, which was shedding off-white fibers that appeared to match the one they'd found at the Whitleys' death scene.

This was *some* connection, though a tenuous one.

"Sir, I found something outside!" a cop called up the stairs.

They went out to the garage, where the officer was standing over a suitcase, hidden under stacks of boxes. Inside were two large bottles of Luminux, with only a few pills remaining in each. There were no personal prescription labels attached but they seemed to be the containers that were sold directly to hospitals. This one had been sold to the Cardiac Support Center. Also in the suitcase were articles cut from magazines and newspapers—one was from several years ago. It was about a nurse who'd killed elderly patients in a nursing home in Ohio with lethal drugs. The woman was quoted as saying, "I did a good thing, helping those people die with dignity. I never got a penny from their deaths. I only wanted them to be at peace. My worst crime is I'm an Angel of Mercy." There were a half-dozen others, too, the theme being the kindness of euthanasia. Some actually gave practical advice on "transitioning" people from life.

Tal stepped back, arms crossed, staring numbly at the find.

Another officer walked outside. "Found these hidden behind the desk downstairs."

In his latex-gloved hands Tal took the documents. They were the Bensons' files from the Cardiac Support Center. He opened and read through the first pages.

LaTour said something but the statistician didn't hear. He'd hoped up until now that the facts were wrong, that this was all a huge misunderstanding. But true mathematicians will always accept where the truth leads, even if it shatters their most heart-felt theorem.

There was no doubt that Mac McCaffrey was the killer.

She'd been the person who'd just bought the suicide book. And it was here, in her house, that they'd found the jacket, the Luminux bottles and the euthanasia articles. As for the Bensons' files, her name was prominently given as the couple's nurse/counselor. She'd lied about working with them.

The homicide cop spoke again.

"What'd you say?" Tal muttered.

"Where is she, you think?"

"At the hospital, I'd guess. The Cardiac Support Center."

"So you ready?" LaTour asked.

"For what?"

"To make your first collar."

∞

The blue cheese, in fact, turned out to be a bust.

But Nurse Mac—the only way Robert Covey could think of her now—seemed to enjoy the other food he'd laid out.

"Nobody's ever made appetizers for me," she said, touched.

"They don't make gentlemen like me anymore."

And bless her, here was a woman who didn't whine about her weight. She smeared a big slab of paté on a cracker and ate it right down, then went for the shrimp.

Covey sat back on the couch in the den, a bit perplexed. He recalled her feistiness from their first meeting and was anticipating—and looking forward to—a fight about diet and exercise. But she made only one exercise comment—after she'd opened the back door.

"Beautiful yard."

"Thanks. Ver was the landscaper."

"That's a nice pool. You like to swim?"

He told her he loved to, though since he'd been diagnosed with the heart prob-

lem he didn't swim alone, worried he'd faint
or have a heart attack and drown.

Nurse Mac had nodded. But there was
something else on her mind. She finally
turned away from the pool. "You're probably wondering what's on the agenda for this
session?"

"Yes'm, I am."

"Well, I'll be right up front. I'm here to
talk you into doing something you might
not want to do."

"Ah, negotiating, are we? This involve the
fourth glass of port?"

She smiled. "It's a little more important
than that. But now that you've brought it
up . . ." She rose and walked to the bar. "You
don't mind, do you?" She picked up a bottle
of old Taylor-Fladgate, lifted an eyebrow.

"I'll mind if you pour it down the drain. I
don't mind if we drink some."

"Why don't you refill the food," she said.
"I'll play bartender."

When Covey returned from the kitchen
Nurse Mac had poured him a large glass of
port. She handed it to him then poured one
for herself. She lifted hers. He did too and
the crystal rang.

They both sipped.

"So what's this all about, you acting so
mysterious?"

"What's it about?" she mused. "It's about eliminating pain, finding peace. And sometimes you just can't do that alone. Sometimes you need somebody to help you."

"Can't argue with the sentiment. What've you got in mind? Specific, I mean."

Mac leaned forward, tapped her glass to his. "Drink up." They downed the ruby-colored liquor.

∞

"Go, go, go!"

"You wanna drive?" LaTour shouted over the roar of the engine. They skidded sharply around the parkway, over the curb and onto the grass, nearly scraping the side of the unmarked car against a jutting rock.

"At least I know *how* to drive," Tal called. Then: "Step on it!"

"Shut the fuck up. Let me concentrate."

As the wheel grated against another curb Tal decided that shutting up was a wise idea and fell silent.

Another squad car was behind them.

"There, that's the turn-off." Tal pointed.

LaTour controlled the skid and somehow managed to keep them out of the oncoming traffic lane.

Another three hundred yards. Tal directed the homicide cop down the winding road then up a long driveway, at the end of which was a small, dark-blue sedan. The same car the witnesses had seen outside the Bensons' house, the same car that had left the tread marks at the Whitley's the day they died.

Killing the siren, LaTour skidded to a stop in front of the car. The squad car parked close behind, blocking the sedan in.

All four officers leapt out. As they ran past the vehicle Tal glanced in the backseat and saw the tan baseball cap that the driver of the car, Mac McCaffrey, had worn outside the Bensons' house, the day she'd engineered their deaths.

In a movement quite smooth for such a big man LaTour unlatched the door and shoved inside, not even breaking stride. He pulled his gun from his holster.

They and the uniformed officers charged into the living room and then the den.

They stopped, looking at the two astonished people on the couch.

One was Robert Covey, who was unharmed.

The other, the woman who'd been about to kill him, was standing over him, eyes wide. Mac was just offering the old man one of the tools of her murderous trade: a glass undoubtedly laced with enough Luminux to render him half conscious and suggestible to suicide. Tal noticed that the back door was open, revealing a large swimming pool. So, not a gun or carbon monoxide. Death by drowning this time.

"Tal!" she gasped.

But he said nothing. He let LaTour step forward to cuff her and arrest her. The homicide cop was, of course, much better versed in such matters of protocol.

∞

The homicide detective looked through her purse and found the suicide book inside.

Robert Covey was in the ambulance outside, being checked out by the medics. He'd seemed okay but they were taking their time, just to make sure.

After they found the evidence at Mac's house, Tal and LaTour had sped to the hospital. She was out but Dr. Dehoeven at the CRC had pulled her client list and they'd gone through her calendar, learning that she was meeting with Covey at that moment. He hadn't answered the phone, and they'd raced to the elderly man's house.

LaTour would've been content to ship Mac off to Central Booking but Tal was a bit out of control; he couldn't help confronting her. "You *did* know Don and Sy Benson. Don was your client. You lied to me."

Mac started to speak then looked down, her tearful eyes on the floor.

"We found Benson's files in your house. And the computer logs at CSC showed you erased his records. You *were* at their house the day they died. It was you the witness saw in the hat and sunglasses. And the Whitleys? You killed them too."

"I didn't kill anybody!"

"Okay, fine—you *helped* them kill themselves. You drugged them and talked them into it. And then cleaned up after." He turned to the uniformed deputy. "Take her to Booking."

And she was led away, calling, "I didn't do anything wrong!"

"Bullshit," LaTour muttered.

Though, staring after her as the car eased down the long drive, Tal reflected that in a way—some abstract, moral sense—she truly *did* believe she hadn't done anything wrong.

But to the people of the state of New York, the evidence was irrefutable. Nurse Claire "Mac" McCaffrey had murdered four people and undoubtedly intended to murder scores of others. She'd gotten the Bensons doped up on Friday and helped them kill themselves. Then on Sunday she'd called the Whitleys from a pay phone, made sure they were home then went over there and arranged for their suicides too. She'd cleaned up the place, taken the Luminux and hadn't left until *after* they died. (Tal had learned that the opera show she listened to wasn't on until 7:00 P.M. Not 4:00, as she'd told him. That's why he hadn't been able to find it when he'd surfed the frequencies in LaTour's car.)

She'd gone into this business to ease the suffering of patients—because her own mother had had such a difficult time dying. But what she'd meant by "easing suffering" was putting them down like dogs.

Robert Covey returned to his den. He was badly shaken but physically fine. He had some Luminux in his system but not a dangerously high dosage. "She seemed so nice, so normal," he whispered.

Oh, you bet, Tal thought bitterly. A goddamn perfect member of the Four Percent Club.

He and LaTour did some paperwork—Tal so upset that he didn't even think about his own questionnaire—and they walked back to LaTour's car. Tal sat heavily in the front seat, staring straight ahead. The homicide cop didn't start the engine. He said, "Sometimes closing a case is harder than not closing it. That's something they don't teach you at the academy. But you did what you had to. People'll be alive now because of what you did."

"I guess," he said sullenly. He was picturing Mac's office. Her crooked smile when she'd look over the park. Her laugh.

"Let's file the papers. Then we'll go get a beer. Hey, you do drink beer, don'tcha?"

"Yeah, I drink beer," Tal said.

"We'll make a cop outta you yet, Einstein."

Tal clipped his seatbelt on, deciding that being a real cop was the last thing in the world he wanted.

∞

A beep on the intercom. "Mr. Covey's here, sir."

"I'll be right there." Dr. William Farley rose from his desk, a glass-sheet-covered Victorian piece his business partner had bought for him in New England on one of the man's buying sprees. Farley would have been content to have a metal desk or even a card table.

But in the *business* of medicine, not the *practice*, appearances count. The offices of the Lotus Research Foundation, near the mall containing Neiman Marcus and Saks Fifth Avenue, were filled with many antiques. Farley had been amused when they'd moved here three years ago to see the fancy furniture, paintings, objets d'art. Now, they were virtually invisible to him. What he greatly preferred was the huge medical facility itself behind the offices. As a doctor and researcher, that was the only place he felt truly at home.

Forty-eight, slim to the point of being scrawny, hair with a mind of its own, Farley had nonetheless worked hard to rid himself of his backroom medical researcher's image. He now pulled on his thousand-dollar suit jacket and applied a comb. He paused at the door, took a deep breath, exhaled and stepped into a lengthy corridor to the foundation's main lobby. It was deserted except for the receptionist and one elderly man, sitting in a deep plush couch.

"Mr. Covey?" the doctor asked, extending his hand.

The man set down the coffee cup he'd been given by the receptionist and they shook hands.

"Dr. Farley?"

A nod.

"Come on into my office."

They chatted about the weather as Farley led him down the narrow corridor to his office. Sometimes the patients here talked about sports, about their families, about the paintings on the walls.

Sometimes they were so nervous they said nothing at all.

Entering the office, Farley gestured toward a chair and then sat behind the massive desk. Covey glanced at it, unimpressed. Farley looked him over. He didn't appear particularly wealthy—an off-the-rack suit, a tie with stripes that went one way while those on his shirt went another. Still, the director of the Lotus Foundation had learned enough about rich people to know that the wealthiest were those who drove hybrid Toyota gas-savers and wore raincoats until they were threadbare.

Farley poured more coffee and offered Covey a cup.

"Like I said on the phone yesterday, I know a little about your condition. Your cardiologist is Jennifer Lansdowne, right?"

"That's right."

"And you're seeing someone from the Cardiac Support Center at the hospital."

Covey frowned. "I *was.*"

"You're not any longer?"

"A problem with the nurse they sent me. I haven't decided if I'm going back. But that's a whole 'nother story."

"Well, we think you might be a good candidate for our services here, Mr. Covey. We offer a special program to patients in certain cases."

"What kind of cases?"

"Serious cases."

"The Lotus Research Foundation for *Alternative* Treatment," Covey recited. "Correct me if I'm wrong but I don't think ginseng and acupuncture work for serious cases."

"That's not what we're about." Farley looked him over carefully. "You a businessman, sir?"

"Was. For half a century."

"What line?"

"Manufacturing. Then venture capital."

"Then I imagine you generally like to get straight to the point."

"You got that right."

"Well, then let me ask you this, Mr. Covey. How would you like to live forever?"

∞

"How's that?"

In the same way that he'd learned to polish his shoes and speak in words of fewer than four syllables, Farley had learned how to play potential patients like trout. He knew how to pace the pitch. "I'd like to tell you about the foundation. But first would you mind signing this?" He opened the drawer of his desk and passed a document to Covey.

He read it. "A nondisclosure agreement."

"It's pretty standard."

"I know it is," the old man said. "I've written 'em. Why do you want me to sign it?"

"Because what I'm going to tell you can't be made public."

He was intrigued now, the doctor could tell, though trying not to show it.

"If you don't want to, I understand. But then I'm afraid we won't be able to pursue our conversation further."

Covey read the sheet again. "Got a pen?"

Farley handed him a Mont Blanc; Covey took the heavy barrel with a laugh suggesting he didn't like ostentation very much. He signed and pushed the document back.

Farley put it into his desk. "Now, Dr. Lansdowne's a good woman. And she'll do whatever's humanly possible to fix your heart and give you a few more years. But there're limits to what medical science can do. After all, Mr. Covey, we all die. You, me, the children being born at this minute. Saints and sinners . . . we're all going to die."

"You got an interesting approach to medical services, Doctor. You cheer up all your patients this way?"

Dr. Farley smiled. "We hear a lot about aging nowadays."

"Can't turn on the TV without it."

"And about people trying to stay young forever."

"Second time you used that word. Keep going."

"Mr. Covey, you ever hear about the Hayflick rule?"

"Nope. Never have."

"Named after the man who discovered that human cells can reproduce themselves a limited number of times. At first, they make perfect reproductions of themselves. But after a while they can't keep up that level of quality control, you could say; they become more and more inefficient."

"Why?"

Covey, he reflected, was a sharp one. Most people sat there and nodded with stupid smiles on their faces. He continued. "There's an important strand of DNA that gets shorter and shorter each time the cells reproduce. When it gets too short, the cells go haywire and they don't duplicate properly. Sometimes they stop altogether."

"I'm following you in general. But go light on the biology bullshit. Wasn't my strong suit."

"Fair enough, Mr. Covey. Now, there're some ways to cheat the Hayflick limit. In the future it may be possible to extend life span significantly, dozens, maybe hundreds of years."

"That ain't forever."

"No, it's not."

"So cut to the chase."

"We'll never be able to construct a human body that will last more than a few hundred years at the outside. The laws of physics and nature just don't allow it. And even if we could we'd still have disease and illness and accidents that shorten life spans."

"This's getting cheerier and cheerier."

"Now, Dr. Lansdowne'll do what she can medically and the Cardiac Support Center will give you plenty of help."

"Depending on the nurse," Covey muttered. "Go on."

"And you might have another five, ten, fifteen years. . . . Or you can consider our program." Farley handed Covey a business card and tapped the logo of the Lotus Foundation, a golden flower. "You know what the lotus signifies in mythology?"

"Not a clue."

"Immortality."

"Does it now?"

"Primitive people'd see lotuses grow up out of the water in riverbeds that'd been dry for years. They assumed the plants were immortal."

"You said you can't keep people from dying."

"We can't. You will die. What we offer is what you might call a type of reincarnation."

Covey sneered. "I stopped going to church thirty years ago."

"Well, Mr. Covey. I've never gone to church. I'm not talking about spiritual reincarnation. No, I mean scientific, provable reincarnation."

The old man grunted. "This's about the time you start losing people, right?"

Farley laughed hard. "That's right. Pretty much at that sentence."

"Well, you ain't lost me yet. Keep going."

"It's very complex but I'll give it to you in a nutshell—just a little biology."

The old man sipped more coffee and waved his hand for the doctor to continue.

"The foundation holds the patent on a process that's known as neuro stem cell regenerative replication. . . . I know, it's a mouthful. Around here we just call it consciousness cloning."

"Explain that."

"What is consciousness?" Farley asked. "You look around the room, you see things, smell them, have reactions. Have thoughts. I sit in the same room, focus on different things, or focus on the same things, and have different reactions. Why? Because our brains are unique."

A slow nod. This fish was getting close to the fly.

"The foundation's developed a way to genetically map your brain and then program embryonic cells to grow in a way that duplicates it perfectly. After you die your identical consciousness is recreated in a fetus. You're—" A slight smile. "—born again. In a secular, biological sense, of course. The sensation you have is as if your brain were transplanted into another body."

Farley poured more coffee, handed it to Covey, who was shaking his head.

"How the hell do you do this?" Covey whispered.

"It's a three-step process." The doctor was always delighted to talk about his work. "First, we plot the exact structure of your brain as it exists now—the parts where the consciousness resides. We use supercomputers and micro-MRI machines."

"MRI. . . . that's like a fancy X-ray, right?"

"Magnetic resonance. We do a perfect schematic of your consciousness. Then step two: you know about genes, right? They're the blueprints for our bodies, every cell in your body contains them. Well, genes decide not only what your hair color is and your height and susceptibility to certain diseases but also how your brain develops. After a certain age the brain development gene shuts off; your brain's structure is determined and doesn't change—that's why brain tissue doesn't regenerate if it's destroyed. The second step is to extract and reactivate the development gene. Then we implant it into a fetus."

"You clone me?"

"No, not your body. We use donor sperm and egg and a surrogate mother. There's an in vitro clinic attached to the foundation. You're 'placed,' we call it, with a good family from the same social-economic class as you live in now."

Covey wanted to be skeptical, it seemed, but he was still receptive.

"The final part is to use chemical and electromagnetic intervention to make sure the brain develops identically to the map we made of your present one. Stimulate some cells' growth, inhibit others'. When you're born again, your perceptions will be exactly what they are from your point of view now. Your sensibilities, interests, desires."

Covey blinked.

"You won't look like you. Your body type will be different. Though you will be male. We insist on that. It's not our job to work out gender-identity issues."

"Not a problem," he said shortly, frowning at the absurdity of the idea. Then: "Can you eliminate health problems? I had skin cancer. And the heart thing, of course."

"We don't do that. We don't make supermen or superwomen. We simply boost your consciousness into another generation, exactly as you are now."

Covey considered this for a moment. "Will I remember meeting you, will I have images of this life?"

"Ah, memories . . . We didn't quite know about those at first. But it seems that, yes, you will remember, to some extent— because memories are hard-wired into some portions of the brain. We aren't sure how many yet, since our first clients are only three or four years old now—in their second lives, of course—and we haven't had a chance to fully interview them yet."

"You've actually *done* this?" he whispered.

Farley nodded. "Oh, yes, Mr. Covey. We're up and running."

"What about will I go wacko or anything? That sheep they cloned died? She was a mess, I heard."

"No, that can't happen because we control development, like I was explaining. Every step of the way."

"Jesus," he whispered. "This isn't a joke?"

"Oh, no, not at all."

"You said, 'Forever.' So, how does it work—we do the same thing in seventy years or whatever?"

"It's literally a lifetime guarantee, even if that lifetime lasts ten thousand years. The Lotus Foundation will stay in touch with all our clients over the years. You can keep going for as many generations as you want."

"How do I know you'll still be in business?"

A slight chuckle. "Because we sell a product there's an infinite demand for. Companies that provide that don't ever go out of business."

Covey eyed Farley and the old man said coyly, "Which brings up your fee."

"As you can imagine . . ."

"Forever don't come cheap. Gimme a number."

"One half of your estate with a minimum of ten million dollars."

"One half? That's about twenty-eight million. But it's not liquid. Real estate, stocks, bonds. I can't just write you a check for it."

"We don't want you to. We're keeping this procedure very low-key. In the future we hope to offer our services to more people but now our costs are so high we can work only with the ones who can cover the expenses. . . . And, let's be realistic, we prefer people like you in the program."

"Like me?"

"Let's say higher in the gene pool than others."

Covey grunted. "Well, how *do* you get paid?"

"You leave the money to one of our charities in your will."

"Charities?"

"The foundation owns dozens of them. The money gets to us eventually."

"So you don't get paid until I die."

"That's right. Some clients wait until they actually die of their disease. Most, though, do the paperwork and then transition themselves."

"Transition?"

"They end their own life. That way they avoid a painful end. And, of course, the sooner they leave, the sooner they come back."

"How many people've done this?"

"Eight."

Covey looked out the window for a moment, at the trees in Central Park, waving slowly in a sharp breeze. "This's crazy. The whole thing's nuts."

Farley laughed. "*You'd* be nuts if you didn't think that at first. . . . Come on, I'll give you a tour of the facility."

Setting down his coffee, Covey followed

the doctor out of the office. They walked down the hallway through an impressive-looking security door into the laboratory portion of the foundation. Farley pointed out first the massive supercomputers used for brain mapping and then the genetics lab and cryogenic facility itself, which they couldn't enter but could see from windows in the corridor. A half dozen white-coated employees dipped pipettes into tubes, grew cultures in petri dishes and hunched over microscopes.

Covey was intrigued but not yet sold, Farley noted.

"Let's go back to the office."

When they'd sat again the old man finally said, "Well, I'll think about it."

Sheldon nodded with a smile and said, "You bet. A decision like this . . . Some people just can't bring themselves to sign on. You take your time." He handed Covey a huge binder. "Those're case studies, genetic data for comparison with the transitioning clients and their next-life selves, interviews with them. There's nothing identifying them but you can read about the children and the process itself." Farley paused and let Covey flip through the material. He seemed to be reading it carefully. The doctor added, "What's so nice about this is that you never have to say good-bye to your loved ones. Say you've got a son or daughter . . . we could contact them when they're older and propose our services to them. You could reconnect with them a hundred years from now."

At the words *son or daughter*, Covey had looked up, blinking. His eyes drifted off and finally he said, "I don't know. . . ."

"Mr. Covey," Farley said, "let me just add one thing. I understand your skepticism. But you tell me you're a businessman? Well, I'm going to treat you like one. Sure, you've got doubts. Who wouldn't? But even if you're not one hundred percent sure, even if you think I'm trying to sell you a load of hooey, what've you got to lose? You're going to die anyway. Why don't you just roll the dice and take the chance?"

He let this sink in for a minute and saw that the words—as so often—were having an effect. Time to back off. He said, "Now, I've got some phone calls to make, if you'll excuse me. There's a lounge through that door. Take your time and read through those things."

Covey picked up the files and stepped into the room the doctor indicated. The door closed.

Farley had pegged the old man as shrewd and deliberate. And accordingly the doctor gave him a full forty-five minutes to examine the materials. Finally he rose and walked to the doorway. Before he could say anything Covey looked up from the leather couch he was sitting in and said, "I'll do it. I want to do it."

"I'm very happy for you," Farley said sincerely.

"What do I need to do now?"

"All you do is an MRI scan and then give us a blood sample for the genetic material."

"You don't need part of my brain?"

"That's what's so amazing about genes. All of us is contained in a cell of our own blood."

Covey nodded.

"Then you change your will and we take it from there." He looked in a file and pulled out a list of the charities the foundation had set up recently.

"Any of these appeal? You should pick three or four. And they ought to be something in line with interests or causes you had when you were alive."

"There." Covey circled three of them. "I'll leave most to the Metropolitan Arts Assistance Association." He looked up. "Veronica, my wife, was an artist. That okay?"

"It's fine." Farley copied down the names and some other information and then handed a card to Covey. "Just take that to your lawyer."

The old man nodded. "His office is only a few miles from here. I could see him today."

"Just bring us a copy of the will." He didn't add what Covey, of course, a savvy businessman, knew. That if the will was not altered, or if he changed it later, the foundation wouldn't do the cloning. They had the final say.

"What about the . . . transition?"

Farley said, "That's your choice. Entirely up to you. Tomorrow or next year. Whatever you're comfortable with."

At the door Covey paused and turned back, shook Farley's hand. He gave a faint laugh. "Who would've thought? Forever."

∞

In Greek mythology Eos was the goddess of dawn and she was captivated with the idea of having human lovers. She fell deeply in love with a mortal, Tithonos, the son of the king of Troy, and convinced Zeus to let him live forever.

The god of gods agreed. But he neglected one small detail: granting him youth as well as immortality. While Eos remained unchanged Tithonos grew older and more decrepit with each passing year until he was so old he was unable to move or speak. Horrified, Eos turned him into an insect and moved on to more suitable paramours.

Dr. William Farley thought of this myth now, sitting at his desk in the Lotus Research Foundation. The search for immortality's always been tough on us poor humans, he reflected. But how doggedly we ignore the warning in Tithonos's myth—and the logic of science—and continue to look for ways to cheat death.

Farley glanced at a picture on his desk. It showed a couple, arm in arm—younger versions of those in a second picture on his credenza. His parents, who'd died in an auto accident when Farley was in medical school.

An only child, desperately close to them, he took months to recover from the shock. When he was able to resume his studies, he decided he'd specialize in emergency medicine—devoting his to saving lives threatened by trauma.

But the young man was brilliant—too smart for the repetitious mechanics of ER work. Lying awake nights he would reflect about his parents' deaths and he took some reassurance that they were, in a biochemical way, still alive within him. He developed an interest in genetics, and that was the subject he began to pursue in earnest.

Months, then years, of manic twelve-hour days doing research in the field resulted in many legitimate discoveries. But this also led to some ideas that were less conventional, even bizarre—consciousness cloning, for instance.

Not surprisingly, he was either ignored or ridiculed by his peers. His papers were rejected by professional journals, his grant requests turned down. The rejection didn't discourage him, though he grew more and more desperate to find the millions of dollars needed to research his theory. One day—about seven years ago—nearly penniless and living in a walk-up beside one of Westbrook's commuter train lines, he'd gotten a call from an old acquaintance. The man had heard about Farley's plight and had an idea.

"You want to raise money for your research?" he'd asked the impoverished medico. "It's easy. Find really sick, really wealthy patients and sell them immortality."

"What?"

"Listen," the man had continued. "Find patients who're about to die anyway. They'll be desperate. You package it right, they'll buy it."

"I can't sell them anything yet," Farley had replied. "I *believe* I can make this work. But it could take years."

"Well, sometimes sacrifices have to be made. You can pick up ten million overnight, twenty. That'd buy some pretty damn nice research facilities."

Farley had been quiet, considering those words. Then he'd said, "I *could* keep tissue samples, I suppose, and then when we actually can do the cloning, I could bring them back then."

"Hey, there you go," said the doctor. Something in the tone suggested to Farley that he didn't think the process would ever work. But the man's disbelief was irrelevant if he could help Farley get the money he needed for research.

"Well, all right," Farley said to his colleague—whose name was Anthony Sheldon, of the cardiology department at Westbrook Hospital, a man who was as talented an entrepreneur as he was a cardiovascular surgeon.

Six years ago they'd set up the Lotus Research Foundation, an in vitro clinic and a network of bogus charities. Dr. Sheldon, whose office was near the Cardiac Support Center, would finagle a look at the files of patients there and would find the richest and sickest. Then he'd arrange for them to be contacted by the Lotus Foundation and Farley would sell them the program.

Farley had truly doubted that anybody would buy the pitch but Sheldon had coached him well. The man had thought of everything. He found unique appeals for each potential client and gave Farley this information to snare them. In the case of the Bensons, for instance, Sheldon had learned how much they loved each other. His pitch to them was that this was the chance to be together forever, as they so poignantly noted in their suicide note. With Robert Covey, Sheldon had learned about his estranged son, so Farley added the tactical mention that a client could have a second chance to connect with children.

Sheldon had also come up with one vital part of the selling process. He made sure the patients got high doses of Luminux (even the coffee that Covey had just been drinking, for instance, was laced with the drug). Neither doctor believed that anyone would sign up for such a far-fetched idea without the benefit of some mind-numbing Mickey Finn.

The final selling point was, of course, the desperate desire of people facing death to believe what Farley promised them.

And that turned out to be one hell of a hook. The Lotus Research Foundation had earned almost 93 million in the past six years.

Everything had gone fine—until recently, when their greed got the better of them. Well, got the better of Sheldon. They'd decided that the cardiologist would never refer his own patients to the foundation—and would wait six months or a year between clients. But Tony Sheldon apparently had a mistress with very expensive taste and had lost some serious money in the stock market recently. Just after the Bensons signed up, the Whitleys presented themselves. Although Sam Whitley was a patient, they were far too wealthy to pass up and so Farley reluctantly yielded to Sheldon's pressure to go ahead with the plan.

But they learned that, though eager to proceed, Sam Whitley had wanted to reassure himself that this wasn't pure quackery and he'd tracked down some technical literature about the computers used in the technique and genetics in general. After the patients had died, Farley and Sheldon had to find this information in his house, burn it and scour the place for any other evidence that might lead back to the foundation.

The intrusion, though, must've alerted the police to the possibility that the families' deaths were suspicious. Officers had actually interviewed Sheldon, sending a jolt of panic through Farley. But then a scapegoat stumbled into the picture: Mac McCaffrey, a young nurse/counselor at the Cardiac Support Center. She was seeing their latest recent prospect—Robert Covey—as she'd been working with the Bensons and the Whitleys. This made her suspect to start with. Even better was her reluctance to admit she'd seen the Bensons; after their suicide the nurse had apparently lied about them and had stolen their files from the CSC. A perfect setup. Sheldon had used his ample resources to bribe a pharmacist at the CSC to doctor the logs and give him a couple of wholesale bottles containing a few Luminux tablets, to make it look like she'd been drugging patients for some time. Farley, obsessed with death and dying, had a vast library of articles on euthanasia and suicide. He copied several dozen of these. The drugs and the articles they planted in the nurse's garage—insurance in case they needed somebody to take the fall.

Which they had. And now the McCaffrey woman had just been hauled off to jail.

A whole 'nother story, as Covey had said.

The nurse's arrest had troubled Farley. He'd speculated out loud about telling the police that she was innocent. But Sheldon reminded him coolly what would happen to them and the foundation if Farley did that and he relented.

Sheldon had said, "Look, we'll do one more—this Covey—and then take a break. A year. Two years."

"No. Let's wait."

"I checked him out," Sheldon said, "He's worth over fifty million."

"I think it's too risky."

"I've thought about that." With the police still looking into the Benson and Whitley suicides, Sheldon explained, it'd be better to have the old man die in a mugging or hit and run, rather than killing himself.

"But," Farley had whispered, "you mean murder?"

"A suicide'll be way too suspicious."

"We can't."

But Sheldon had snapped, "Too late for morality, Doctor. You made your deal with the devil. You can't renegotiate now." And hung up.

Farley stewed for a while but finally realized the man was right; there was no going back. And, my, what he could do with another $25 million. . . .

His secretary buzzed him on the intercom.

"Mr. Covey's back, sir."

"Show him in."

Covey walked into the office. They shook hands again and Covey sat. As cheerful and blinky as most patients on seventy-five milligrams of Luminux. He happily took another cup of special brew then reached into his jacket pocket and displayed a copy of the codicil to the will. "Here you go."

Though Farley wasn't a lawyer he knew what to look for; the document was in proper form.

They shook hands formally.

Covey finished his coffee and Farley escorted him to the lab, where he would undergo the MRI and give a blood sample, making the nervous small talk that the clients always made at this point in the process.

The geneticist shook his hand and told him he'd made the right decision. Covey thanked Farley sincerely, with a hopeful smile on his face that was, Farley knew, only partly from the drug. He returned to his office and the doctor picked up the phone, called Anthony Sheldon. "Covey's changed the will. He'll be leaving here in about fifteen minutes."

"I'll take care of him now," Sheldon said and hung up.

Farley sighed and dropped the received into the cradle. He stripped off his suit jacket then pulled on a white lab coat. He left his office and fled up the hall to the research lab, where he knew he would find solace in the honest world of science, safe from all his guilt and sins, as if they were barred entry by the double-sealed doors of the airlock.

∞

Robert Covey was walking down the street, feeling pretty giddy, odd thoughts going through his head.

Thinking of his life—the way he'd lived it. And the people who'd touched him and whom he'd touched. A foreman in the Bedford plant, who'd worked for the company for forty years . . . The men in his golfing foursome . . . Veronica . . . His brother . . .

His son, of course.

Still no call from Randy. And for the first time it occurred to him that maybe there *was* a reason the boy—well, young man— had been ignoring him. He'd always assumed he'd been such a good father. But maybe not.

Nothing makes you question your life more closely than when somebody's trying to sell you immortality.

Walking toward the main parking garage, Covey noted that the area was largely deserted. He saw only a few grungy kids on skateboards, a pretty redhead across the street, two men getting out of a white van parked near an alley.

He paid attention only to the men, because they were large, dressed in what looked like cheap suits and, with a glance up and down, started in his direction.

Covey soon forgot them, though, and concentrated again on his son. Thinking about his decision not to tell the boy about his illness. Maybe withholding things like this had been a pattern in Covey's life. Maybe the boy had felt excluded.

He laughed to himself. Maybe he should leave a message about what he and Farley had just been talking about. Lord have mercy, what he wouldn't give to see Randy's reaction when he listened to that! He could—

Covey slowed, frowning.

What was this?

The two men from the van were now jogging—directly toward him. He hesitated and shied back. Suddenly the men split up. One stopped and turned his back to Covey, scanning the sidewalk, while the other sped up, springing directly toward the old man. Then simultaneously they both pulled guns from under their coats.

No!

He turned to run, thinking that sprinting would probably kill him faster than the bullets. Not that it mattered. The man approaching him was fast and before Covey had a chance to take more than a few steps he was being pulled roughly into the alleyway behind him.

∞

"No, what are you doing? Who are—"

"Quiet!"

The man pressed Covey against the wall.

The other joined them but continued to gaze out over the street as he spoke into a walkie-talkie. "We've got him. No sign of hostiles. Move in, all units, move in!"

From out on the street came the rushing sound of car engines and the bleats of siren.

"Sorry, Mr. Covey. We had a little change of plans." The man speaking was the one who'd pulled him into the alley. They both produced badges and ID cards of the Westbrook County Sheriff's Department. "We work with Greg LaTour."

Oh, LaTour . . . He was the burly officer who, along with that skinny young officer named Talbot Simms, had come to his house early this morning with a truly bizarre story. This outfit called the Lotus Research Foundation might be running some kind of scam, targeting sick people, but the police weren't quite sure how it worked. Had he been contacted by anyone there? When Covey had told them, yes, and that he was in fact meeting with its director, Farley, that afternoon, they wondered if he'd be willing to wear a wire to find out what it was all about.

Well, what it was all about was immortality . . . and it *had* been one hell of a scam.

The plan was that after he stopped at Farley's office and dropped off the fake codicil to his will (he executed a second one at the same time, voiding the one he'd given Farley), he was going to meet LaTour and Simms at a Starbucks not far away.

But now the cops had something else in mind.

"Who're you?" Covey now asked. "Where're Laurel and Hardy?" Meaning Simms and LaTour.

The young officer who'd shoved him into the alley had blinked, not understanding the reference. He said, "Well, sir, what happened was we had a tap on the phone in Farley's office. He called Sheldon to tell him about you and it seems they weren't going to wait to try to talk you into killing yourself. Sheldon was going to kill you right away— make it look like a mugging or hit and run, we think."

Covey muttered, "You might've thought about that possibility up front."

There was a crackle in the mike/speaker
of one of the officers. Covey couldn't hear
too well but the gist of it was that they'd arrested Dr. Anthony Sheldon just outside his
office. They now stepped out of the alley
and Covey observed a half dozen police officers escorting William Farley and three men
in lab coats out of the Lotus Foundation offices in handcuffs.

Covey observed the procession coolly,
feeling contempt for the depravity of the
foundation's immortality scam, though also
with a grudging admiration. A businessman
to his soul, Robert Covey couldn't help be
impressed by someone who'd identified an
inexhaustible market demand. Even if that
product he sold was completely bogus.

∞

The itch had yet to be scratched. Tal's office
was still as sloppy as LaTour's. The mess was
driving him crazy, though Shellee seemed to
think it was a step up on the evolutionary
chain—for him to have digs that looked like
everyone else's.

Captain Dempsey was sitting in the office,
playing with one rolled-up sleeve, then the
other. Greg LaTour too, his booted feet on
the floor for a change, though the reason
for this propriety seemed to be that Tal's

desk was piled too high with paper to find a place to rest them.

"How'd you tip to this scam of theirs?" the captain asked. "The Lotus Foundation?"

Tal said, "Some things just didn't add up."

"Haw." From LaTour.

Both the captain and Tal glanced at him.

LaTour stopped smiling. "He's the math guy. He says something didn't *add* up. I thought it was a joke." He grumbled, "Go on."

Tal explained that after he'd returned to the office following Mac's arrest, he couldn't get her out of his head.

"Women do that," LaTour said.

"No, I mean there was something odd about the whole case," he continued. "Issues I couldn't reconcile. So I checked with Crime Scene—there *was* no Luminux in the port Mac was giving Covey. Then I went to see her in the lockup. She admitted she'd lied about not being the Bensons' nurse. She said she destroyed their records at the Cardiac Support Center and that she was the one that the witnesses had seen the day they died. But she lied because she was afraid she'd lose her job—two of her patients killing themselves? When, to her, they seemed to be doing fine? It shook her up bad. That's why she bought the suicide book. She bought it *after* I told her about it—she got the title from me. She

wanted to know what to look for, to make
sure nobody else died."

"And you believed her?" the captain
asked.

"Yes, I did. I asked Covey if she'd ever
brought up suicide. Did he have any sense
that she was trying to get him to kill himself.
But he said, no. All she'd talked about at
that meeting—when we arrested her—was
how painful and hard it is to go through a
tough illness alone. She'd figured that he
hadn't called his son, Randall, and told him,
like he'd said. She gave him some port, got
him relaxed and was trying to talk him into
calling the boy."

"You said something about an opera
show?" Dempsey continued, examining both
sleeves and making sure they were rolled up
to within a quarter inch of each other. Tal
promised himself never to compulsively play
with his tie knot again. His boss continued,
"You said she lied about the time it was on."

"Oh. Right. Oops."

"Oops?"

"The Whitleys died on Sunday. The
show's on at four then. But it's on at *seven*
during the week, just after the business report. I checked the NPR program guide."

The captain asked, "And the articles

about euthanasia? The ones they found in her house?"

"Planted. Her fingerprints weren't on them. Only glove-print smudges. The stolen Luminux bottle too. No prints. And, according to the inventory, those drugs disappeared from the clinic when Mac was out of town. Naw, she didn't have anything to do with the scam. It was Farley and Sheldon."

LaTour continued, "Quite a plan. Slipping the patients drugs, getting them to change their wills, then kill themselves and clean up afterwards.

"They did it all themselves? Farley and Sheldon?"

LaTour shook his head. "They must've hired muscle or used somebody in the foundation for the dirty work. We got four of 'em in custody. But they clammed up. Nobody's saying anything." LaTour sighed. "And they got the best lawyers in town. Big surprise, with all the fucking money they've got."

Tal said, "So, anyway, I knew Mac was being set up. But we still couldn't figure what was going on. You know, in solving an algebra problem you look for common denominators and—"

"Again with the fucking math," LaTour grumbled.

"Well, what was the denominator? We had two couples committing suicide and leaving huge sums of money to charities—more than half their estates. I looked up the statistics from the NAEPP."

"The—"

"The National Association of Estate Planning Professionals. When people have children, only two percent leave that much of their estate to charities. And even when they're childless, only twelve percent leave significant estates—that's over ten million dollars—to charities. So that made me wonder what was up with these nonprofits. I called the guy at the SEC I've been working with and he put me in touch with the people in charge of registering charities in New York, New Jersey, Massachusetts, and Delaware. I followed the trail of the nonprofits and found they were all owned ultimately by the Lotus Research Foundation. It's controlled by Farley and Sheldon. I checked them out. Sheldon was a rich cardiologist who'd been sued for malpractice a couple of times and been investigated for some securities fraud and insider trading. Farley? . . . Okay, now *he* was interesting. A crackpot. Trying to get funding for some weird cloning theory. I'd found his name on a card for the Lotus Foundation at the Whitleys'. It had something to do with alternative medical treatment but it didn't say what specifically."

LaTour explained about checking with Mac and the other Cardiac Support Center patients to see if they'd heard from the foundation. That led them to Covey.

"Immortality," Dempsey said slowly. "And people fell for it."

Together forever. . . .

"Well, they were pretty doped up on Luminux, remember," Tal said.

But LaTour offered what was perhaps the more insightful answer. "People always fall for shit they wanta fall for."

"That McCaffrey woman been released yet?" Dempsey asked uneasily. Arresting the wrong person was probably as embarrassing as declaring a bum 2124 (and as expensive; Sandra Whitley's lawyer—a guy as harsh as she was—had already contacted the Sheriff's Department, threatening suit).

"Oh, yeah. Dropped all charges," Tal said. Then he looked over his desk. "I'm going to finish up the paperwork and ship it off to the prosecutor. Then I've got some spreadsheets to get back to."

He glanced up to see a cryptic look pass between LaTour and the captain. He wondered what it meant.

∞

Naiveté.

The tacit exchange in Tal's office between the two older cops was a comment on Tal's naiveté. The paperwork didn't get "finished up" at all. Over the next few days it just grew and grew and grew.

As did his hours. His working day expanded from an average 8.3 hours to 12 plus.

LaTour happily pointed out, "You call a twenty-one-twenty-four, you're the case officer. You stay with it all the way till the end. Ain't life sweet?"

And the end was nowhere in sight. Analyzing the evidence—the hundreds of cartons removed from the Lotus Foundation and from Sheldon's office—Tal learned that the Bensons hadn't been the first victims. Farley and Sheldon had engineered other suicides, going back several years, and had stolen tens of millions of dollars. The prior suicides were like the Bensons and the Whitleys— upper class and quite ill, though not necessarily terminally. Tal was shocked to find that he was familiar with one of the earlier victims: Mary Stemple, a physicist who'd taught at the Princeton Institute for Advanced Study, the famed think-tank where Einstein had worked. Tal had read some of her papers. A trained mathematician, she'd done most of her work in physics and astronomy and made important discoveries about the size and nature of the universe. It was a true shame that she'd been tricked into taking her life; she might have had years of important discoveries ahead of her.

He was troubled by the deaths, yes, but he was even more shocked to find that the foundation had actually supervised the in vitro fertilization of six eggs, which had been implanted in surrogate mothers, three of whom had already given birth to children. They were ultimately placed with parents who could not otherwise conceive.

This had been done, Tal, LaTour, and the district attorney concluded, so that Farley and Sheldon could prove to potential clients that they were actually doing the cloning (though another reason, it appeared, was to make an additional fee from childless couples).

The main concern was for the health of the children and the county hired several legitimate genetics doctors and pediatricians to see if the three children who'd been born and the three fetuses within the surrogate mothers were healthy. They were examined and found to be fine and, despite the immortality scam, the surrogate births and the adoption placements were completely legal, the attorney general concluded.

One of the geneticists Tal and LaTour had consulted said, "So Bill Farley was behind this?" The man had shaken his head. "We've been hearing about his crazy ideas for years. A wacko."

"There any chance," Tal wondered, "that someday somebody'll actually be able to do what he was talking about?"

"Cloning consciousness?" The doctor laughed. "You said you're a statistician, right?"

"That's right."

"You know what the odds are of being able to perfectly duplicate the structure of any given human brain?"

"Small as a germ's ass?" LaTour suggested.

The doctor considered this and said, "That sums it up pretty well."

∞

The day was too nice to be inside so Mac McCaffrey and Robert Covey were in the park. Tal spotted them on a bench overlooking a duck pond. He waved and veered toward them.

She appeared to be totally immersed in the sunlight and the soft breeze; Tal remem-

bered how much this member of the Four
Percent Club loved the out-of-doors.

Covey, Mac had confided to Tal, was doing pretty well. His blood pressure was
down and he was in good spirits as he approached his surgery. She was breaching
confidentiality rules by telling Tal this but
she justified it on the grounds that Tal was a
police officer investigating a case involving
her patient. Another reason was simply that
Tal liked the old guy and was concerned
about him.

Mac also told him that Covey had finally
called his son and left a message about his
condition and the impending surgery.
There'd been no reply, though Covey'd gotten a hang-up on his voice mail, the caller
ID on the phone indicating "Out of Area."
Mac took the optimistic position that it had
indeed been his son on the other end of the
line and the man hadn't left a message because he preferred to talk to his father in
person. Time would tell.

In his office an hour ago, on the phone,
Tal had been distracted as he listened to
Mac's breathy, enthusiastic report about her
patient. He'd listened attentively but was
mostly waiting for an appropriate lull in the
conversation to leap in with a dinner invita-

tion. None had presented itself, though, before she explained she had to get to a meeting. He'd hurriedly made plans to meet here.

Tal now joined them and she looked up with that charming crooked smile that he really liked (and was more than just a little sexy).

"Hey," he said.

"Officer," Robert Covey said. They warmly shook hands. Tal hesitated for a moment in greeting Mac but then thought, hell with it, bent down and kissed her on the cheek. This seemed unprofessional on several levels—his as well as hers—but she didn't seem to care; he knew *he* certainly didn't have a problem with the lapse.

Tal proceeded to explain to Covey that since he was the only victim who'd survived the Lotus Foundation scam the police needed a signed and notarized copy of his statement.

"In case I croak when I'm under the knife you'll still have the evidence to put the pricks away."

That was it exactly. Tal shrugged. "Well . . ."

"Don'tcha worry," the old man said. "I'm happy to."

Tal handed him the statement. "Look it

over, make any changes you want. I'll print
out a final version and we'll get it notarized."

"Will do." Covey skimmed it and then
looked up. "How 'bout something to drink?
There's a bar—"

"Coffee, tea or soda," Mac said ominously.
"It's not even noon yet."

"She claims she negotiates," Covey muttered to Tal. "But she don't."

The old man pointed toward the park's
concession stand at the top of a hill some
distance away. "Coffee's not bad there—for
an outfit that's not named for a whaler."

"I'll get it."

"I'll have a large with cream."

"He'll have a medium, skim milk," Mac
said. "Tea for me, please. Sugar." She fired a
crooked smile Tal's way.

∞

About a hundred yards from the bench
where the old man sat chatting away with his
friend, a young woman walked along the
park path. The redhead was short, busty, at-
tractive, wearing a beautiful tennis bracelet
and a diamond/emerald ring, off which the
sunlight glinted fiercely.

She kept her eyes down as she walked, so
nobody could see her abundant tears.

Margaret Ludlum had been crying on

and off for several days. Ever since her boss and lover, Dr. Anthony Sheldon, had been arrested.

Margaret had greeted the news of his arrest—and Farley's too—with horror, knowing that she'd probably be the next to be picked up. After all, she'd been the one that Sheldon and Farley had sent as a representative of the Lotus Research Foundation to the couples who were planning to kill themselves. It was she who'd slipped them plenty of Luminux during their last few weeks on earth, then suggested they buy the blueprint for their deaths—the suicide books—and coerced them into killing themselves and afterwards cleaned up any evidence linking them to the Foundation or its two principals.

But the police had taken her statement—denying everything, of course—and let her go. It was clear they suspected Sheldon and Farley had an accomplice but seemed to think that it was one of Farley's research assistants. Maybe they thought that only a man was capable of killing defenseless people.

Wrong. Margaret had been completely comfortable with assisted suicide. And more: She'd been only a minute away from murdering Robert Covey the other day as he walked down the street after leaving the Lotus Research Foundation. But just as she

started toward him a van stopped nearby
and two men jumped out, pulling him to
safety. Other officers had raided the foundation. She'd veered down a side street and
called Sheldon to warn him. But it was too
late. They got him outside his office at the
hospital as he'd tried to flee.

Oh, yes, she'd been perfectly willing to
kill Covey then.

And was perfectly willing to kill him now.

She watched that detective who'd initially
come to interview Tony Sheldon walk away
from the bench and up the path toward the
refreshment stand. It didn't matter that he
was leaving; he wasn't her target.

Only Covey. With the old man gone it
would be much harder to get a conviction,
Sheldon explained. He might get off altogether or serve only a few years—that's what
they doled out in most cases of assisted suicides. The cardiologist promised he'd finally get divorced and he and Margaret
would move to Europe. . . . They'd taken
some great trips to the south of France and
the weeks there had been wonderful. Oh,
how she missed him.

Missed the money too, of course. That was
the other reason she had to get Tony out of
jail, of course. The doctor had been meaning to set up an account for her but hadn't

gotten around to it. She'd let it slide for too
long and the paperwork never materialized.

In her purse, banging against her hip, she
felt the heavy pistol, the one she'd been planning to use on Covey several days ago. She
was familiar with guns—she'd helped several
of the other foundation clients "transition"
by shooting themselves. And though she'd
never actually pulled the trigger and murdered someone, she knew she could do it.

The tears were gone now. She was thinking of how best to handle the shooting.
Studying the old man and that woman—
who'd have to die too, of course; she'd be a
witness against Margaret herself for the
murder today. Anyway, the double murder
would make the scenario more realistic. It
would look like a mugging. Margaret would
demand the wallet and the woman's purse
and when they handed the items over, she'd
shoot them both in the head.

Pausing now, next to a tree, Margaret
looked over the park. A few passersby, but
no one was near Covey and the woman. The
detective—Simms, she recalled—was still
hiking up the hill to the concession stand.
He was two hundred yards from the bench;
she could kill them both and be in her car
speeding away before he could sprint back
to the bench.

She waited until he disappeared into a stand of trees then reached into her purse, cocking the pistol. Margaret stepped out from behind the tree and moved quickly down the path that led to the bench. A glance around her. Nobody was present.

Closer now, closer. Along the asphalt path, damp from an earlier rain and the humid spring air.

She was twenty feet away . . . ten . . .

She stepped quickly up behind them. They looked up. The woman gave a faint smile in greeting—a smile that faded as she noted Margaret's cold eyes.

"Who are you?" the woman asked, alarm in her voice.

Margaret Ludlum said nothing. She pulled the gun from her purse.

∞

"Wallet!" Pointing the pistol directly at the old man's face.

"What?"

"Give me your wallet!" Then turning to the woman, "And the purse! Now!"

"You want—?"

They were confused, being mugged by someone outfitted by Neiman Marcus.

"Now!" Margaret screamed.

The woman thrust the purse forward and

stood, holding her hands out. "Look, just calm down."

The old man was frantically pulling his wallet from his pocket and holding it out unsteadily.

Margaret grabbed the items and shoved them into her shoulder bag. Then she looked at the man's eyes and—rather than feel any sympathy, she felt that stillness she always did when slipping someone drugs or showing them how to grip the gun or seal the garage with duct tape to make the most efficient use of the carbon monoxide.

The woman was saying, "Please, don't do anything stupid. Just take everything and leave!"

Then Robert Covey squinted. He was looking at Margaret with certain understanding. He knew what this was about. "Leave her alone," he said. "Me, it's okay. It's all right. Just let her go."

But she thrust the gun forward at Covey as the woman with him screamed and dropped to the ground. Margaret began to pull the trigger, whispering the phrase she always did when helping transition the foundation's clients, offering a prayer for a safe journey. "God be with—"

A flash of muddy light filled her vision as

she felt, for a tiny fragment of a second, a fist or rock slam into her chest.

"But . . . what . . ."

Then nothing but numb silence.

∞

A thousand yards away, it seemed.

If not miles.

Talbot Simms squinted toward the bench, where he could see the forms of Robert Covey and Mac on their feet, backing away from the body of the woman he'd just shot. Mac was pulling out her cell phone, dropping it, picking it up again, looking around in panic.

Tal lowered the gun and stared.

A moment before, Tal had paid the vendor and was turning from the concession stand, holding the tray of drinks. Frowning, he saw a woman standing beside the bench, pointing something toward Mac and Covey, Mac rearing away then handing her purse over, the old man giving her something, his wallet, it seemed.

And then Tal had noticed that what she held was a gun.

He knew that she was in some way connected to Sheldon or Farley and the Lotus Foundation. The red hair . . . Yes! Sheldon's

secretary, unsmiling Celtic Margaret. He'd
known too that she'd come here to shoot
the only living eyewitness to the scam—and
probably Mac too.

Dropping the tray of tea and coffee, he'd
drawn his revolver. He'd intended to sprint
back toward them, calling for her to stop,
threatening her. But when he saw Mac fall to
the ground, futilely covering her face, and
Margaret shoving the pistol forward, he'd
known she was going to shoot.

Tal had cocked his own revolver to single-
action and stepped into a combat firing
stance, left hand curled under and around
his right, weight evenly distributed on both
feet, aiming high and slightly to the left,
compensating for gravity and a faint breeze.

He'd fired, felt the kick of the recoil and
heard the sharp report, followed by screams
behind him of bystanders diving for cover.

Remaining motionless, he'd cocked the
gun again and prepared to fire a second
time in case he'd missed.

But he saw immediately that another shot
wouldn't be necessary.

Tal Simms carefully lowered the hammer
of his weapon, replaced it in his holster and
began running down the path.

∞

"Excuse me, you were standing *where?*"

Tal ignored Greg LaTour's question and asked them both one more time, "You're okay? You're sure?"

The bearded cop persisted. "You were on *that* hill. Way the fuck up *there?*"

Mac told Tal that she was fine. He instinctively put his arm around her. Covey too said that he was unhurt, though he added that, as a heart patient, he could do without scares like that one.

Margaret Ludlum's gun had fired but it was merely a reflex after Tal's bullet had struck her squarely in the chest. The slug from her pistol had buried itself harmlessly in the ground.

Tal glanced at her body, now covered with a green tarp from the Medical Examiner's Office. He waited to feel upset, or shocked or guilty, but he was only numb. Those feelings would come later, he supposed. At the moment he was just relieved to find that Mac and Robert Covey were all right—and that the final itch in the case had been alleviated: The tough Irish girl, Margaret, was the missing link.

They must've hired muscle or used somebody in the foundation for the dirty work.

As the Crime Scene techs picked up evidence around the body and looked through the woman's purse, LaTour persisted. "That hill up there? No fucking way."

Tal glanced up. "Yeah. Up there by the concession stand. Why?"

The bearded cop glanced at Mac. "He's kidding. He's jerking my chain, right?"

"No, that's where he was."

"That's a fucking long shot. Wait . . . how big's your barrel?"

"What?"

"On your service piece."

"Three inch."

LaTour said. "You made that shot with a three-inch barrel?"

"We've pretty much established that, Greg. Can we move on?" Tal turned back to Mac and smiled, feeling weak, he was so relieved to see her safe.

But LaTour said, "You told me you don't shoot."

"I didn't say that at all. You *assumed* I don't shoot. I just didn't want to go the range the other day. I've shot all my life. I was captain of the rifle team at school."

LaTour squinted at the distant concession stand. He shook his head. "No way."

Tal glanced at him and asked, "Okay, you want to know how I did it? There's a trick."

"What?" the big cop asked eagerly.

"Easy. Just calculate the correlation be-

tween gravity as a constant and the esti-
mated mean velocity of the wind over the
time it takes the bullet to travel from points
A to B—that's the muzzle to the target. Got
that? Then you just multiply distance times
that correlated factor divided by the mass of
the bullet times its velocity squared."

"You—" The big cop squinted again.
"Wait, you—"

"It's a joke, Greg."

"You son of a bitch. You had me."

"Haven't you noticed it's not that hard to
do?"

The cop mouthed words that Mac couldn't
see but Tal had no trouble deciphering.

LaTour squinted one last time toward the
knoll and exhaled a laugh. "Let's get statements." He nodded to Robert Covey and escorted him toward his car, calling back to Tal,
"You get hers. That okay with you, Einstein?"

"Sure."

Tal led Mac to a park bench out of sight of
Margaret's body and listened to what she
had to say about the incident, jotting down
the facts in his precise handwriting. An officer drove Covey home and Tal found himself
alone with Mac. There was silence for a moment and he asked, "Say, one thing? Could
you help me fill out this questionnaire?"

"I'd be happy to."

He pulled one out of his briefcase, looked at it, then back to her. "How 'bout dinner tonight?"

"Is that one of the questions?"

"It's one of *my* questions. Not a police question."

"Well, the thing is I've got a date tonight. Sorry."

He nodded. "Oh, sure." Couldn't think of anything to follow up with. He pulled out his pen and smoothed the questionnaire, thinking: Of *course* she had a date. Women like her, high-ranking members of the Four Percent Club, always had dates. He wondered if it'd been the Pascal-sex comment that had knocked him out of the running. Note for the future: Don't bring that one up too soon.

Mac continued, "Yeah, tonight I'm going to help Mr. Covey find a health club with a pool. He likes to swim but he shouldn't do it alone. So we're going to find a place that's got a lifeguard."

"Really? Good for him." He looked up from Question 1.

"But I'm free Saturday," Mac said.

"Saturday? Well, I am too."

Silence. "Then how's Saturday?" she asked.

"I think it's great ... Now how 'bout those questions?"

∞

A week later the Lotus Research Foundation case was nearly tidied up—as was Tal's office, much to his relief—and he was beginning to think about the other tasks awaiting him: the SEC investigation, the statistical analysis for next year's personnel assignments and, of course, hounding fellow officers to get their questionnaires in on time.

The prosecutor still wanted some final statements for the Farley and Sheldon trials, though, and he'd asked Tal to interview the parents who'd adopted the three children born following the in vitro fertilization at the foundation.

Two of the three couples lived nearby and he spent one afternoon taking their statements. The last couple was in Warwick, a small town outside of Albany, over an hour away. Tal made the drive on a Sunday afternoon, zipping down the picturesque roadway along the Hudson River, the landscape punctuated with blooming azaleas, forsythia, and a billion spring flowers, the car filling with the scent of mulch and hot loam and sweet asphalt.

He found both Warwick and the couple's bungalow with no difficulty. The husband

and wife, in their late twenties, were identically pudgy and rosy skinned. Uneasy too, until Tal explained that his mission there had nothing to do with any challenges to the adoption. It was merely a formality for a criminal case.

Like the other parents they provided good information that would be helpful in prosecuting Farley and Sheldon. For a half hour Tal jotted careful notes and then thanked them for their time. As he was leaving he walked past a small, cheery room decorated in a circus motif.

A little girl, about four, stood in the doorway. It was the youngster the couple had adopted from the foundation. She was adorable—blond, gray-eyed, with a heart-shaped face.

"This is Amy," the mother said.

"Hello, Amy," Tal offered.

She nodded shyly.

Amy was clutching a piece of paper and some crayons. "Did you draw that?" he asked.

"Uh-huh. I like to draw."

"I can tell. You've got lots of pictures." He nodded at the girl's walls.

"Here," she said, holding the sheet out. "You can have this. I just drew it."

"For me?" Tal asked. He glanced at her

mother, who nodded her approval. He studied the picture for a moment. "Thank you, Amy. I love it. I'll put it up on my wall at work."

The girl's face broke into a beaming smile.

Tal said good-bye to her parents and ten minutes later he was cruising south on the parkway. When he came to the turnoff that would take him to his house and his Sunday retreat into the world of mathematics, though, Tal continued on. He drove instead to his office at the County Building.

A half hour later he was on the road again. En route to an address in Chesterton, a few miles away.

He pulled up in front of a split-level house surrounded by a small but immaculately trimmed yard. Two plastic tricycles and other assorted toys sat in the driveway.

But this wasn't the right place, he concluded with irritation. Damn. He must've written the address down wrong.

The house he was looking for had to be nearby and Tal decided to ask the owner here where it was. Walking to the door, Tal pushed the bell then stood back.

A pretty blonde in her thirties greeted him with a cheerful, "Hi. Help you?"

"I'm looking for Greg LaTour's house."

"Well, you found it. Hi, I'm his wife, Joan."

"He lives *here*?" Tal asked, glancing past her into a suburban home right out of a Hollywood sitcom. Thinking too: *And he's married?*

She laughed. "Hold on. I'll get him."

A moment later Greg LaTour came to the door, wearing shorts, sandals, and a green Izod shirt. He blinked in surprise and looked back over his shoulder into the house. Then he stepped outside and pulled the door shut after him. "What're you doing here?"

"Needed to tell you something about the case. . . ." But Tal's voice faded. He was staring at two cute blond girls, twins, about eight years old, who'd come around the side of the house and were looking at Tal curiously.

One said, "Daddy, the ball's in the bushes. We can't get it."

"Honey, I've got to talk to my friend here," he said in a sing-song, fatherly voice. "I'll be there in a minute."

"Okay." They disappeared.

"You've got two kids?"

"*Four* kids."

"How long you been married?"

"Eighteen years."

"But I thought you were single. You never mentioned family. You didn't wear a ring.

Your office, the biker posters, the bars after work . . ."

"That's who I need to be to do my job," LaTour said in a low voice. "That life—" He nodded vaguely in the direction of the Sheriff's Department. "—and this life I keep separate. Completely."

That's something else . . .

Tal now understood the meaning of the phrase. It wasn't about tragedies in his life, marital breakups, alienated children. And there was nothing LaTour was hiding from Tal. This was a life kept separate from everybody in the department.

"So you're mad I'm here," Tal said.

A shrug. "Just wish you'd called first."

"Sorry."

LaTour shrugged. "You go to church today?"

"I don't go to church. Why?"

"Why're you wearing a tie on Sunday?"

"I don't know. I just do. Is it crooked?"

The big cop said, "No it's not crooked. So. What're you doing here?"

"Hold on a minute."

Tal got his briefcase out of the car and returned to the porch. "I stopped by the office and checked up on the earlier suicides Sheldon and Farley arranged."

"You mean from a few years ago?"

"Right. Well, one of them was a professor named Mary Stemple. I'd heard of her—she was a physicist at Princeton. I read some of her work a while ago. She was brilliant. She spent the last three years of her life working on this analysis of the luminosity of stars and measuring blackbody radiation—"

"I've got burgers about to go on the grill," LaTour grumbled.

"Okay. Got it. Well, this was published just before she killed herself." He handed La-Tour what he'd downloaded from the *Journal of Advanced Astrophysics* Web site:

THE INFINITE JOURNEY OF LIGHT:
A NEW APPROACH TO MEASURING
DISTANT STELLAR RADIATION
BY PROF. MARY STEMPLE, PH.D.

He flipped to the end of the article, which consisted of several pages of complicated formulae. They involved hundreds of numbers and Greek and English letters and mathematical symbols. The one that occurred most frequently was the sign for infinity: ∞

LaTour looked up. "There a punch line to all this?"

"Oh, you bet there is." He explained

about his drive to Warwick to interview the adoptive couple.

And then he held up the picture that their daughter, Amy, had given him. It was a drawing of the earth and the moon and a spaceship—and all around them, filling the sky, were infinity symbols, growing smaller and smaller as they receded into space.

Forever . . .

Tal added, "And this wasn't the only one. Her walls were *covered* with pictures she'd done that had infinity signs in them. When I saw this I remembered Stemple's work. I went back to the office and I looked up her paper."

"What're you saying?" LaTour frowned.

"Mary Stemple killed herself five years ago. The girl who drew this was conceived at the foundation's clinic a month after she died."

"Jesus . . ." The big cop stared at the picture. "You don't think . . . Hell, it can't be real, that cloning stuff. That doctor we talked to, he said it was impossible."

Tal said nothing, continued to stare at the picture.

LaTour shook his head. "Naw, naw. You know what they did, Sheldon or that girl of his? Or Farley? They showed the kid pictures of that symbol. You know, so they could prove to other clients that the cloning worked. That's all."

"Sure," Tal said. "That's what happened. . . . Probably."

Still, they stood in silence for a long moment, this trained mathematician and this hardened cop, staring, captivated, at a clumsy, crayon picture drawn by a cute four-year-old.

"It can't be," LaTour muttered. "Germ's ass, remember?"

"Yeah, it's impossible," Tal said, staring at the symbol. He repeated: "Probably."

"Daddy!" Came a voice from the backyard.

LaTour called, "Be there in a minute, honey!" Then he looked up at Tal and said, "Hell, as long as you're here, come on in. Have dinner. I make great burgers."

Tal considered the invitation but his eyes were drawn back to the picture, the stars, the moon, the infinity signs. "Thanks but think I'll pass. I'm going back to the office for a while. All that evidence we took out of the foundation? I wanta look over the data a little more."

"Suit yourself, Einstein," the homicide cop said. He started back into the house but paused and turned back. "Data plural," he said, pointing a huge finger at Tal's chest.

"Data plural," Tal agreed.

LaTour vanished inside, the screen door swinging shut behind him with a bang.

LAWRENCE BLOCK

There are two kinds of stylists: the show-off who wants to be congratulated every time he turns a nice phrase and the kind who quietly turns a nice phrase but just gets on with the story. **Lawrence Block** is one of the latter. Even at the outset of his career, when he was turning out books at a furious pace, he managed to bring elegance and taste to even minor assignments, particularly with a knowing, wry take on the relationships and interactions between his characters: men with women, men with men, fathers and sons, husbands and wives. His hard work paid off. Not only is he one of the premier crime novelists of our time—with two bestselling series: the Matt Scudder novels (dark), including *Eight Million Ways to Die*, *The Devil Knows You're Dead*, and the Edgar-winning *A Dance at the Slaughterhouse*; and the Bernie Rhodenbarr mysteries (humorous), including *The Burglar Who Thought He Was Bogart* and *The Burglar Who Traded Ted Williams*—he is also one of our most accomplished short story writers. No wonder the Mystery Writers of America hailed him as one of the Grand Masters. Recently he turned to editing books, with seven stellar anthologies published: *Master's Choice, Vol. 1 and 2*, *Opening Shots, Vol. 1 and 2*, *Speaking of Lust* and *Speaking of Greed*, and the MWA anthology *Blood on Their Hands*. His latest novels are *Hit Parade* and *All the Flowers Are Dying*.

KELLER'S ADJUSTMENT

Lawrence Block

Keller, waiting for the traffic light to turn from red to green, wondered what had happened to the world. The traffic light wasn't the problem. There'd been traffic lights for longer than he could remember, longer than he'd been alive. For almost as long as there had been automobiles, he supposed, although the automobile had clearly come first, and would in fact have necessitated the traffic light. At first they'd have made do without them, he supposed, and then, when there were enough cars around for them to start slamming into one another, someone would have figured out that some form of control was necessary, some device to stop east-west traffic while allowing north-south traffic to proceed, and then switching.

He could imagine an early motorist fulminating against the new regimen. *Whole world's going to hell. They're taking our rights away one after another. Light turns red because some damn timer tells it to turn red, a man's supposed to stop what he's doing and hit the brakes. Don't matter if there ain't another car around for fifty miles, he's gotta stop and stand there like a goddam fool until the light turns green and tells him he can go again. Who wants to live in a country like that? Who wants to bring children into a world where that kind of crap goes on?*

A horn sounded, jarring Keller abruptly from the early days of the twentieth century to the early days of the twenty-first. The light, he noted, had turned from red to green, and the fellow in the SUV just behind him felt a need to bring this fact to Keller's attention. Keller, without feeling much in the way of actual irritation or anger, allowed himself a moment of imagination in which he shifted into park, engaged the emergency brake, got out of the car and walked back to the SUV, whose driver would already have begun to regret leaning on the horn. Even as the man (pig-faced and jowly in Keller's fantasy) was reaching for the button to lock the door, Keller was opening the door, taking hold of the man (sweating now, stammering, making simultaneous threats and excuses) by the shirtfront, yanking him out of the car, sending him sprawling on the pavement. Then, while the man's child (no, make it his wife, a fat shrew with dyed hair and rheumy eyes) watched in horror, Keller bent from the waist and dispatched the man with a movement learned from the Burmese master U Minh U, one in which the adept's hands barely appeared to touch the subject, but death, while indescribably painful, was virtually instantaneous.

Keller, satisfied by the fantasy, drove on. Behind him, the driver of the SUV—an unaccompanied young woman, Keller now noted, her hair secured by a bandana, and a sack of groceries on the seat beside her— followed along for half a block, then turned off to the right, seemingly unaware of her close brush with death.

How you do go on, he thought.

It was all the damned driving. Before everything went to hell, he wouldn't have had to drive clear across the country. He'd have taken a cab to JFK and caught a flight to Phoenix, where he'd have rented a car, driven it around for the day or two it would take to do the job, then turned it in and flown back to New York. In and out, case closed, and he could get on with his life.

And leave no traces behind, either. They made you show ID to get on the plane, they'd been doing that for a few years now, but it didn't have to be terribly good ID. Now they all but fingerprinted you before they let you board, and they went through your checked baggage and gave your carry-on luggage a lethal dose of radiation. God help you if you had a nail clipper on your key ring.

He hadn't flown at all since the new security procedures had gone into effect, and he didn't know that he'd ever get on a plane again. Business travel was greatly reduced, he'd read, and he could understand why. A business traveler would rather hop in his car and drive five hundred miles than get to the airport two hours early and go through all the hassles the new system imposed. It was bad enough if your business consisted of meeting with groups of salesmen and giving them pep talks. If you were in Keller's line of work, well, it was out of the question.

Keller rarely traveled other than for business, but sometimes he'd go somewhere for a stamp auction, or because it was the middle of a New York winter and he felt the urge to lie in the sun somewhere. He supposed he could still fly on such occasions, showing valid ID and clipping his nails before departure, but would he want to? Would it still be pleasure travel if you had to go through all that in order to get there?

He felt like that imagined motorist, griping about red lights. *Hell, if that's what they're gonna make me do, I'll just walk. Or I'll stay home. That'll show them!*

It all changed, of course, on a September morning, when a pair of airliners flew into the twin towers of the World Trade Center. Keller, who lived on First Avenue not far from the UN building, had not been home at the time. He was in Miami, where he had already spent a week, getting ready to kill a man named Rubén Olivares. Olivares was a Cuban, and an important figure in one of the Cuban exile groups, but Keller wasn't sure that was why someone had been willing to spend a substantial amount of money to have him killed. It was possible, certainly, that he was a thorn in the side of the Castro government, and that someone had decided it would be safer and more cost-effective to hire the work done than to send a team of agents from Havana. It was also possible that Olivares had turned out to be a spy for Havana, and it was his fellow exiles who had it in for him.

Then too, he might be sleeping with the wrong person's wife, or muscling in on the wrong person's drug trade. With a little investigative work, Keller might have managed to find out who wanted Olivares dead, and why, but he'd long since determined that such considerations were none of his business. What difference did it make? He had a job to do, and all he had to do was do it.

Monday night, he'd followed Olivares around, watched him eat dinner at a steakhouse in Coral Gables, then tagged along when Olivares and two of his dinner companions hit a couple of titty bars in Miami Beach. Olivares left with one of the dancers, and Keller tailed him to the woman's apartment and waited for him to come out. After an hour and a half, Keller decided the man was spending the night. Keller, who'd watched lights go on and off in the apartment house, was reasonably certain he knew which apartment the couple was occupying, and didn't think it would prove difficult to get into the building. He thought about going in and getting it over with. It was too late to catch a flight to New York, it was the middle of the night, but he could get the work done and stop at his motel to shower and collect his luggage, then go straight to the airport and catch an early morning flight to New York.

Or he could sleep late and fly home sometime in the early afternoon. Several airlines flew from New York to Florida, and there were flights all day long. Miami International was not his favorite airport—it was not anybody's favorite airport—but he could skip it if he wanted, turning in his rental car at Fort Lauderdale or West Palm Beach and flying home from there.

No end of options, once the work was done.

But he'd have to kill the woman, the topless dancer.

He'd do that if he had to, but he didn't like the idea of killing people just because they were in the way. A higher body count drew more police and media attention, but that wasn't it, nor was the notion of slaughtering the innocent. How did he know the woman was innocent? For that matter, who was to say Olivares was guilty of anything?

Later, when he thought about it, it seemed to him that the deciding factor was purely physical. He'd slept poorly the night before, rising early and spending the whole day driving around unfamiliar streets. He was tired, and he didn't much feel like forcing a door and climbing a flight of stairs and killing one person, let alone two. And suppose she had a roommate, and suppose the roommate had a boyfriend, and—

He went back to his motel, took a long hot shower, and went to bed.

When he woke up he didn't turn on the TV, but went across the street to the place where he'd been having his breakfast every morning. He walked in the door and saw that something was different. They had a television set on the back counter, and everybody was staring at it. He watched for a few minutes, then picked up a container of coffee and took it back to his room. He sat in front of his own TV and watched the same scenes, over and over and over.

If he'd done his work the night before, he realized, he might have been in the air when it happened. Or maybe not, because he'd probably have decided to get some sleep instead, so he'd be right where he was, in his motel room, watching the plane fly into the building. The only certain difference was that Rubén Olivares, who as things stood was probably watching the same footage everybody else in America was watching (except that he might well be watching it on a Spanish-language station)—well, Olivares wouldn't be watching TV. Nor would he be

on it. A garden-variety Miami homicide
wasn't worth airtime on a day like this, not
even if the deceased was of some importance in the Cuban exile community, not
even if he'd been murdered in the apartment of a topless dancer, with her own
death a part of the package. A newsworthy
item any other day, but not on this day.
There was only one sort of news today, one
topic with endless permutations, and Keller
watched it all day long.

It was Wednesday before it even occurred to
him to call Dot, and late Thursday before he
finally got a call through to her in White
Plains. "I've been wondering about you,
Keller," she said. "There are all these planes
on the ground in Newfoundland, they were
in the air when it happened and got
rerouted there, and God knows when
they're gonna let them come home. I had
the feeling you might be there."

"In Newfoundland?"

"The local people are taking the stranded
passengers into their homes," she said. "Making them welcome, giving them cups of beef
bouillon and ostrich sandwiches, and—"

"Ostrich sandwiches?"

"Whatever. I just pictured you there,

Keller, making the best of a bad situation, which I guess is what you're doing in Miami. God knows when they're going to let you fly home. Have you got a car?"

"A rental."

"Well, hang on to it," she said. "Don't give it back, because the car rental agencies are emptied out, with so many people stranded and trying to drive home. Maybe that's what you ought to do."

"I was thinking about it," he said. "But I was also thinking about, you know. The guy."

"Oh, him."

"I don't want to say his name, but—"

"No, don't."

"The thing is, he's still, uh . . ."

"Doing what he always did."

"Right."

"Instead of doing like John Brown."

"Huh?"

"Or John Brown's body," Dot said. "Moldering in the grave, as I recall."

"Whatever *moldering* means."

"We can probably guess, Keller, if we put our minds to it. You're wondering is it still on, right?"

"It seems ridiculous even thinking about it," he said. "But on the other hand—"

"On the other hand," she said, "they sent

half the money. I'd just as soon not have to give it back."

"No."

"In fact," she said, "I'd just as soon have them send the other half. If they're the ones to call it off, we keep what they sent. And if they say it's still on, well, you're already in Miami, aren't you? Sit tight, Keller, while I make a phone call."

Whoever had wanted Olivares dead had not changed his mind as a result of several thousand deaths fifteen hundred miles away. Keller, thinking about it, couldn't see why he should be any less sanguine about the prospect of killing Olivares than he had been Monday night. On the television news, there was a certain amount of talk about the possible positive effects of the tragedy. New Yorkers, someone suggested, would be brought closer together, aware as never before of the bonds created by their common humanity.

Did Keller feel a bond with Rubén Olivares of which he'd been previously unaware? He thought about it and decided he did not. If anything, he was faintly aware of a grudging resentment against the man. If Olivares had spent less time over dinner and hurried through the foreplay of the titty bar, if he'd gone directly to the topless dancer's apartment and left the premises in the throes of post-coital bliss, Keller could have taken him out in time to catch the last flight back to the city. He might have been in his own apartment when the attack came.

And what earthly difference would that have made? None, he had to concede. He'd have watched the hideous drama unfold on his own television set, just as he'd watched on the motel's unit, and he'd have been no more capable of influencing events whatever set he watched.

Olivares, with his steak dinners and topless dancers, made a poor surrogate for the heroic cops and firemen, the doomed office workers. He was, Keller conceded, a fellow member of the human race. If all men were brothers, a possibility Keller, an only child, was willing to entertain, well, brothers had been killing one another for a good deal longer than Keller had been on the job. If Olivares was Abel, Keller was willing to be Cain.

If nothing else, he was grateful for something to do.

And Olivares made it easy. All over America, people were writing checks and inundating blood banks, trying to do something for the victims in New York. Cops and firemen and ordinary citizens were piling into cars and heading north and east, eager to join in the rescue efforts. Olivares, on the other hand, went on leading his life of self-indulgence, going to an office in the morning, making a circuit of bars and restaurants in the afternoon and early evening, and finishing up with rum drinks in a room full of bare breasts.

Keller tagged him for three days and three nights, and by the third night he'd decided not to be squeamish about the topless dancer. He waited outside the titty bar, until a call of nature led him into the bar, past Olivares's table (where the man was chatting up three silicone-enhanced young ladies) and on to the men's room. Standing at the urinal, Keller wondered what he'd do if the Cuban took all three of them home.

He washed his hands, left the restroom, and saw Olivares counting out bills to settle his tab. All three women were still at the table, and playing up to him, one clutching his arm and leaning her breasts against it, the others just as coquettish. Keller, who'd been ready to sacrifice one bystander, found himself drawing the line at three.

But wait—Olivares was on his feet, his body language suggesting he was excusing himself for a moment. And yes, he was on his way to the men's room, clearly aware of the disadvantage of attempting a night of love on a full bladder.

Keller slipped into the room ahead of him, ducked into an empty stall. There was an elderly gentleman at the urinal, talking soothingly in Spanish to himself, or perhaps to his prostate. Olivares entered the room, stood at the adjoining urinal, and began chattering in Spanish to the older man, who spoke slow sad sentences in response.

Shortly after arriving in Miami, Keller had gotten hold of a gun, a .22-caliber revolver. It was a small gun with a short barrel, and fit easily in his pocket. He took it out now, wondering if the noise would carry.

If the older gentleman left first, Keller might not need the gun. But if Olivares finished first, Keller couldn't let him leave, and would have to do them both, and that would mean using the gun, and a minimum of two shots. He watched them over the top of the stall, wishing that something would happen before some other drunken voyeur felt a need to pee. Then the older man finished up, tucked himself in, and headed for the door.

And paused at the threshold, returning to wash his hands, and saying something to Olivares, who laughed heartily at it, what-

ever it was. Keller, who'd returned the gun
to his pocket, took it out again, and replaced it a moment later when the older
gentleman left. Olivares waited until the
door closed after him, then produced a little blue glass bottle and a tiny spoon. He
treated each of his cavernous nostrils to two
quick hits of what Keller could only pre-
sume to be cocaine, then returned the bottle and spoon to his pocket and turned to
face the sink.

Keller burst out of the stall. Olivares,
washing his hands, evidently couldn't hear
him with the water running; in any event he
didn't react before Keller reached him, one
hand cupping his jowly chin, the other taking hold of his greasy mop of hair. Keller
had never studied the martial arts, not even
from a Burmese with an improbable name,
but he'd been doing this sort of thing long
enough to have learned a trick or two. He
broke Olivares's neck and was dragging him
across the floor to the stall he'd just vacated
when, damn it to hell, the door burst open
and a little man in shirtsleeves got halfway
to the urinal before he suddenly realized
what he'd just seen. His eyes widened, his
jaw dropped, and Keller got him before he
could make a sound.

The little man's bladder, unable to relieve

itself in life, could not be denied in death. Olivares, having emptied his bladder in his last moments of life, voided his bowels. The men's room, no garden spot to begin with, stank to the heavens. Keller stuffed both bodies into one stall and got out of there in a hurry, before some other son of a bitch could rush in and join the party.

Half an hour later he was heading north on I-95. Somewhere north of Stuart he stopped for gas, and in the men's room— empty, spotless, smelling of nothing but pine-scented disinfectant—he put his hands against the smooth white tiles and vomited. Hours later, at a rest area just across the Georgia line, he did so again.

He couldn't blame it on the killing. It had been a bad idea, lurking in the men's room. The traffic was too heavy, with all those drinkers and cocaine-sniffers. The stench of the corpses he'd left there, on top of the reek that had permeated the room to start with, could well have turned his stomach, but it would have done so then, not a hundred miles away when it no longer existed outside of his memory.

Some members of his profession, he knew, typically threw up after a piece of work, just as some veteran actors never failed to vomit before a performance. Keller had known a man once, a cheerfully cold-blooded little murderer with dainty little-girl wrists and a way of holding a cigarette between his thumb and forefinger. The man would chatter about his work, excuse himself, throw up discreetly into a basin, and resume his conversation in midsentence.

A shrink would probably argue that the body was expressing a revulsion which the mind was unwilling to acknowledge, and that sounded about right to Keller. But it didn't apply to him, because he'd never been one for puking. Even early on, when he was new to the game and hadn't found ways to deal with it, his stomach had remained serene.

This particular incident had been unpleasant, even chaotic, but he could if pressed recall others that had been worse.

But there was a more conclusive argument, it seemed to him. Yes, he'd thrown up outside of Stuart, and again in Georgia, and he'd very likely do so a few more times before he reached New York. But it hadn't begun with the killings.

He'd thrown up every couple of hours ever since he sat in front of his television set and watched the towers fall.

———

A week or so after he got back, there was a message on his answering machine. Dot, wanting him to call. He checked his watch, decided it was too early. He made himself a cup of coffee, and when he'd finished it he dialed the number in White Plains.

"Keller," she said. "When you didn't call back, I figured you were out late. And now you're up early."

"Well," he said.

"Why don't you get on a train, Keller? My eyes are sore, and I figure you're a sight for them."

"What's the matter with your eyes?"

"Nothing," she said. "I was trying to express myself in an original fashion, and it's a mistake I won't make again in a hurry. Come see me, why don't you?"

"Now?"

"Why not?"

"I'm beat," he said. "I was up all night, I need to get to sleep."

"What were you . . . never mind, I don't need to know. All right, I'll tell you what. Sleep all you want and come out for dinner. I'll order something from the Chinese. Keller? You're not answering me."

"I'll come out sometime this afternoon," he said.

He went to bed, and early that afternoon

he caught a train to White Plains and a cab from the station. She was on the porch of the big old Victorian on Taunton Place, with a pitcher of iced tea and two glasses on the tin-topped table. "Look," she said, pointing to the lawn. "I swear the trees are dropping their leaves earlier than usual this year. What's it like in New York?"

"I haven't really been paying attention."

"There was a kid who used to come around to rake them, but I guess he must have gone to college or something. What happens if you don't rake the leaves, Keller? You happen to know?"

He didn't.

"And you're not hugely interested, I can see that. There's something different about you, Keller, and I've got a horrible feeling I know what it is. You're not in love, are you?"

"In love?"

"Well, are you? Out all night, and then when you get home all you can do is sleep. Who's the lucky girl, Keller?"

He shook his head. "No girl," he said. "I've been working nights."

"Working? What the hell do you mean, working?"

He let her drag it out of him. A day or two after he got back to the city and turned in his rental car, he'd heard something on the news and went to one of the Hudson River piers, where they were enlisting volunteers to serve food for the rescue workers at Ground Zero. Around ten every evening they'd all get together at the pier, then sail down the river and board another ship anchored near the site. Top chefs supplied the food, and Keller and his fellows dished it out to men who'd worked up prodigious appetites laboring at the smoldering wreckage.

"My God," Dot said. "Keller, I'm trying to picture this. You stand there with a big spoon and fill their plates for them? Do you wear an apron?"

"Everybody wears an apron."

"I bet you look cute in yours. I don't mean to make fun, Keller. What you're doing's a good thing, and of course you'd wear an apron. You wouldn't want to get marinara sauce all over your shirt. But it seems strange to me, that's all."

"It's something to do," he said.

"It's heroic."

He shook his head. "There's nothing heroic about it. It's like working in a diner, dishing out food. The men we feed, they work long shifts doing hard physical work and breathing in all that smoke. That's heroic, if anything is. Though I'm not sure there's any point to it."

"What do you mean?"

"Well, they call them rescue workers," he said, "but they're not rescuing anybody, because there's nobody to rescue. Everybody's dead."

She said something in response but he didn't hear it. "It's the same as with the blood," he said. "The first day, everybody mobbed the hospitals, donating blood for the wounded. But it turned out there weren't any wounded. People either got out of the buildings or they didn't. If they got out, they were okay. If they didn't, they're dead. All that blood people donated? They've been throwing it out."

"It seems like a waste."

"It's all a waste," he said, and frowned. "Anyway, that's what I do every night. I dish out food, and they try to rescue dead people. That way we all keep busy."

"The longer I know you," Dot said, "the more I realize I don't."

"Don't what?"

"Know you, Keller. You never cease to amaze me. Somehow I never pictured you as Florence Nightingale."

"I'm not nursing anybody. All I do is feed them."

"Betty Crocker, then. Either way, it seems like a strange role for a sociopath."

"You think I'm a sociopath?"

"Well, isn't that part of the job description, Keller? You're a hit man, a contract killer. You leave town and kill strangers and get paid for it. How can you do that without being a sociopath?"

He thought about it.

"Look," she said, "I didn't mean to bring it up. It's just a word, and who even knows what it means? Let's talk about something else, like why I called you and got you to come out here."

"Okay."

"Actually," she said, "there's two reasons. First of all, you've got money coming. Miami, remember?"

"Oh, right."

She handed him an envelope. "I thought you'd want this," she said, "although it couldn't have been weighing on your mind, because you never asked about it."

"I hardly thought about it."

"Well, why would you want to think about blood money while you were busy doing good works? But you can probably find a use for it."

"No question."

"You can always buy stamps with it. For your collection."

"Sure."

"It must be quite a collection by now."

"It's coming along."

"I'll bet it is. The other reason I called, Keller, is somebody called me."

"Oh?"

She poured herself some more iced tea, took a sip. "There's work," she said. "If you want it. In Portland, something to do with labor unions."

"Which Portland?"

"You know," she said, "I keep forgetting there's one in Maine, but there is, and I suppose they've got their share of labor problems there, too. But this is Portland, Oregon. As a matter of fact, it's Beaverton, but I think it's a suburb. The area code's the same as Portland."

"Clear across the country," he said.

"Just a few hours in a plane."

They looked at each other. "I can remember," he said, "when all you did was step up to the counter and tell them where you wanted to go. You counted out bills, and they were perfectly happy to be paid in cash. You had to give them a name, but you could make it up on the spot, and the only way they asked for identification was if you tried to pay them by check."

"The world's a different place now, Keller."

"They didn't even have metal detectors," he remembered, "or scanners. Then they brought in metal detectors, but the early ones didn't work all the way down to the ground. I knew a man who used to stick a gun into his sock and walk right onto the plane with it. If they ever caught him at it, I never heard about it."

"I suppose you could take a train."

"Or a clipper ship," he said. "Around the Horn."

"What's the matter with the Panama Canal? Metal detectors?" She finished the tea in her glass, heaved a sigh. "I think you answered my question. I'll tell Portland we have to pass."

After dinner she gave him a lift to the station and joined him on the platform to wait for his train. He broke the silence to ask her if she really thought he was a sociopath.

"Keller," she said, "it was just an idle remark, and I didn't mean anything by it. Anyway, I'm no psychologist. I'm not even sure what the word means."

"Someone who lacks a sense of right and wrong," he said. "He understands the difference but doesn't see how it applies to him personally. He lacks empathy, doesn't have any feeling for other people."

She considered the matter. "It doesn't

sound like you," she said, "except when you're working. Is it possible to be a part-time sociopath?"

"I don't think so. I've done some reading on the subject. Case histories, that sort of thing. The sociopaths they write about, almost all of them have the same three things in their childhood background. Setting fires, torturing animals, and wetting the bed."

"You know, I heard that somewhere. Some TV program about FBI profilers and serial killers. Do you remember your childhood, Keller?"

"Most of it," he said. "I knew a woman once who claimed she could remember being born. I don't go back that far, and some of it's spotty, but I remember it pretty well. And I didn't do any of those three things. Torture animals? God, I loved animals. I told you about the dog I had."

"Nelson. No, sorry, that was the one you had a couple of years ago. You told me the name of the other one, but I can't remember it."

"Soldier."

"Soldier, right."

"I loved that dog," he said. "And I had other pets from time to time, the ways kids do. Goldfish, baby turtles. They all died."

"They always do, don't they?"

"I suppose so. I used to cry."

"When they died."

"When I was little. When I got older I took it more in stride, but it still made me sad. But torture them?"

"How about fires?"

"You know," he said, "when you talked about the leaves, and what happens if you don't rake them, I remembered raking leaves when I was a kid. It was one of the things I did to make money."

"You want to make twenty bucks here and now, there's a rake in the garage."

"What we used to do," he remembered, "was rake them into a pile at the curb, and then burn them. It's illegal nowadays, because of fire laws and air pollution, but back then it's what you were supposed to do."

"It was nice, the smell of burning leaves on the autumn air."

"And it was satisfying," he said. "You raked them up and put a match to them and they were gone. Those were the only fires I remember setting."

"I'd say you're oh-for-two. How'd you do at wetting the bed?"

"I never did, as far as I can recall."

"Oh-for-three. Keller, you're about as much of a sociopath as Albert Schweitzer. But if that's the case, how come you do what you do? Never mind, here's your train. Have fun dishing out the lasagna tonight. And don't torture any animals, you hear?"

Two weeks later he picked up the phone on his own and told her not to turn down jobs automatically. "Now you tell me," she said. "You at home? Don't go anywhere, I'll make a call and get back to you." He sat by the phone, and picked it up when it rang. "I was afraid they'd found somebody by now," she said, "but we're in luck, if you want to call it that. They're sending us something by Airborne Express, which always sounds to me like paratroopers ready for battle. They swear I'll have it by nine tomorrow morning, but you'll just be getting home around then, won't you? Do you figure you can make the 2:04 from Grand Central? I'll pick you up at the station."

"There's a 10:08," he said. "Gets to White Plains a few minutes before eleven. If you're not there I'll figure you had to wait for the paratroopers, and I'll get a cab."

It was a cold, dreary day, with enough rain so that she needed to use the windshield wipers but not enough to keep the blades from squeaking. She put him at the kitchen table, poured him a cup of coffee, and let

him read the notes she'd made and study
the Polaroids that had come in the Airborne
Express envelope, along with the initial pay-
ment in cash. He held up one of the pictures, which showed a man in his seventies,
with a round face and a small white mustache, holding up a golf club as if in the
hope that someone would take it from him.

He said the fellow didn't look much like a
labor leader, and Dot shook her head. "That
was Portland," she said. "This is Phoenix.
Well, Scottsdale, and I bet it's nicer there today than it is here. Nicer than Portland, too,
because I understand it always rains there.
In Portland, I mean. It never rains in Scottsdale. I don't know what's the matter with
me, I'm starting to sound like the Weather
Channel. You could fly, you know. Not all
the way, but to Denver, say."

"Maybe."

She tapped the photo with her fingernail.
"Now according to them," she said, "the
man's not expecting anything, and not taking any security precautions. Other hand,
his life is a security precaution. He lives in a
gated community."

"Sundowner Estates, it says here."

"There's an eighteen-hole golf course,
with individual homes ranged around it.
And each of them has a state-of-the-art

home security system, but the only thing that ever triggers an alarm is when some clown hooks his tee shot through your living room picture window, because the only way into the compound is past a guard. No metal detector, and they don't confiscate your nail clippers, but you have to belong there for him to let you in."

"Does Mr. Egmont ever leave the property?"

"He plays golf every day. Unless it rains, and we've already established that it never does. He generally eats lunch at the clubhouse, they've got their own restaurant. He has a housekeeper who comes in a couple of times a week—they know her at the guard shack, I guess. Aside from that, he's all alone in his house. He probably gets invited out to dinner a lot. He's unattached, and there's always six women for every man in those Geezer Leisure communities. You're staring at his picture, and I bet I know why. He looks familiar, doesn't he?"

"Yes, and I can't think why."

"You ever play Monopoly?"

"By God, that's it," he said. "He looks like the drawing of the banker in Monopoly."

"It's the mustache," she said, "and the round face. Don't forget to pass Go, Keller. And collect two hundred dollars."

She drove him back to the train station, and because of the rain they waited in her car instead of on the platform. He said he'd pretty much stopped working on the food ship. She said she hadn't figured it was something he'd be doing for the rest of his life.

"They changed it," he said. "The Red Cross took it over. They do this all the time, their specialty's disaster relief, and they're pros at it, but it transformed the whole thing from a spontaneous New York affair into something impersonal. I mean, when we started we had name chefs knocking themselves out to feed these guys something they'd enjoy eating, and then the Red Cross took over and we were filling their plates with macaroni and cheese and chipped beef on toast. Overnight we went from Bobby Flay to Chef Boy-Ar-Dee."

"Took the joy out of it, did it?"

"Well, would you like to spend ten hours shifting scrap metal and collecting body parts and then tuck into something you'd expect to find in an army chow line? I got so I couldn't look them in the eye when I ladled the slop onto their plates. I skipped a night and felt guilty about it, and I went in the next night and felt worse, and I haven't been back since."

"You were probably ready to give it up, Keller."

"I don't know. I still felt good doing it, until the Red Cross showed up."

"But that's why you were there," she said. "To feel good."

"To help out."

She shook her head. "You felt good because you were helping out," she said, "but you kept coming back and doing it because it made you feel good."

"Well, I suppose so."

"I'm not impugning your motive, Keller. You're still a hero, as far as I'm concerned. All I'm saying is that volunteerism only goes so far. When it stops feeling good, it tends to run out of steam. That's when you need the professionals. They do their job because it's their job, and it doesn't matter whether they feel good about it or not. They buckle down and get it done. It may be macaroni and cheese, and the cheese may be Velveeta, but nobody winds up holding an empty plate. You see what I mean?"

"I guess so," Keller said.

———

Back in the city, he called one of the airlines, thinking he'd take Dot's suggestion
and fly to Denver. He worked his way
through their automated answering system,
pressing numbers when prompted, and
wound up on hold, because all of their
agents were busy serving other customers.
The music they played to pass the time was
bad enough all by itself, but they kept inter-
rupting it every fifteen seconds to tell him
how much better off he'd be using their
Web site. After a few minutes of this he
called Hertz, and the phone was answered
right away by a human being.

He picked up a Ford Taurus first thing the
next morning and beat the rush hour traffic
through the tunnel and onto the New Jersey
Turnpike. He'd rented the car under his
own name, showing his own driver's license
and using his own American Express card,
but he had a cloned card in another name
that Dot had provided, and he used it in the
motels where he stopped along the way.

It took him four long days to drive to Tucson. He would drive until he was hungry, or
the car needed gas, or he needed a restroom, then get behind the wheel again and
drive some more. When he got tired he'd
find a motel and register under the name
on his fake credit card, take a shower, watch

a little TV, and go to bed. He'd sleep until
he woke up, and then he'd take another
shower and get dressed and look for someplace to have breakfast. And so on.

While he drove he played the radio until
he couldn't stand it, then turned it off until
he couldn't stand the silence. By the third
day the solitude was getting to him, and he
couldn't figure out why. He was used to being alone, he lived his whole life alone, and
he certainly never had or wanted company
while he was working. He seemed to want it
now, though, and at one point turned the
car's radio to a talk show on a Clear Channel station in Omaha. People called in and
disagreed with the host, or a previous caller,
or some schoolteacher who'd given them a
hard time in the fifth grade. Gun control
was the announced topic for the day, but the
real theme, as far as Keller could tell, was resentment, and there was plenty of it to go
around.

Keller listened, fascinated at first, and before very long he reached the point where
he couldn't stand another minute of it. If
he'd had a gun handy, he might have put a
bullet in the radio, but all he did was switch
it off.

The last thing he wanted, it turned out,
was someone talking to him. He had the

thought, and realized a moment later that he'd not only thought it but had actually spoken the words aloud. He was talking to himself, and wondered—wondered in silence, thank God—if this was something new. It was like snoring, he thought. If you slept alone, how would you know if you did it? You wouldn't, not unless you snored so loudly that you woke yourself up.

He started to reach for the radio, stopped himself before he could turn it on again. He checked the speedometer, saw that the cruise control was keeping the car at three miles an hour over the posted speed limit. Without cruise control you found yourself going faster or slower than you wanted to, wasting time or risking a ticket. With it, you didn't have to think about how fast you were going. The car did the thinking for you.

The next step, he thought, would be steering control. You got in the car, keyed the ignition, set the controls, and leaned back and closed your eyes. The car followed the turns in the road, and a system of sensors worked the brake when another car loomed in front of you, swung out to pass when such action was warranted, and knew to take the next exit when the gas gauge dropped below a certain level.

It sounded like science fiction, but no less

so in Keller's boyhood than cruise control, or auto-response telephone answering systems, or a good ninety-five percent of the things he nowadays took for granted. Keller didn't doubt for a minute that right this minute some bright young man in Detroit or Osaka or Bremen was working on steering control. There'd be some spectacular head-on collisions before they got the bugs out of the system, but before long every car would have it, and the accident rate would plummet and the state troopers wouldn't have anybody to give tickets to, and everybody would be crazy about technology's newest breakthrough, except for a handful of cranks in England who were convinced you had more control and got better mileage the old-fashioned way.

Meanwhile, Keller kept both hands on the steering wheel.

Sundowner Estates, home of William Wallis Egmont, was in Scottsdale, an upscale suburb of Phoenix. Tucson, a couple hundred miles to the east, was as close as Keller wanted to bring the Taurus. He followed the signs to the airport and left the car in long-term parking. Over the years he'd left other cars in long-term parking, but they'd been other men's cars, with their owners stuffed in the trunk, and Keller, having no need to find the cars again, had gotten rid of the claim checks at the first opportunity. This time was different, and he found a place in his wallet for the check the gate attendant had supplied, and noted the lot section and the number of the parking space.

He went into the terminal, found the car rental counters, and picked up a Toyota Camry from Avis, using his fake credit card and a matching Pennsylvania driver's license. It took him a few minutes to figure out the cruise control. That was the trouble with renting cars, you had to learn a new system with every car, from lights and windshield wipers to cruise control and seat adjustment. Maybe he should have gone to the Hertz counter and picked up another Taurus. Was there an advantage in driving the same model car throughout? Was there a disadvantage that offset it, and was some intuitive recognition of that disadvantage what had led him to the Avis counter?

"You're thinking too much," he said, and realized he'd spoken the words aloud. He shook his head, not so much annoyed as amused, and a few miles down the road realized that what he wanted, what he'd been wanting all along, was not someone to talk to him but someone to listen.

A little ways past an exit ramp, a kid with a duffel bag had his thumb out, trying to hitch a ride. For the first time that he could recall, Keller had the impulse to stop for him. It was just a passing thought; if he'd had his foot on the gas, he'd have barely begun to ease up on the gas pedal before he'd overruled the thought and sped onward. Since he was running on cruise control, his foot didn't even move, and the hitchhiker slipped out of sight in the rearview mirror, unaware what a narrow escape he'd just had.

Because the only reason to pick him up was for someone to talk to, and Keller would have told him everything. And, once he'd done that, what choice would he have?

Keller could picture the kid, listening wide-eyed to everything Keller had to tell him. He pictured himself, his soul unburdened, grateful to the youth for listening, but compelled by circumstance to cover his tracks. He imagined the car gliding to a stop, imagined the brief struggle, imagined the body left in a roadside ditch, the Camry heading west at a thoughtful three miles an hour above the speed limit.

The motel Keller picked was an independent mom-and-pop operation in Tempe, which was another suburb of Phoenix. He counted out cash and paid a week in advance, plus a twenty-dollar deposit for phone calls. He didn't plan to make any calls, but if he needed to use the phone he wanted it to work.

He registered as David Miller of San Francisco, and fabricated an address and zip code. You were supposed to include your license plate number, and he mixed up a couple of digits and put CA for the state instead of AZ. It was hardly worth the trouble, nobody was going to look at the registration card, but there were certain things he did out of habit, and this was one of them.

He always traveled light, never took along more than a small carry-on bag with a shirt or two and a couple changes of socks and underwear. That made sense when you were flying, and less sense when you had a car with an empty trunk and back seat at your disposal. By the time he got to Phoenix, he'd run through his socks and underwear. He picked up two three-packs of briefs and a six-pack of socks at a strip mall, and was looking for a trash bin for his dirty clothes when he spotted a Goodwill Industries collection box. He felt good dropping his soiled socks and underwear in the box, though not quite as good as he'd felt dishing out designer food to the smoke-stained rescue workers at Ground Zero.

Back at his motel, he called Dot on the prepaid cell phone he'd picked up on 23rd Street. He'd paid cash for it, and hadn't even been asked his name, so as far as he could tell it was completely untraceable. At best someone could identify calls made from it as originating with a phone manufactured in Finland and sold at Radio Shack. Even if they managed to pin down the specific Radio Shack outlet, so what? There was nothing to tie it to Keller, or to Phoenix.

On the other hand, cell phone communications were about as secure as shouting. Any number of listening devices could pick up your conversation, and whatever you said was very likely being heard by half a dozen people on their car radios and one old fart who was catching every word on the fillings in his teeth. That didn't bother Keller, who figured every phone was tapped, and acted accordingly.

He phoned Dot, and the phone rang seven or eight times, and he broke the connection. She was probably out, he decided, or in the shower. Or had he misdialed? Always a chance, he thought, and pressed redial, then caught himself and realized that, if he had in fact misdialed, redialing would just repeat the mistake. He broke the connection again in midring and punched in the number afresh, and this time he got a busy signal.

He tried it again, got another busy signal, frowned, waited, and tried again. It had barely begun to ring when she picked up, barking "Yes?" into the phone, and somehow fitting a full measure of irritation into the single syllable.

"It's me," he said.

"What a surprise."

"Is something wrong?"

"I had somebody at the door," she said, "and the teakettle was whistling, and I finally got to the phone and picked it up in time to listen to the dial tone."

"I let it ring a long time."

"That's nice. So I put it down and turned away, and it rang again, and I picked it up in the middle of the first ring, and I was just in time to hear you hang up."

He explained about pressing redial, and realizing that wouldn't work.

"Except it worked just fine," she said, "since you hadn't misdialed in the first place. I figured it had to be you, so I pressed star sixty-nine. But whatever phone you're on, star sixty-nine doesn't work. I got one of those weird tones and a canned message saying return calls to your number were blocked."

"It's a cell phone."

"Say no more. . . . Hello? Where'd you go?"

"I'm here. You said *Say no more*, and . . ."

"It's an expression. Tell me it's all wrapped up and you're heading for home."

"I just got here."

"That's what I was afraid of. How's the weather?"

"Hot."

"Not here. They say it might snow, but then again it might not. You're just calling to check in, right?"

"Right."

"Well, it's good to hear your voice, and I'd love to chat, but you're on a cell phone."

"Right."

"Call anytime," she said. "It's always a treat to hear from you."

Keller didn't know the population or acreage of Sundowner Estates, although he had a hunch neither figure would be hard to come by. But what good would the information do him? The compound was large enough to contain a full-size eighteen-hole golf course, and enough homes adjacent to it to support the operation.

And there was a ten-foot adobe wall encircling the entire affair. Keller supposed it was easier to sell homes if you called it Sundowner Estates, but Fort Apache would have better conveyed the stockadelike feel of the place.

He drove around the compound a couple of times, establishing that there were in fact two gates, one at the east and the other not quite opposite, at the southwest corner. He parked where he could keep an eye on the southwest gate, and couldn't tell much beyond the fact that every vehicle entering or leaving the compound had to stop for some sort of exchange with the uniformed guard. Maybe you flashed a pass at him, maybe he called to make sure you were expected, maybe they wanted a thumbprint and a semen sample. No way to tell, not from where Keller was watching, but he was pretty sure he couldn't just drive up and bluff his way through. People who willingly lived behind a thick wall almost twice their own height probably expected a high level of security, and a guard who failed to provide that would be looking for a new job.

He drove back to his motel, sat in front of the TV and watched a special on the Discovery Channel about scuba diving at Australia's Great Barrier Reef. Keller didn't think it looked like something he wanted to do. He'd tried snorkeling once, on a vacation in Aruba, and kept having to stop because he was getting water in his snorkel, and under his mask. And he hadn't been able to see much of anything, anyhow.

The divers on the Discovery Channel were having much better luck, and there were plenty of colorful fish for them (and Keller) to look at. After fifteen minutes, though, he'd seen as much as he wanted to, and was ready to change the channel. It seemed like a lot of trouble to go through, flying all the way to Australia, then getting in the water with a mask and fins. Couldn't you get pretty much the same effect staring into a fish tank at a pet shop, or a Chinese restaurant?

"I'll tell you this," the woman said. "If you do make a decision to buy at Sundowner, you won't regret it. Nobody ever has."

"That's quite a recommendation," Keller said.

"Well, it's quite an operation, Mr. Miller. I don't suppose I have to ask if you play golf."

"It's somewhere between a pastime and an addiction," he said.

"I hope you brought your clubs. Sundowner's a championship course, you know. Robert Walker Wilson designed it, and Clay Bunis was a consultant. We're in the middle of the desert, but you wouldn't know it inside the walls at Sundowner. The course is as green as a pasture in the Irish midlands."

Her name, Keller learned, was Michelle Prentice, but everyone called her Mitzi. And what about him? Did he prefer Dave or David?

That was a stumper, and Keller realized he was taking too long to answer it. "It depends," he said, finally. "I answer to either one."

"I'll bet business associates call you Dave," she said, "and really close friends call you David."

"How on earth did you know that?"

She smiled broadly, delighted to be right. "Just a guess," she said. "Just a lucky guess, David."

So they were going to be close friends, he thought. Toward that end she proceeded to tell him a few things about herself, and by the time they reached the guard shack at the east gate of Sundowner Estates, he learned that she was thirty-nine years old, that she'd divorced her rat bastard of a husband three years ago and moved out here from Frankfort, Kentucky, which happened to be the state capital, although most people would guess it was Louisville. She'd sold houses in Frankfort, so she'd picked up an Arizona Realtor's license first chance she got, and it was a lot better selling houses here than it had ever been in Kentucky, because they just about sold themselves. The entire Phoenix area was growing like a house on fire, she assured him, and she was just plain excited to be a part of it all.

At the east gate she moved her sunglasses up onto her forehead and gave the guard a big smile. "Hi, Harry," she said. "Mitzi Prentice, and this here's Mr. Miller, come for a look at the Lattimore house on Saguaro Circle."

"Miz Prentice," he said, returning her smile and nodding at Keller. He consulted a clipboard, then slipped into the shack and picked up a telephone. After a moment he emerged and told Mitzi she could go ahead. "I guess you know how to get there," he said.

"I guess I ought to," she told Keller, after they'd driven away from the entrance. "I showed the house two days ago, and he was there to let me by. But he's got his job to do, and they take it seriously, let me tell you. I know not to joke with him, or with any of them, because they won't joke back. They can't, because it might not look good on camera."

"There are security cameras running?"

"Twenty-four hours a day. You don't get in unless your name's on the list, and the camera's got a record of when you came and went, and what car you were driving, license plate number and all."

"Really."

"There are some very affluent people at Sundowner," she said, "and some of them are getting along in years. That's not to say you won't find plenty of people your age here, especially on the golf course and around the pool, but you do get some older folks, too, and they tend to be a little more concerned about security. Now just look, David. Isn't that a beautiful sight?"

She pointed out her window at the golf course, and it looked like a golf course to him. He agreed it sure looked gorgeous.

The living room of the Lattimore house had a cathedral ceiling and a walk-in fireplace. Keller thought the fireplace looked nice, but he didn't quite get it. A walk-in closet was one thing, you could walk into it and pick what you wanted to wear, but why would anybody want to walk into a fireplace?

For that matter, who'd want to hold a prayer service in the living room?

He thought of raising the point with Mitzi. She might find either question provocative, but would it fit the Serious Buyer image he was trying to project? So he asked instead what he figured were more typical questions, about heating and cooling systems and financing, good basic home-buyer questions.

There was, predictably enough, a big picture window in the living room, and it afforded the predictable view of the golf course, overlooking what Mitzi told him were the fifth green and the sixth tee. There was a man taking practice swings who might have been W. W. Egmont himself, although from this distance and angle it was hard to say one way or the other. But if the guy turned a little to his left, and if Keller could look at him not with his naked eye but through a pair of binoculars—

Or, he thought, a telescopic sight. That would be quick and easy, wouldn't it? All he had to do was buy the place and set up in the living room with a high-powered rifle, and Egmont's state-of-the-art home burglar alarm wouldn't do him a bit of good. Keller could just perch there like a vulture, and sooner or later Egmont would finish up the fifth hole by four-putting for a triple bogey, and Keller could take him right there and save the poor duffer a stroke or wait until he came even closer and teed up his ball for the sixth hole (525 yards, par 5). Keller was no great shakes as a marksman, but how hard could it be to center the crosshairs on a target and squeeze the trigger?

"I bet you're picturing yourself on that golf course right now," Mitzi said, and he grinned and told her she got that one right.

From the bedroom window in the back of the house, you could look out at a desert garden, with cacti and succulents growing in sand. The plantings, like the bright green lawn in front, were all the responsibility of the Sundowners Estates association, who took care of all maintenance. They kept it beautiful year-round, she told him, and you never had to lift a finger.

"A lot of people think they want to garden when they retire," she said, "and then they find out how much work it can be. And what happens when you want to take off for a couple of weeks in Maui? At Sundowner,

you can walk out the door and know everything's going to be beautiful when you
come back."

He said he could see how that would be a
comfort. "I can't see the fence from here,"
he said. "I was wondering about that, if
you'd feel like you were walled in. I mean,
it's nice looking, being adobe and earth-
colored and all, but it's a pretty high fence."

"Close to twelve feet," she said.

Even higher than he'd thought. He said
he wondered what it would be like living
next to it, and she said none of the houses
were close enough to the fence for it to be a
factor.

"The design was very well thought out,"
she said. "There's the twelve-foot fence, and
then there's a big space, anywhere from ten
to twenty yards, and then there's an inner
fence, also of adobe, that stands about five
feet tall, and there's cactus and vines in
front of it for landscaping, so it looks nice
and decorative."

"That's a great idea," he said. And he
liked it; all he had to do was clear the first
fence and follow the stretch of no-
man's-land around to wherever he felt like
vaulting the shorter wall. "About the taller
fence, though. I mean, it's not really terribly
secure, is it?"

"What makes you say that?"

"Well, I don't know. I guess it's because I'm used to the Northeast, where security's pretty up front and obvious, but it's just a plain old mud fence, isn't it? No razor wire on top, no electrified fencing. It looks as though all a person would have to do is lean a long ladder up against it and he'd be over the top in a matter of seconds."

She laid a hand on his arm. "David," she said, "you asked that very casually, but I have the sense that security's a real concern of yours."

"I have a stamp collection," he said. "It's not worth a fortune, and collections are hard to sell, but the point is I've been collecting since I was a kid and I'd hate to lose it."

"I can understand that."

"So security's a consideration, yes. And the fellow at the gate's enough to put anybody's mind at rest, but if any jerk with a ladder can just pop right over the fence—"

It was, she told him, a little more complicated than that. There was no razor or concertina wire, because that made a place look like a concentration camp, but there were sensors that set up some kind of force field, and no one could begin to climb the fence without setting off all kinds of alarms. Nor were you home free once you cleared the

fence, because there were dogs that pa-
trolled the belt of no-man's-land, Dobermans, swift and silent.

"And there's an unmarked patrol car that
circles the perimeter at regular intervals
twenty-four hours a day," she said, "so if they
spotted you on your way to the fence with a
ladder under your arm—"

"It wouldn't be me," he assured her. "I
like dogs okay, but I'd just as soon not meet
those Dobermans you just mentioned."

It was, he decided, a good thing he'd
asked. Earlier, he'd found a place to buy an
aluminum extension ladder. He could have
been over the fence in a matter of seconds,
just in time to keep a date with Mr. Swift and
Mr. Silent.

In the Lattimore kitchen, they sat across a
table topped with butcher block and Mitzi
went over the fine points with him. The furniture was all included, she told him, and as
he could see it was in excellent condition.
He might want to make some changes, of
course, as a matter of personal taste, but the
place was in turnkey condition. He could
buy it today and move in tomorrow.

"In a manner of speaking," she said, and
touched his arm again. "Financing takes a

little time, and even if you were to pay cash it would take a few days to push the paperwork through. Were you thinking in terms of cash?"

"It's always simpler," he said.

"It is, but I'm sure you wouldn't have trouble with a mortgage. The banks love to write mortgages on Sundowner properties, because the prices only go up." Her fingers encircled his wrist. "I'm not sure I should tell you this, David, but now's a particularly good time to make an offer."

"Mr. Lattimore's eager to sell?"

"Mr. Lattimore couldn't care less," she said. "About selling or anything else. It's his daughter who'd like to sell. She had an offer of ten percent under the asking price, but she'd just listed the property and she turned it down, thinking the buyer'd boost it a little, but instead the buyer went and bought something else, and that woman's been kicking herself ever since. What *I* would do, I'd offer fifteen percent under what she's asking. You might not get it for that, but the worst you'd do is get it for ten percent under, and that's a bargain in this market."

He nodded thoughtfully, and asked what happened to Lattimore. "It was very sad," she said, "although in another sense it wasn't, because he died doing what he loved."

"Playing golf," Keller guessed.

"He hit a very nice tee shot on the thir-teenth hole," she said, "which is a par four with a dogleg to the right. 'That's a sweet shot,' his partner said, and Mr. Lattimore said, 'Well, I guess I can still hit one now and then, can't I?' And then he just went and dropped dead."

"If you've got to go . . ."

"That's what everyone said, David. The body was cremated, and then they had a nice nondenominational service in the club-house, and afterward his daughter and son-in-law rode golf carts to the sixteenth hole and put his ashes in the water hazard." She laughed involuntarily, and let go of his wrist to cover her mouth with her hand. "Pardon me for laughing, but I was thinking what somebody said. How his balls were already there, and now he could go look for them."

Her hand returned to his wrist. He looked at her, and her eyes were looking back at him. "Well," he said. "My car's at your office, so you'd better run me back there. And then I'll want to get back to where I'm staying and freshen up, but after that I'd love to take you to dinner."

"Oh, I wish," she said.

"You have plans?"

"My daughter lives with me," she said, "and I like to be home with her on school nights, and especially tonight because there's a program on television we never miss."

"I see."

"So you're on your own for dinner," she said, "but what do you and I care about dinner, David? Why don't you just take me into old Mr. Lattimore's bedroom and fuck me senseless?"

She had a nice body and used it eagerly and imaginatively. Keller, his mind on his work, had been only vaguely aware of the sexual possibilities, and had in fact surprised himself by asking her to dinner. In the Lattimore bedroom he surprised himself further.

Afterward she said, "Well, I had high expectations, but I have to say they were exceeded. Isn't it a good thing I'm busy tonight? Otherwise it'd be a couple of hours before we even got to the restaurant, and ages before we got to bed. I mean, why waste all that time?"

He tried to think of something to say, but

she didn't seem to require comment. "For all those years," she said, "I was the most faithful wife since Penelope. And it's not like nobody was interested. Men used to hit on me all the time. David, I even had girls hitting on me."

"Really."

"But I was never interested, and if I was, if I felt a little itch, a little tickle, well, I just pushed it away and put it out of my mind. Because of a little thing called marriage. I'd made some vows, and I took them seriously.

"And then I found out the son of a bitch was cheating on me, and it turned out it was nothing new. On our wedding day? It was years before I knew it, but that son of a bitch got lucky with one of my bridesmaids. And over the years he was catting around all the time. Not just my friends, but my sister."

"Your sister?"

"Well, my half-sister, really. My daddy died when I was little, and my mama remarried, and that's where she came from." She told him more than he needed to know about her childhood, and he lay there with his eyes closed and let the words wash over him. He hoped there wasn't going to be a test, because he wasn't paying close attention. . . .

———

"So I decided to make up for lost time," she said.

He'd dozed off, and after she woke him they'd showered in separate bathrooms. Now they were dressed again, and he'd followed her into the kitchen, where she opened the refrigerator and seemed surprised to find it empty.

She closed it and turned to him and said, "When I meet someone I feel like sleeping with, well, I go ahead and do it. I mean, why wait?"

"Works for me," he said.

"The only thing I don't like to do," she said, "is mix business and pleasure. So I made sure not to commit myself until I knew you weren't going to buy this place. And you're not, are you?"

"How did you know?"

"A feeling I got, when I said how you should make an offer. Instead of trying to think how much to offer, you were looking for a way out—or at least that was what I picked up. Which was okay with me, because by then I was more interested in getting laid than in selling a house. I didn't have to tell you about a whole lot of tax advantages, and how easy it is to rent the place out during the time you spend somewhere else. It's all pretty persuasive, and I could give you that whole rap now, but you don't really want to hear it, do you?"

"I might be in the market in a little while," he said, "but you're right, I'm nowhere near ready to make an offer at the present time. I suppose it was wrong of me to drag you out here and waste your time, but—"

"Do you hear me complaining, David?"

"Well, I just wanted to see the place," he said. "So I exaggerated my interest somewhat. Whether or not I'll be interested in settling in here depends on the outcome of a couple of business matters, and it'll be a while before I know how they're going to turn out."

"Sounds interesting," she said.

"I wish I could talk about it, but you know how it is."

"You could tell me," she said, "but then you'd have to kill me. In that case, don't you say a word."

He ate dinner by himself in a Mexican restaurant that reminded him of another Mexican restaurant. He was lingering over a second cup of café con leche before he figured it out. Years ago work had taken him to

Roseburg, Oregon, and before he got out of there he'd picked out a real estate agent and spent an afternoon driving around looking at houses for sale.

He hadn't gone to bed with the Oregon realtor, or even considered it, nor had he used her as a way to get information on an approach to his quarry. That man, whom the Witness Protection Program had imperfectly protected, had been all too easy to find, but Keller, who ordinarily knew well enough to keep his business and personal life separate, had somehow let himself befriend the poor bastard. Before he knew it he was having fantasies about moving to Roseburg himself, buying a house, getting a dog, settling down.

He'd looked at houses, but that was as far as he'd let it go. The night came when he got a grip on himself, and the next thing he got a grip on was the man who'd brought him there. He used a garrote, and what he got a grip on was on the guy's throat, and then it was time to go back to New York.

He remembered the Mexican café in Roseburg now. The food had been good, though he didn't suppose it was all that special, and he'd had a mild crush on the waitress, about as realistic as the whole idea of moving there. He thought of the man he'd killed, an accountant who'd become the proprietor of a quick-print shop.

You could learn the business in a couple of hours, the man had said of his new career. *You could buy the place and move in the same day*, Mitzi had said of the Lattimore house.

Patterns . . .

You could tell me, she'd said, thinking she was joking, *but then you'd have to kill me.* Oddly, in the languor that followed their lovemaking, he'd had the impulse to confide in her, to tell her what had brought him to Scottsdale.

Yeah, right.

He drove around for a while, then found his way back to his motel and surfed the TV channels without finding anything that caught his interest. He turned off the set and sat there in the dark.

He thought of calling Dot. There were things he could talk about with her, but others he couldn't, and anyway he didn't want to do any talking on a cell phone, not even an untraceable one.

He found himself thinking about the guy in Roseburg. He tried to picture him and couldn't. Early on he'd worked out a way to keep people from the past from flooding the

present with their faces. You worked with
their images in your mind, leached the color
out of them, made the features grow dimmer,
shrank the picture as if viewing it through
the wrong end of a telescope. You made
them grow smaller and darker and hazier until they disappeared, and if you did it correctly you forgot everything but the barest of
facts about them. There was no emotional
charge, no weight to them, and they became
more and more difficult to recall to mind.

But now he'd bridged a gap and closed a
circuit, and the man's face was there in his
memory, the face of an aging chipmunk. Jesus, Keller thought, get out of my memory,
will you? You've been dead for years. Leave
me the hell alone.

If you were here, he told the face, I could
talk to you. And you'd listen, because what
the hell else could you do? You couldn't talk
back, you couldn't judge me, you couldn't
tell me to shut up. You're dead, so you
couldn't say a goddam word.

He went outside, walked around for a
while, came back in and sat on the edge of
the bed. Very deliberately he set about getting rid of the man's face, washing it of
color, pushing it farther and farther away,
making it disappear. The process was more
difficult than it had been in years, but it

worked, finally, and the little man was gone to wherever the washed-out faces of dead people went. Wherever it was, Keller prayed he'd stay there.

He took a long hot shower and went to bed.

In the morning he found someplace new to have breakfast. He read the paper and had a second cup of coffee, then drove pointlessly around the perimeter of Sundowner Estates.

Back at the motel, he called Dot on his cell phone. "Here's what I've been able to come up with," he said. "I park where I can watch the entrance. Then, when some resident drives out, I follow them."

"Them?"

"Well, him or her, depending which it is. Or them, if there's more than one in the car. Sooner or later, they stop somewhere and get out of the car."

"And you take them out, and you keep doing this, and sooner or later it's the right guy."

"They get out of the car," he said, "and I hang around until nobody's watching, and I get in the trunk."

"The trunk of their car."

"If I wanted to get in the trunk of my own car," he said, "I could go do that right now. Yes, the trunk of their car."

"I get it," she said. "Their car morphs into the Trojan Chrysler. They sail back into the walled city, and you're in there, and hoping they'll open the trunk eventually and let you out."

"Car trunks have a release mechanism built in these days," he said. "So kidnap victims can escape."

"You're kidding," she said. "The auto makers added something for the benefit of the eight people a year who get stuffed into car trunks?"

"I think it's probably more than eight a year," he said, "and then there are the people, kids mostly, who get locked in accidentally. Anyway, it's no problem getting out."

"How about getting in? You real clever with auto locks?"

"That might be a problem," he admitted. "Does everybody lock their car nowadays?"

"I bet the ones who live in gated communities do. Not when they're home safe, but when they're out and about in a dangerous place like the suburbs of Phoenix. How crazy are you about this plan, Keller?"

"Not too," he admitted.

"Because how would you even know they were going back? Your luck, they're on their way to spend two weeks in Las Vegas."

"I didn't think of that."

"Of course you'd know right away," she said, "when you tried to get in the trunk and it was full of suitcases and copies of *Beat the Dealer.*"

"It's not a great plan," he allowed, "but you wouldn't believe the security. The only other thing I can think of is to buy a place."

"Buy a house there, you mean. I don't think the budget would cover it."

"I could keep it as an investment," he said, "and rent it out when I wasn't using it."

"Which would be what, fifty-two weeks a year?"

"But if I could afford to do all that," he said, "I could also afford to tell the client to go roll his hoop, which I'm thinking I might have to go and do anyway."

"Because it's looking difficult."

"It's looking impossible," he said, "and then on top of everything else . . ."

"Yes? Keller? Where'd you go? Hello?"

"Never mind," he said. "I just figured out how to do it."

"As you can see," Mitzi Prentice said, "the view's nowhere near as nice as the Lattimore house. And there's just two bedrooms instead of three, and the furnishing's a little on the generic side. But compared to spending the next two weeks in a motel—"

"It's a whole lot more comfortable," he said.

"And more secure," she said, "just in case you've got your stamp collection with you."

"I don't," he said, "but a little security never hurt anybody. I'd like to take it."

"I don't blame you, it's a real good deal, and nice income for Mr. and Mrs. Sundstrom, who're in the Galapagos Islands looking at blue-footed boobies. That's where all the crap on their walls comes from. Not the Galapagos, but other places they go to on their travels."

"I was wondering."

"Well, they could tell you about each precious piece, but they're not here, and if they were then their place wouldn't be available, would it? We'll go to the office and fill out the paperwork, and then you can give me a check and I'll give you a set of keys and some ID to get you past the guard at the gate. And a pass to the clubhouse, and information on greens fees and all. I hope you'll have some time for golf."

"Oh, I should be able to fit in a few rounds."

"No telling what you'll be able to fit in,"

she said. "Speaking of which, let's fit in a quick stop at the Lattimore house before we start filling out lease agreements. And no, silly, I'm not trying to get you to buy that place. I just want you to take me into that bedroom again. I mean, you don't expect me to do it in Cynthia Sundstrom's bed, do you? With all those weird masks on the wall? It'd give me the jimjams for sure. I'd feel like primitive tribes were watching me."

The Sundstrom house was a good deal more comfortable than his motel, and he found he didn't mind being surrounded by souvenirs of the couple's travels. The second bedroom, which evidently served as Harvey Sundstrom's den, had a collection of edged weapons hanging on the walls, knives and daggers and what he supposed were battle-axes, and there was no end of carved masks and tapestries in the other rooms. Some of the masks looked godawful, he supposed, but they weren't the sort of things to give him the jimjams, whatever the jimjams might be, and he got in the habit of acknowledging one of them, a West African mask with teeth like tombstones and a lot of rope fringe for hair. He found himself giving it a nod when he passed it, even raising a hand in a salute.

Pretty soon, he thought, he'd be talking to it.

Because it was becoming clear to him that he felt the need to talk to someone. It was, he supposed, a need he'd had all his life, but for years he'd led an existence that didn't much lend itself to sharing confidences. He'd spent virtually all his adult life as a paid assassin, and it was no line of work for a man given to telling his business to strangers—or to friends, for that matter. You did what they paid you to do and you kept your mouth shut, and that was about it. You didn't talk about your work, and it got so you didn't talk about much of anything else, either. You could go to a sports bar and talk about the game with the fellow on the next barstool, you could gripe about the weather to the woman standing alongside you at the bus stop, you could complain about the mayor to the waitress at the corner coffee shop, but if you wanted a conversation with a little more substance to it, well, you were pretty much out of luck.

Once, a few years ago, he'd let someone talk him into going to a psychotherapist. He'd taken what struck him as reasonable precautions, paying cash, furnishing a false name and address, and essentially limiting disclosures to his childhood. It was productive, too, and he developed some useful insights, but in the end it went bad, with the therapist drawing some unwelcome inferences and eventually following Keller, and learning things he wasn't supposed to know about him. The man wanted to become a client himself, and of course Keller couldn't allow that, and made him a quarry instead. So much for therapy. So much for shared confidences.

Then, for some months after the therapist's exit, he'd had a dog. Not Soldier, the dog of his boyhood years, but Nelson, a fine Australian cattle dog. Nelson had turned out to be not only the perfect companion but the perfect confidante. You could tell him anything, secure in the knowledge that he'd keep it to himself, and it wasn't like talking to yourself or talking to the wall, because the dog was real and alive and gave every indication of paying close attention. There were times when he could swear Nelson understood every word.

He wasn't judgmental, either. You could tell him anything and he didn't love you any the less for it.

If only it had stayed that way, he thought. But it hadn't, and he supposed it was his own fault. He'd found someone to take care of Nelson when work took him out of town, and that was better than putting him in a kennel, but then he wound up falling for the dog walker, and she moved in, and he only really got to talk to Nelson when Andria was somewhere else. That wasn't too bad, and she was fun to have around, but then one day it was time for her to move on, and on she moved. He'd bought her no end of earrings during their time together, and she took the earrings along with her when she left, which was okay. But she also took Nelson, and there he was, right back where he started.

Another man might have gone right out and got himself another dog—and then, like as not, gone looking for a woman to walk it for him. Keller figured enough was enough. He hadn't replaced the therapist, and he hadn't replaced the dog, and, although women drifted in and out of his life, he hadn't replaced the girlfriend. He had, after all, lived alone for years, and it worked for him.

Most of the time, anyway.

"Now this is nice," Keller said. "The suburbs go on for a ways, but once you get past them you're out in the desert, and as long as you stay off the Interstate you've pretty much got the whole place to yourself. It's pleasant, isn't it?"

There was no answer from the passenger seat.

"I paid cash for the Sundstrom house," he went on. "Two weeks, a thousand dollars a week. That's more than a motel, but I can cook my own meals and save on restaurant charges. Except I like to go out for my meals. But I didn't drag you all the way out here to listen to me talk about stuff like that."

Again, his passenger made no response, but then he hadn't expected one.

"There's a lot I have to figure out," he said. "Like what I'm going to do with the rest of my life, for starters. I don't see how I can keep on doing what I've been doing all these years. If you think of it as killing people, taking lives, well, how could a person go on doing it year after year after year?

"But the thing is, see, you don't have to dwell on that aspect of the work. I mean, face it, that's what it is. These people are walking around, doing what they do, and then I come along, and whatever it is they've been doing, they don't get to do it anymore. Because they're dead, because I killed them."

He glanced over, looking for a reaction. Yeah, right.

"What happens," he said, "is you wind up thinking of each subject not as a person to be killed but as a problem to be solved. Here's this piece of work you have to do, and how do you get it done? How do you carry out the contract as expediently as possible, with the least stress all around?

"Now there are guys doing this," he went on, "who cope with it by making it personal. They find a reason to hate the guy they have to kill. They're mad at him, they're angry with him, because it's his fault that they've got to do this bad thing. If it weren't for him, they wouldn't be committing this sin. He's going to be the cause of them going to hell, the son of a bitch, so of course they're mad at him, of course they hate him, and that makes it easier for them to kill him, which is what they made up their minds to do in the first place.

"But that always struck me as silly. I don't know what's a sin and what isn't, or if one person deserves to go on living and another deserves to have his life ended. Sometimes I think about stuff like that, but as far as working it all out in my mind, well, I never seem to get anywhere.

"I could go on like this, but the thing is I'm okay with the moral aspects of it, if you want to call it that. I just think I'm getting a little old to be still at it, that's part of it, and the other's that the business has changed. It's the same in that there are still people who are willing to pay to have other people killed. You never have to worry about running out of clients. Sometimes business drops off for a while, but it always comes back again. Whether it's a guy like that Cuban in Miami, who must have had a hundred guys with a reason to want him dead, or this Egmont with his pot belly and his golf clubs, who you'd think would be unlikely to inspire strong feelings in anybody. All kinds of subjects, and all kinds of clients, and you never run out of either one."

The road curved, and he took the curve a little too fast, and had to reach over with his right hand to reposition his silent companion.

"You should be wearing your seat belt," he said. "Where was I? Oh, the way the business is changing. It's the world, really. Airport security, having to show ID everywhere you go. And gated communities, and all the rest of it. You think of Daniel Boone, who knew it was time to head west when he couldn't cut down a tree without giving some thought to which direction it was going to fall.

"I don't know, it seems to me that I'm just

running off at the mouth, not making any sense. Well, that's okay. What do you care? Just so long as I take it easy on the curves so you don't wind up on the floor, you'll be perfectly willing to sit there and listen as long as I want to talk. Won't you?"

No response.

"If I played golf," he said, "I'd be out on the course every day, and I wouldn't have to burn up a tankful of gas driving around the desert. I'd spend all my time within the Sundowner walls, and I wouldn't have been walking around the mall, wouldn't have seen you in the display next to the cash register. A batch of different breeds on sale, and I'm not sure what you're supposed to be, but I guess you're some kind of terrier. They're good dogs, terriers. Feisty, lots of personality.

"I used to have an Australian cattle dog. I called him Nelson. Well, that was his name before I got him, and I didn't see any reason to change it. I don't think I'll give you a name. I mean, it's nutty enough, buying a stuffed animal, taking it for a ride and having a conversation with it. It's not as if you're going to answer to a name, or as if I'll relate to you on a deeper level if I hang a name on you. I mean, I may be crazy but I'm not stupid. I realize I'm talking to polyester and foam rubber, or whatever the hell you're made out of. Made in China, it says on the tag. That's another thing, everything's made in China or Indonesia or the Philippines, nothing's made in America anymore. It's not that I'm paranoid about it, it's not that I'm worried about all the jobs going overseas. What do I care, anyway? It's not affecting my work. As far as I know, nobody's flying in hired killers from Thailand and Korea to take jobs away from good homegrown American hit men.

"It's just that you have to wonder what people in this country are doing. If they're not making anything, if everything's imported from someplace else, what the hell do Americans do when they get to the office?"

He talked for a while more, then drove around some in silence, then resumed the one-sided conversation. Eventually he found his way back to Sundowner Estates, circling the compound and entering by the southwestern gate.

Hi, Mr. Miller. Hello, Harry. Hey, whatcha got there? Cute little fella, isn't he? A present for my sister's little girl, my niece. I'll ship it to her tomorrow.

The hell with that. Before he got to the guard shack, he reached into the back seat for a newspaper and spread it over the stuffed dog in the passenger seat.

In the clubhouse bar, Keller listened sympathetically as a fellow named Al went over his round of golf, stroke by stroke. "What kills me," Al said, "is that I just can't put it all together. Like on the seventh hole this afternoon, my drive's smack down the middle of the fairway, and my second shot with a three-iron is hole-high and just off the edge of the green on the right. I'm not in the bunker, I'm past it, and I've got a good lie maybe ten, twelve feet from the edge of the green."

"Nice," Keller said, his voice carefully neutral. If it wasn't nice, Al could assume he was being ironic.

"Very nice," Al agreed, "and I'm lying two, and all I have to do is run it up reasonably close and sink the putt for a par. I could use a wedge, but why screw around? It's easier to take this little chipping iron I carry and run it up close."

"Uh-huh."

"So I run it up close, all right, and it doesn't miss the cup by more than two inches, but I played it too strong, and it picks up speed and rolls past the pin and all the way off the green, and I wind up farther from the cup than when I started."

"Hell of a thing."

"So I chip again, and pass the hole again, though not quite as badly. And by the time I'm done hacking away with my goddam putter I'm three strokes over par with a seven. Takes me two strokes to cover four hundred and forty yards and five more strokes to manage the last fifty feet."

"Well, that's golf," Keller said.

"By God, you said a mouthful," Al said. "That's golf, all right. How about another round of these, Dave, and then we'll get ourselves some dinner? There's a couple of guys you ought to meet."

He wound up at a table with four other fellows. Al and a man named Felix were residents of Sundowner Estates, while the other two men were Felix's guests, seasonal residents of Scottsdale who belonged to one of the other local country clubs. Felix told a long joke, involving a hapless golfer driven to suicide by a bad round of golf. For the punch line, Felix held his wrists together and said, "What time?" and everybody roared. They all ordered steaks and drank beer and talked about golf and politics and how screwed-up the stock market was these days, and Keller managed to keep up his end of the conversation without anybody seeming to notice that he didn't know what the hell he was talking about.

"So how'd you do out there today?" someone asked him, and Keller had his reply all ready.

"You know," he said thoughtfully, "it's a hell of a thing. You can hack away like a man trying to beat a ball to death with a stick, and then you hit one shot that's so sweet and true that it makes you feel good about the whole day."

He couldn't even remember when or where he'd heard that, but it evidently rang true with his dinner companions. They all nodded solemnly, and then someone changed the subject and said something disparaging about Democrats, and it was Keller's turn to nod in agreement.

Nothing to it.

"So we'll go out tomorrow morning," Al said to Felix. "Dave, if you want to join us . . ."

Keller pressed his wrists together, said, "What time?" When the laughter died down he said, "I wish I could, Al. I'm afraid tomorrow's out. Another time, though."

"You could take a lesson," Dot said. "Isn't there a club pro? Doesn't he give lessons?"

"There is," he said, "and I suppose he does, but why would I want to take one?"

"So you could get out there and play golf. Protective coloration and all."

"If anyone sees me swinging a golf club," he said, "with or without a lesson, they'll wonder what the hell I'm doing here. But this way they just figure I fit in a round earlier in the day. Anyway, I don't want to spend too much time around the clubhouse. Mostly I get the hell out of here and go for drives."

"On the driving range?"

"Out in the desert," she said.

"You just ride around and look at the cactus."

"There's a lot of it to look at," he said, "although they have a problem with poachers."

"You're kidding."

"No," he said, and explained how the cacti were protected, but criminals dug them up and sold them to florists.

"Cactus rustlers," Dot said. "That's the damnedest thing I ever heard of. I guess they have to be careful of the spines."

"I suppose so."

"Serve them right if they get stuck. You just drive around, huh?"

"And think things out."

"Well, that's nice. But you don't want to lose sight of the reason you moved in there in the first place."

He stayed away from the clubhouse the next day, and the day after. Then, on a Tuesday afternoon, he got in his car and drove around, staying within the friendly confines of Sundowner. He passed the Lattimore house and wondered if Mitzi Prentice had shown it to anyone lately. He drove past William Egmont's house, which looked to be pretty much the same model as the Sundstrom place. Egmont's Cadillac was parked in the carport, but the man owned his own golf cart, and Keller couldn't see it there. He'd probably motored over to the first tee on his cart, and might be out there now, taking big divots, slicing balls deep into the rough.

Keller went home, parked his Toyota in the Sundstrom carport. He'd worried, after taking the house for two weeks, that Mitzi would call all the time, or, worse, start turning up without calling first. But in fact he hadn't heard a word from her, for which he'd been deeply grateful, and now he found himself thinking about calling her, at work or at home, and figuring out a place to meet. Not at his place, because of the masks, and not at her place, because of her daughter, and—

That settled it. If he was starting to think like that, well, it was time he got on with it. Or the next thing you knew he'd be taking golf lessons, and buying the Lattimore house, and trading in the stuffed dog on a real one.

He went outside. The afternoon had already begun fading into early evening, and it seemed to Keller that the darkness came quicker here than it did in New York. That stood to reason, it was a good deal closer to the equator, and that would account for it. Someone had explained why to him once, and he'd understood it at the time, but now all that remained was the fact: the farther you were from the equator, the more extended twilight became.

In any event, the golfers were through for the day. He took a walk along the edge of the golf course, and passed Egmont's house. The car was still there, and the golf cart was not. He walked on for a while, then turned around and headed toward the house again, coming from the other direction, and saw someone gliding along on a motorized golf cart. Was it Egmont, on his way home? No, as the cart came closer he saw that the rider was thinner than Keller's quarry, and had a fuller head of hair. And the cart turned off before it reached Egmont's house, which pretty much cinched things.

Besides, he was soon to discover, Egmont had already returned. His cart was parked in the carport, alongside his car, and the bag of golf clubs was slung over the back of the cart. Something about that last touch reminded Keller of a song, though he couldn't pin down the song or figure out how it hooked up to the golf cart. Something mournful, something with bagpipes, but Keller couldn't put his finger on it.

There were lights on in Egmont's house. Was he alone? Had he brought someone home with him?

One easy way to find out. He walked up the path to the front door, poked the doorbell. He heard it ring, then didn't hear anything and considered ringing it again. First he tried the door, and found it locked, which was no great surprise, and then he heard footsteps, but just barely, as if someone was walking lightly on deep carpet. And then the door opened a few inches until the chain stopped it, and William Wallis Egmont looked out at him, a puzzled expression on his face.

"Mr. Egmont?"

"Yes?"

"My name's Miller," he said. "David Miller. I'm staying just over the hill, I'm renting the Sundstrom house for a couple of weeks . . ."

"Oh, of course," Egmont said, visibly relaxing. "Of course, Mr. Miller. Someone was mentioning you just the other day. And I do believe I've seen you around the club. And out on the course, if I'm not mistaken."

It was a mistake Keller saw no need to correct. "You probably have," he said. "I'm out there every chance I get."

"As am I, sir. I played today and I expect to play tomorrow."

Keller pressed his wrists together, said, "What time?"

"Oh, very good," Egmont said. " 'What time?' That's a golfer for you, isn't it? Now how can I help you?"

"It's delicate," Keller said. "Do you suppose I could come in for a moment?"

"Well, I don't see why not," Egmont said, and slipped the chain lock to let him in.

The keypad for the burglar alarm was mounted on the wall, just to the right of the front door. Immediately adjacent to it was a sheet of paper headed HOW TO SET THE BURGLAR ALARM with the instructions hand-printed in block capitals large enough to be read easily by elderly eyes. Keller read the directions, followed them, and let himself out of Egmont's house. A few minutes later he was back in his own house—the Sundstrom house. He made himself a cup of coffee in the Sundstrom kitchen and sat with it in the Sundstrom living room, and while it cooled he let himself remember the last moments of William Wallis Egmont.

He practiced the exercises that were automatic for him by now, turning the images that came to mind from color to black and white, then watching them fade to gray, willing them farther and farther away so that they grew smaller and smaller until they were vanishing pinpoints, gray dots on a gray field, disappearing into the distance, swallowed up by the past.

When his coffee cup was empty he went into the Sundstrom bedroom and undressed, then showered in the Sundstrom bathroom, only to dry off with a Sundstrom towel. He went into the den, Harvey Sundstrom's den, and took a Fijian battle-axe from the wall. It was fashioned of black wood, and heavier than it looked, and its elaborate geometric shape suggested it would be of more use as wall decoration than weapon. But Keller worked out how to grip it and swing it, and took a few experimental whiffs with it, and he could see how the islanders would have found it useful.

He could have taken it with him to Egmont's house, and he let himself imagine it now, saw himself clutching the device in both hands and swinging around in a 360-degree arc, whipping the business end of the axe into Egmont's skull. He shook his head, returned the battle-axe to the wall, and resumed where he'd left off earlier, summoning up Egmont's image, reviewing the last moments of Egmont's life, and making it all gray and blurry, making it all smaller and smaller, making it all go away.

In the morning he went out for breakfast, returning in time to see an ambulance leaving Sundowner Estates through the east gate. The guard recognized Keller and waved him through, but he braked and rolled down the window to inquire about the ambulance. The guard shook his head soberly and reported the sad news.

He went home and called Dot. "Don't tell me," she said. "You've decided you can't do it."

"It's done."

"It's amazing how I can just sense these

things," she said. "You figure it's psychic powers or old-fashioned feminine intuition? That was a rhetorical question, Keller. You don't have to answer it. I'd say I'll see you tomorrow, but I won't, will I?"

"It'll take me a while to get home."

"Well, no rush," she said. "Take your time, see the sights. You've got your clubs, haven't you?"

"My clubs?"

"Stop along the way, play a little golf. Enjoy yourself, Keller. You deserve it."

The day before his two-week rental was up, he walked over to the clubhouse, settled his account, and turned in his keys and ID card. He walked back to the Sundstrom house, where he put his suitcase in the trunk and the little stuffed dog in the passenger seat. Then he got behind the wheel and drove slowly around the golf course, leaving the compound by the east gate.

"It's a nice place," he told the dog. "I can see why people like it. Not just the golf and the weather and the security. You get the feeling nothing really bad could happen to you there. Even if you die, it's just part of the natural order of things."

He set cruise control and pointed the car

toward Tucson, lowering the visor against the morning sun. It was, he thought, good weather for cruise control. Just the other day, he'd had NPR on the car radio, and listened as a man with a professionally mellow voice cautioned against using cruise control in wet weather. If the car were to hydroplane on the slick pavement, cruise control would think the wheels weren't turning fast enough, and would speed up the engine to compensate. And then, when the tires got their grip again, wham!

Keller couldn't recall the annual cost in lives from this phenomenon, but it was higher than you'd think. At the time all he did was resolve to make sure he took the car out of cruise control whenever he switched on the windshield wipers. Now, cruising east across the Arizona desert, he found himself wondering if there might be any practical application for this new knowledge. Accidental death was a useful tool, it had most recently claimed the life of William Wallis Egmont, but Keller couldn't see how cruise control in inclement weather could become part of his bag of tricks. Still, you never knew, and he let himself think about it.

In Tucson he stuck the dog in his suitcase before he turned in the car, then walked out into the heat and managed to locate his original car in long-term parking. He tossed his suitcase in the back seat and stuck the key in the ignition, wondering if the car would start. No problem if it wouldn't, all he'd have to do was talk to somebody at the Hertz counter, but suppose they'd just noticed him at the Avis counter, turning in another car. Would they notice something like that? You wouldn't think so, but airports were different these days. There were people standing around noticing everything.

He turned the key, and the engine turned over right away. The woman at the gate figured out what he owed and sounded apologetic when she named the figure. He found himself imagining what the charges would have added up to on other cars he'd left in long-term lots, cars he'd never returned to claim, cars with bodies in their trunks. Probably a lot of money, he decided, and nobody to pay it. He figured he could afford to pick up the tab for a change. He paid cash, took the receipt, and got back on the Interstate.

As he drove, he found himself figuring out just how he'd have handled it if the car hadn't started. "For God's sake," he said, "look at yourself, will you? Something could have happened but didn't, it's over and done with, and you're figuring out what you would have done, developing a coping strategy when there's nothing to cope with. What the hell's the matter with you?"

He thought about it. Then he said, "You want to know what's the matter with you? You're talking to yourself, that's what's the matter with you."

He stopped doing it. Twenty minutes down the road he pulled into a rest area, leaned over the seat back, opened his suitcase, and returned the dog to its position in the passenger seat.

"And away we go," he said.

In New Mexico he got off the Interstate and followed the signs to an Indian pueblo. A plump woman, her hair braided and her face expressionless, sat in a room with pots she had made herself. Keller picked out a little black pot with scalloped edges. She wrapped it carefully for him, using sheets of newspaper, and put the wrapped pot in a brown paper bag, and the paper bag into a plastic bag. Keller tucked the whole thing away in his suitcase and got back behind the wheel.

"Don't ask," he told the dog.

Just over the Colorado state line it started to rain. He drove through the rain for ten or twenty miles before he remembered the guy on NPR. He tapped the brake, which made the cruise control cut out, but just to make sure he used the switch, too.

"Close one," he told the dog.

In Kansas he took a state road north and visited a roadside attraction, a house that had once been a hideout of the Dalton boys. They were outlaws, he knew, contemporaries of the Jesse James and the Youngers. The place was tricked out as a mini museum, with memorabilia and news clippings, and there was an underground passage leading from the house to the barn in back, so that the brothers, when surprised by the law, could hurry through the tunnel and escape that way. He'd have liked to see the passage, but it was sealed off.

"Still," he told the woman attendant, "it's nice to know it's there."

If he was interested in the Daltons, she told him, there was another museum at the other end of the state. At Coffeyville, she said, where as he probably knew most of the Daltons were killed, trying to rob two banks in one day. He had in fact known that, but only because he'd just read it on the information card for one of the exhibits.

He stopped at a gas station, bought a state

map, and figured out the route to Coffeyville. Halfway there he stopped for the
night at a Red Roof Inn, had a pizza delivered, and ate it in front of the television set.
He ran the cable channels until he found a
western that looked promising, and
damned if it didn't turn out to be about the
Dalton boys. Not just the Daltons—Frank
and Jesse James were in it, too, and Cole
Younger and his brothers.

They seemed like real nice fellows, too,
the kind of guys you wouldn't mind hanging
out with. Not a sadist or pyromaniac in the
lot, as far as he could tell. And did you think
Jesse James wet the bed? Like hell he did.

In the morning he drove on to Coffeyville
and paid the admission charge and took his
time studying the exhibits. It was a pretty
bold act, robbing two banks at once, but it
might not have been the smartest move in
the history of American crime. The local citizens were just waiting for them, and they rid-
dled the brothers with bullets. Most of them
were dead by the time the shooting stopped,
or died of their wounds before long.

Emmett Dalton wound up with something
like a dozen bullets in him, and went off to
prison. But the story didn't end there. He
recovered, and eventually got released, and
wound up in Los Angeles, where he wrote

films for the young motion picture industry and made a small fortune in real estate.

Keller spent a long time taking that in, and it gave him a lot to think about.

Most of the time he was quiet, but now and then he talked to the dog.

"Take soldiers," he said, on a stretch of I-40 east of Des Moines. "They get drafted into the army, they go through basic training, and before you know it they're aiming at other soldiers and pulling the trigger. Maybe they have to force themselves the first couple of times, and maybe they have bad dreams early on, but then they get used to it, and before you know it they sort of enjoy it. It's not a sex thing, they don't get that kind of a thrill out of it, but it's sort of like hunting. Except you just pull the trigger and leave it at that. You don't have to track wounded soldiers to make sure they don't suffer. You don't have to dress your kill and pack it back to camp. You just pull the trigger and get on with your life.

"And these are ordinary kids," he went on. "Eighteen-year-old boys, drafted fresh out of high school. Or I guess it's volunteers now, they don't draft them anymore, but it amounts to the same thing. They're just ordinary American boys. They didn't grow up torturing animals or starting fires. Or wetting the bed.

"You know something? I still don't see what wetting the bed has to do with it."

Coming into New York on the George Washington Bridge, he said, "Well, they're not there."

The towers, he meant. And of course they weren't there, they were gone, and he knew that. He'd been down to the site enough times to know it wasn't trick photography, that the twin towers were in fact gone. But somehow he'd half expected to see them, half expected the whole thing to turn out to have been a dream. You couldn't make part of the skyline disappear, for God's sake.

He drove to the Hertz place, returned the car. He was walking away from the office with his suitcase in hand when an attendant rushed up, brandishing the little stuffed dog. "You forgot somethin'," the man said, smiling broadly.

"Oh, right," Keller said. "You got any kids?"

"Me?"

"Give it to your kid," Keller told him. "Or some other kid."

"You don't want him?"

He shook his head, kept walking. When he got home he showered and shaved and looked out the window. His window faced east, not south, and had never afforded a view of the towers, so it was the same as it had always been. And that's why he'd looked, to assure himself that everything was still there, that nothing had been taken away.

It looked okay to him. He picked up the phone and called Dot.

She was waiting for him on the porch, with the usual pitcher of iced tea. "You had me going," she said. "You didn't call and you didn't call and you didn't call. It took you the better part of a month to get home. What did you do, walk?"

"I didn't leave right away," he said. "I paid for two weeks."

"And you wanted to make sure you got your money's worth."

"I thought it'd be suspicious, leaving early. 'Oh, I remember that guy, he left four days early, right after Mr. Egmont died.'"

"And you thought it'd be safer to hang around the scene of a homicide?"

"Except it wasn't a homicide," he said. "The man came home after an afternoon at the golf course, locked his door, set the burglar alarm, got undressed and drew a hot bath. He got into the tub and lost consciousness and drowned."

"Most accidents happen in the home," Dot said. "Isn't that what they say? What did he do, hit his head?"

"He may have smacked it on the tile on the way down, after he lost his balance. Or maybe he had a little stroke. Hard to say."

"You undressed him and everything?"

He nodded. "Put him in the tub. He came to in the water, but I picked up his feet and held them in the air, and his head went under, and, well, that was that."

"Water in the lungs."

"Right."

"Death by drowning."

He nodded.

"You okay, Keller?"

"Me? Sure, I'm fine. Anyway, I figured I'd wait the four days, leave when my time was up."

"Just like Egmont."

"Huh?"

"He left when his time was up," she said. "Still, how long does it take to drive home from Phoenix? Four, five days?"

"I got sidetracked," he said, and told her about the Dalton boys.

"Two museums," she said. "Most people have never been to one Dalton boys museum, and you've been to two."

"Well, they robbed two banks at once."

"What's that got to do with it?"

"I don't know. Nothing, I guess. You ever hear of Nashville, Indiana?"

"I've heard of Nashville," she said, "and I've heard of Indiana, but I guess the answer to your questions is no. What have they got in Nashville, Indiana? The Grand Ole Hoosier Opry?"

"There's a John Dillinger museum there."

"Jesus, Keller. What were you taking, an outlaw's tour of the Midwest?"

"There was a flyer for the place in the museum in Coffeyville, and it wasn't that far out of my way. It was interesting. They had the fake gun he used to break out of prison. Or it may have been a replica. Either way, it was pretty interesting."

"I'll bet."

"They were folk heroes," he said. "Dillinger and Pretty Boy Floyd and Baby Face Nelson."

"And Bonnie and Clyde. Have those two got a museum?"

"Probably. They were heroes the same as the Daltons and Youngers and Jameses, but they weren't brothers. Back in the nineteenth century it was a family thing, but then that tradition died out."

"Kids today," Dot said. "What about Ma Barker? Wasn't that around the same time as Dillinger? And didn't she have a whole houseful of bank-robbing brats? Or was that just in the movies?"

"No, you're right," he said. "I forgot about Ma Barker."

"Well, let's forget her all over again, so you can get to the point."

He shook his head. "I'm not sure there is one. I just took my time getting back, that's all. I had some thinking to do."

"And?"

He reached for the pitcher, poured himself more iced tea. "Okay," he said. "Here's the thing. I can't do this anymore."

"I can't say I'm surprised."

"I was going to retire a while ago," he said. "Remember?"

"Vividly."

"At the time," he said, "I figured I could afford it. I had money put aside. Not a ton, but enough for a little bungalow somewhere in Florida."

"And you could get to Denny's in time for the early bird special, which helps keep food costs down."

"You said I needed a hobby, and that got

me interested in stamp collecting again. And before I knew it I was spending serious money on stamps."

"And that was the end of your retirement fund."

"It cut into it," he agreed. "And it's kept me from saving money ever since then, because any extra money just goes into stamps."

She frowned. "I think I see where this is going," she said. "You can't keep on doing what you've been doing, but you can't retire, either."

"So I tried to think what else I could do," he said. "Emmett Dalton wound up in Hollywood, writing movies and dealing in real estate."

"You working on a script, Keller? Boning up for the realtor's exam?"

"I couldn't think of a single thing I could do," he said. "Oh, I suppose I could get some kind of minimum-wage job. But I'm used to living a certain way, and I'm used to not having to work many hours. Can you see me clerking in a 7-Eleven?"

"I couldn't even see you sticking up a 7-Eleven, Keller."

"It might be different if I were younger."

"I guess armed robbery is a young man's job."

"If I were just starting out," he said, "I could take some entry-level job and work my way up. But I'm too old for that now. Nobody would hire me in the first place, and the jobs I'm qualified for, well, I wouldn't want them."

" 'Do you want fries with that?' You're right, Keller. Somehow it just doesn't sound like you."

"I started at the bottom once. I started coming around and the old man found things for me to do. 'Richie's gotta see a man, so why don't you ride along with him, keep him company.' Or go see this guy, tell him we're not happy with the way he's been acting. Or he used to send me to the store to pick up candy bars for him. What was that candy bar he used to like?"

"Mars bars."

"No, he switched to those, but early on it was something else. They were hard to find, only a few stores had them. I think he was the only person I ever met who liked them. What the hell was the name of them? It's on the tip of my tongue."

"Hell of a place for a candy bar."

"Powerhouse," he said. "Powerhouse candy bars."

"The dentist's best friend," she said. "I remember them now. I wonder if they still make them."

" 'Do me a favor, kid, see if they got any of my candy bars downtown.' Then one day it was do me a favor, here's a gun, go see this guy and give him two in the head. Out of the blue, more or less, except by then he probably knew I'd do it. And you know something? It never occurred to me not to. 'Here's a gun, do me a favor.' So I took the gun and did him a favor."

"Just like that?"

"Pretty much. I was used to doing what he told me, and I just did. And that let him know I was somebody who could do that kind of thing. Because not everybody can."

"But it didn't bother you."

"I've been thinking about this," he said. "Reflecting, I guess you'd call it. I didn't let it bother me."

"That thing you do, fading the color out of the image and pushing it off in the distance . . ."

"It was later that I taught myself to do that," he said. "Earlier, well, I guess you'd just call it denial. I told myself it didn't bother me and made myself believe it. And then there was this sense of accomplishment. Look what I did, see what a man I am. Bang, and he's dead and you're not, there's a certain amount of exhilaration that comes with it."

"Still?"

He shook his head. "There's the feeling that you've got the job done, that's all. If it was difficult, well, you've accomplished something. If there are other things you'd rather be doing, well, now you can go home and do them."

"Buy stamps, see a movie."

"Right."

"You just pretended it didn't bother you," she said, "and then one day it didn't."

"And it was easy to pretend, because it never bothered me all that much. But yes, I just kept on doing it, and then I didn't have to pretend. This place I stayed in Scottsdale, there were all these masks on the walls. Tribal stuff, I guess they were. And I thought about how I started out wearing a mask, and before long it wasn't a mask, it was my own face."

"I guess I follow you."

"It's just a way of looking at it," he said. "Anyway, how I got here's not the point. Where do I go from here? That's the question."

"You had a lot of time to think up an answer."

"Too much time."

"I guess, with all the stops in Nashville and Coffee Pot."

"Coffeyville."

"Whatever. What did you come up with, Keller?"

"Well," he said, and drew a breath. "One, I'm ready to stop doing this. The business is different, with the airline security and people living behind stockade fences. And I'm different. I'm older, and I've been doing this for too many years."

"Okay."

"Two, I can't retire. I need the money, and I don't have any other way to earn what I need to live on."

"I hope there's a three, Keller, because one and two don't leave you much room to swing."

"What I had to do," he said, "was figure out how much money I need."

"To retire on."

He nodded. "The figure I came up with," he said, "is a million dollars."

"A nice round sum."

"That's more than I had when I was thinking about retirement the last time. I think this is a more realistic figure. Invested right, I could probably get a return of around fifty thousand dollars a year."

"And you can live on that?"

"I don't want that much," he said. "I'm not thinking in terms of around-the-world cruises and expensive restaurants. I don't spend a lot on clothes, and when I buy something I wear it until it's worn out."

"Or even longer."

"If I had a million in cash," he said, "plus what I could get for the apartment, which is probably another half million."

"Where would you move?"

"I don't know. Someplace warm, I suppose."

"Sundowner Estates?"

"Too expensive. And I wouldn't care to be walled in, and I don't play golf."

"You might, just to have something to do."

He shook his head. "Some of those guys loved golf," he said, "but others, you had the feeling they had to keep selling themselves on the idea, telling each other how crazy they were about the game. 'What time?' "

"How's that?"

"It's the punch line of a joke. It's not important. No, I wouldn't want to live there. But there are these little towns in New Mexico north of Albuquerque, up in the high desert, and you could buy a shack there or just pick up a mobile home and find a place to park it."

"And you think you could stand it? Out in the boonies like that?"

"I don't know. The thing is, say I netted

half a million from the apartment, plus the million I saved. Say five percent, comes to seventy-five thousand a year, and yes, I could live fine on that."

"And your apartment's worth half a million?"

"Something like that."

"So all you need is a million dollars, Keller. Now I'd lend it to you, but I'm a little short this month. What are you going to do, sell your stamps?"

"They're not worth anything like that. I don't know what I've spent on the collection, but it certainly doesn't come to a million dollars, and you can't get back what you put into them, anyway."

"I thought they were supposed to be a good investment."

"They're better than spending the money on caviar and champagne," he said, "because you get something back when you sell them, but dealers have to make a profit, too, and if you get half your money back you're doing well. Anyway, I wouldn't want to sell them."

"You want to keep them. And keep on collecting?"

"If I had seventy-five thousand a year coming in," he said, "and if I lived in some little town in the desert, I could afford to spend ten or fifteen thousand a year on stamps."

"I bet northern New Mexico's full of people doing just that."

"Maybe not," he said, "but I don't see why I couldn't do it."

"You could be the first, Keller. Now all you need is a million dollars."

"That's what I was thinking."

"Okay, I'll bite. How're you going to get it?"

"Well," he said, "that pretty much answers itself, doesn't it? I mean, there's only one thing I know how to do."

"I think I get it," Dot said. "You can't do this anymore, so you've got to do it with a vengeance. You have to depopulate half the country in order to get out of the business of killing people."

"When you put it that way . . ."

"Well, there's a certain irony operating, wouldn't you say? But there's a certain logic there, too. You want to grab every high-ticket job that comes along, so that you can salt away enough cash to get out of the business once and for all. You know what it reminds me of?"

"What?"

"Cops," she said. "Their pensions are based on what they make the last year they work, so they grab all the overtime they can get their hands on, and then when they retire they can live in style. Usually we sit back and pick and choose, and you take time off between jobs, but that's not what you want to do now, is it? You want to do a job, come home, catch your breath, then turn around and do another one."

"Right."

"Until you can cash in at an even million."

"That's the idea."

"Or maybe a few dollars more, to allow for inflation."

"Maybe."

"A little more iced tea, Keller?"

"No, I'm fine."

"Would you rather have coffee? I could make coffee."

"No thanks."

"You sure?"

"Positive."

"You took a lot of time in Scottsdale. Did he really look just like the man in Monopoly?"

"In the photo. Less so in real life."

"He didn't give you any trouble?"

He shook his head. "By the time he had a clue what was happening, it was pretty much over."

"He wasn't on his guard at all, then."

"No. I wonder why he got on somebody's list."

"An impatient heir would be my guess.

Did it bother you much, Keller? Before, during, or after?"

He thought about it, shook his head.

"And then you took your time getting out of there."

"I thought it made sense to hang around a few days. One more day and I could have gone to the funeral."

"So you left the day they buried him?"

"Except they didn't," he said. "He had the same kind of funeral as Mr. Lattimore."

"Am I supposed to know who that is?"

"He had a house I could have bought. He was cremated, and after a nondenominational service his ashes were placed in the water hazard."

"Just a five-iron shot from his front door."

"Well," Keller said. "Anyway, yes, I took my time getting home."

"All those museums."

"I had to think it all through," he said. "Figuring out what I want to do with the rest of my life."

"Of which today is the first day, if I remember correctly. Let me make sure I've got this straight. You're done feeding rescue workers at Ground Zero, and you're done going to museums for dead outlaws, and you're ready to get out there and kill one for the Gipper. Is that about it?"

"It's close enough."

"Because I've been turning down jobs left and right, Keller, and what I want to do is get on the horn and spread the word that we're ready to do business. We're not holding any two-for-one sales, but we're very much in the game. Am I clear on that?" She got to her feet. "Which reminds me. Don't go away."

She came back with an envelope and dropped it on the table in front of him. "They paid up right away, and it took you so long to get home I was beginning to think of it as my money. What's this?"

"Something I picked up on the way home."

She opened the package, took the little black clay pot in her hands. "That's really nice," she said. "What is it, Indian?"

"From a pueblo in New Mexico."

"And it's for me?"

"I got the urge to buy it," he said, "and then afterward I wondered what I was going to do with it. And I thought maybe you'd like it."

"It would look nice on the mantel," she said. "Or it would be handy to keep paper-clips in. But it'll have to be one or the other, because there's no point in keeping paper-clips on the mantel. You said you got it in New Mexico? In the town you're figuring to wind up in?"

He shook his head. "It was a pueblo. I think you have to be an Indian."

"Well, they do nice work. I'm very pleased to have it."

"Glad you like it."

"And you take good care of that," she said, pushing the envelope toward him. "It's the first deposit in your retirement fund. Though I suppose you'll want to spend some of it on stamps."

Two days later he was working on his stamps when the phone rang. "I'm in the city," she said. "Right around the corner from you, as a matter of fact."

She told him the name of the restaurant, and he went there and found her in a booth at the back, eating an ice cream sundae. "When I was a kid," she said, "they had these at Wohler's drugstore for thirty-five cents. It was five cents extra if you wanted walnuts on top. I'd hate to tell you what they get for this beauty, and walnuts weren't part of the deal, either."

"Nothing's the way it used to be."

"You're right about that," she said, "and a philosophical observation like that is worth the trip. But it's not why I came in. Here's the waitress, Keller. You want one of these?"

He shook his head, ordered a cup of coffee. The waitress brought it, and when she was out of earshot Dot said, "I had a call this morning."

"Oh?"

"And I was going to call you, but it wasn't anything to discuss on the phone, and I didn't feel right about telling you to come out to White Plains because I was pretty sure you'd be wasting your time. So I figured I'd come in, and have an ice cream sundae while I'm at it. It's worth the trip, incidentally, even if they do charge the earth for it. You sure you don't want one?"

"Positive."

"I got a call," she said, "from a guy we've worked with before, a broker, very solid type. And there's some work to be done, a nice upscale piece of work, which would put a nice piece of change in your retirement fund and one in mine, too."

"What's the catch?"

"It's in Santa Barbara, California," she said, "and there's a very narrow window operating. You'd have to do it Wednesday or Thursday, which makes it impossible, because it would take longer than that for you to drive there even if you left right away and only stopped for gas. I mean, suppose you drove it in three days, which is ridiculous anyway. You'd be wiped out when you got there, and you'd get there when, Thursday afternoon at the earliest? Can't be done."

"No."

"So I'll tell them no," she said, "but I wanted to check with you first."

"Tell them we'll do it," he said.

"Really?"

"I'll fly out tomorrow morning. Or tonight, if I can get something."

"You weren't ever going to fly again."

"I know."

"And then a job comes along . . ."

"Not flying just doesn't seem that important," he said. "Don't ask me why."

"Actually," she said, "I have a theory."

"Oh?"

"When the Towers came down," she said, "it was very traumatic for you. Same as it was for everybody else. You had to adjust to a new reality, and that's not easy to do. Your whole world went tilt, and for a while there you stayed off airplanes, and you went downtown and fed the hungry, and you bided your time and tried to figure out a way to get along without doing your usual line of work."

"And?"

"And time passed," she said, "and things settled down, and you adjusted to the way the world is now. While you were at it, you realized what you'll have to do if you're going to be in a position to retire. You thought things through and came up with a plan."

"Well, sort of a plan."

"And a lot of things which seemed very important a while ago, like not flying with all this security and ID checks and all, turn out to be just an inconvenience and not something to make you change your life around. You'll get a second set of ID, or you'll use real ID and find some other way to cover your tracks. One way or another, you'll work it out."

"I suppose," he said. "Santa Barbara. That's between L.A. and San Francisco, isn't it?"

"Closer to L.A. They have their own airport."

He shook his head. "They can keep it," he said. "I'll fly to LAX. Or Burbank, that's even better, and I'll rent a car and drive up to Santa Barbara. Wednesday or Thursday, you said?" He pressed his wrists together. " 'What time?' "

"What time? What do you mean, what time? What's so funny, anyway?"

"Oh, it's a joke one of the golfers told in the clubhouse in Scottsdale. This golfer goes out and he has the worst round of his life. He loses balls in the rough, he can't get out of sand traps, he hits ball after ball into the water hazard. Nothing goes right for him. By the time he gets to the eighteenth green all he's got left is his putter, because he's broken every other club over his knee, and after he four-putts the final hole he breaks the putter, too, and sends it flying.

"He marches into the locker room, absolutely furious, and he unlocks his locker and takes out his razor and opens it up and gets the blade in his hand and slashes both his wrists. And he stands there, watching the blood flow, and someone calls to him over the bank of lockers. 'Hey, Joe,' the guy says, 'we're getting up a foursome for tomorrow morning. You interested?'"

"And the guy says"—Keller raised his hands to shoulder height, pressed his wrists together—"'What time?'"

"'What time?'"

"Right."

"'What time?'" She shook her head. "I like it, Keller. And any old time you want'll be just fine."